# QUEEN'S DANCE

A.P. THANOS

Copyright © 2018 A.P. Thanos
All rights reserved.
ISBN: 9781729306338

# DEDICATION

Dedicated to all those who fulfilled me.

"Life is a comedy for those who think
and a tragedy for those who feel."
Horace Walpole

# ACKNOWLEDGMENTS

Thank you Francis for teaching me how to feel.
Thank you Franco for teaching me how to accept.
Thank you Frank for teaching me how to think.
Thank you to my editor, Don Macnab-Stark.
Thank you to Maverick Graphics.

# CHAPTER ONE

I TRY TO SCREAM, but can't make a sound. I attempt to break free but his body weight pins me down. Gazing into his dark eyes I desperately gasp for air. His smile is telling. His grip on my neck tightens. Strangely, I notice that his strong hands are surprisingly soft as they slowly squeeze the life out of me. I feel my consciousness slipping away. Time slows and then stops altogether. I'm not sure what comes first...the darkness that envelopes me...or the mind-numbing orgasm that rips through every fiber of my body as I collapse in a heap when he finally releases me.

As I gradually open my eyes Matteo comes into focus, silhouetted against the floor-to-ceiling window of his office, Central Park sprawling beneath us, lush and green. He stands above me zipping up his beautifully tailored dress pants.

It's a typical Saturday morning.

I close my eyes, breathe deep, and try to relax as my heartbeat returns to normal. I eventually open my eyes and look up at him, and with the first full breath of air that returns to my lungs I blurt out, "That was the best orgasm" ...*this week*. Thank you filter. He doesn't need to hear that last part. He is a good lover, above average, and his effort is commendable, but he isn't the best. Not by a long shot, but I won't tell him that. Why would I? Bruising his ego does not serve my purposes - quite the opposite. I do, however, have a barely controllable urge to drop the slightest hint that he is not as good as he thinks he is and that he certainly isn't in charge. Not here anyways. Most definitely not in charge.

"That was great," he grins, looking down at me domineeringly.

*No kidding*, I think to myself, but instead I respond sincerely with, "How do I make it better?"

I want to be the best. Always have. I have been told by many lovers that I am the best. When I ask them, what makes me such a great lover, the typical response is, 'because you love sex'. And that I do.

"You are a strange woman, Zoe," he chuckles.

Strange? Is it strange to enjoy being suffocated or administering a perfectly timed asphyxiation? You have to be perfect with it. Anything less than perfection could mean death. Death, danger and sex…what could be more exciting? A lover's hands caressing my throat, knowing that at any instant he could snap my neck. In 1936, Sada Abe did exactly that. She killed her lover Kichizo Ishida using erotic asphyxiation and, to make matters worse (or better), she severed him, root and stem, and carried the purloined items in her purse for days before her apprehension. *Now that's my kind of gal* and, "Yes Matteo, I am indeed a strange woman."

I have spent the last year becoming acquainted with Matteo. It is an enjoyable yet frightening task. He is fun and sexy, in that dark, Italian, well-dressed, well-mannered, charming sort of way, but with more than a dash of sociopath thrown in. He is attractive and likeable but also unscrupulous, and unfeeling.

"Drink?" he asks.

I check my watch. "Yes," I respond politely as I make my way off the floor and onto the sofa, pulling my dress back down from around my waist.

"Do you have somewhere more important to be?" He walks over to the bar. As always, he is astute and observant.

"No. I just wasn't sure if it was too early for a glass of wine…and a toast."

He smiles. "It's never too early for a glass of good wine." He pulls out a bottle that appears to have a handwritten note on a dark green label. He slowly makes his way back to the couch, bottle-in-hand. Standing over me, he pauses before handing me the bottle. "Do you know what this is?"

I know exactly what it is, but I have to play my part. I look up at him. "Umm, something luscious and complex I hope?"

"You are absolutely right. That's why we have to wait for the right moment to open it."

The attached note reads: *1959 was a fine year. This year will be even finer.* Signed *Sully*.

"That will be soon I hope. Something for us to celebrate?" I hand him back the bottle.

"Yes Zoe…soon." Matteo grins.

I know Matteo well enough now to know that we won't be sipping that very fine vintage today or any day soon; that it is reserved for a very special person, or more precisely, for a very special occasion. As if reading my thoughts Matteo returns the bottle to the bar and pulls out a perfectly respectable Super Tuscan and pours two glasses.

"To you, Zoe." He toasts.

Gazing into his eyes, I reply, "And to our perfectly timed orgasm."

He laughs. "Well said."

Our glasses clink. I look at him as he sips his wine and have to admit that I admire Matteo. We will never be close. I wonder whether we can ever be friends. I certainly don't trust him. In many ways, however, we are the same. His brain works the same way as mine, and I can never truly trust a male version of myself.

"You, Matteo, are a character," I say to him. "You charm me. And I'm not easily charmed." This time I am sincere. That does happen on rare occasions.

He abruptly stands and walks around the coffee table to sit across from me. "You have mere seconds to read people. After those few seconds have passed you must, without hesitation, feed them what they want."

Another one of his teaching moments. Matteo enjoys sharing his stories. It feeds his ego. I give him what he wants, which is my attention. I want so desperately to ask him to read me, but I'm not going to divulge weakness, so I take a different angle...without personalizing it. I am intrigued after all. "How?"

"How what?"

"How do you know what people want?"

"By telling them what they want. To be successful in business you need to control perception."

"And how do you control perception in business?" *Feed his ego, Zoe.*

"You see this room?" He pauses, providing me a moment to observe the space. "How would you characterize it?"

*I laugh inside. Who is the Psychologist here?* But I continue to feed his ego. "I see a room where style trumps functionality, a large space with a great view...and I'm not talking about the man in it."

We both laugh.

"I recently renovated the office next door." He stands. "Follow me."

I grab my purse and my wine and follow him. His rhythm is hypnotizing as he walks into the adjacent room.

"And now?" he asks.

"Now what?"

"Describe this room."

"This being your conference room, you give the illusion of you being powerless within a small space."

"Brava! I make them feel superior. Perception is reality. I intentionally distort theirs."

"Hence why you don't have meetings in your own office."

He beams. "Correct."

I don't want to interrupt him and I won't say what I'm really thinking, but I divert. "Why are people afraid to disappoint you?"

He smiles. "Have a seat."

I obey.

He continues, "One word…vulnerability."

I make myself more comfortable in my seat. "You make people adore you, care for you," I tell him. "They want to please you. They go out of their way to make you happy and they are afraid to disappoint you. You, however, are simply using them to get what you want. You don't care for them and never did. They serve a purpose. You are manipulating them. You are a master of the fine and ancient art of…" I pause for effect and slow my tongue and widen my mouth to annunciate each and every syllable, "…The psycho-fuck."

He just looks at me. He is not agreeing or disagreeing. He just looks right through me. I feel a shiver run up my spine. He knows I'm describing both of us.

Matteo is no ordinary run-of-the-mill businessman. He is a self-made man. He's the son of immigrants, raised in Queens with very little, other than a keen mind and an ambition to become respected and feared by his peers in the hyper-competitive development industry of New York. In this business it's not only what you know, but, to a large extend, who you know. Matteo knows a lot of people – people you want to know, and more than a few that you really don't want to know.

He isn't the biggest, but he is a rising star.

Matteo throws the best parties, drinks the finest wines, and surrounds himself with the sexiest female help. Matteo is currently working on something big, very big. My mission is to find out what that 'thing' is, and my current employer is paying me handsomely for this information.

I am blessed with the equipment necessary to carry out such a mission: the looks, the curves and the attitude. Being attractive, however, is not enough. My best asset is my well-proportioned sexual allure, blended with a devious and analytical mind. My natural passion and mystery fascinates men. I'm a great conversationalist and, in many ways, I'm Matteo's intellectual equal. It is an interesting dance. Matteo knows that I can have any man I set my mind (and body) to and, perhaps most importantly, he knows that I don't need him. If I want him, it's because I chose him, and for me to choose him he has to prove he is worth it. He has to woo me. I am a challenge and a man like Matteo needs a challenge.

Matteo is kind of right, but in this case completely wrong. I need him. More accurately, I need information. Information that is potentially worth millions. Once I had convinced Matteo to decide that he wanted me I mimicked his behavior and became part of his inner circle. Matteo includes me on his nightly outings with partners and friends, but those individuals can't provide me with the information I need.

Fortunately, I enjoy the task. Often, I add a different perspective to the conversation when in the company of his friends...and when that isn't enough I always have my ass to fall back on; or more accurately my pussy.

After slowly consuming most of the wine, Matteo casually turns to me and says, "I was debating whether or not I should share this with you, but I thought what the hell."

Was my one-year investment about to start paying off? Could this be the day?

"You have a secret admirer."

"Really?" I pause, trying not to look disappointed. *This is what I was waiting for?* "Tell me more."

"Last week at the Shangri-La…"

I interrupt. "Dale? He had some interesting dance moves."

Matteo laughs, shaking his head. "Not Dale."

I have an oblivious look on my face. "I didn't spend much time conversing with the other men in the room that night."

"Remember Elias?"

"Who?" I say in a high pitched voice while squinting my eyes in mock confusion.

"Elias. The lawyer. He came back to your place with your girlfriend…what was her name?

"Her name is Blair. I don't recall what he looks like. I may have had a bit too much to drink that night."

"C'mon Zoe. He likes you and is very well connected and it appears that he wasn't so interested in Blair. He asked for your number."

I know who Elias is. Anyone who reads a newspaper in New York knows Elias Macchetta. That is not the issue. I know Matteo well enough to know that he wants something. What is Matteo's intention for pushing me in Elias' direction?

"Are you sure? He didn't so much as look at me."

"Actually," he crosses his arms over his chest, "He thought you were a total bimbo."

"What?" Now I'm confused and curious. "That's a first."

"You didn't let me finish."

"There's more?"

"Initially he thought you were not worth his time…but that's not his current thinking."

"Why the change of heart?"

"At the end of the night when we were at your place he was looking around."

"You mean snooping? Did he find my sex swing?"

"No, Zoe. He saw your degrees hanging on the wall."

I laugh. "I knew I should have gotten rid of those things."

"He wants to get to know you. He thinks he may have misjudged you. He was impressed. Elias is not easily impressed."

Humans are predictable. Egotistical and selfish by nature, when they cling onto something, it's usually for a reason. *What can so-and-so do for me? How can so-and-so further my career? How can I get so-and-so into bed?*

What is Matteo thinking? Frankly, who cares what Matteo or Elias are thinking – I've been doing a little thinking of my own and know exactly how to play this. "Not interested, Matteo. It's very nice of him to give me a second chance, but you know very well I don't give second chances. Does he not recall you and I disappearing into my bedroom for a short time?" *What type of man could this Elias be?* "And besides, do you recollect the last time you set me up with someone you knew?"

"Who? Prince?" He laughs.

"He is an interesting one." I reach over to my purse and pull out my cellphone. "Care to glance at a few of his messages?"

Prince is the CEO of Crown Crane. I was introduced to him by Matteo a few months ago. I played along with Prince and his incessant sexting.

I personally have no interest in sexting. It isn't actionable. Prince's sweet-talking consisted of: *I want you to wear my wife's dirty underwear and I want to lick your pussy; Don't shower for a few days and I will come over and lick your clit.* I hold my cellphone out to Matteo to acknowledge the messages I have received from that sick mother-fucker.

Matteo pauses. I can tell he's curious, but he puts on his poker face, deciding what the best move should be. Does he want to invade his business associates personal space, or does he leave it alone?

I provide Matteo this opportunity to teach me proper etiquette as it pertains to his business associates. Does he satisfy his curiosity or does he ignore the temptation and make his own assumptions as to the character he does business with? Either way, it's a catch twenty-two.

"As tempted as I may be, I am going to politely decline."

"What a diplomatic response. I respect that decision. But may I ask why?"

"Sometimes you are better off not knowing."

I think of that as the cowardly approach. "Is that denial?"

"Perhaps, but I also hope you don't share our intimate moments with others."

"I wouldn't be here if you thought that was the case."

"Smart answer."

"I learn from the best."

Matteo sips his wine. "I can't take full credit." He laughs.

"So, I won't call you guru then?"

Matteo's laughter echoes into the hallway.

I take my last sip of wine. "Am I dismissed?"

"You, Zoe, are a man trapped in a woman's body."

Ignoring that comment, I stand up and begin to gather my belongings. "When am I going to see you again?"

"I am confident that I will see you soon enough. Think about Elias in the meantime".

Matteo leans forward to put his arms around me.

"It was fun," I reply to him as I walk out of his conference room, not turning back for a final glance.

I am confident that Matteo won't spend another moment thinking of me.

I, on the other hand, was thinking about him and our Saturday morning together. The bottle of wine he showed me, but did not serve, is a 59 Château Margaux. It's priceless. There are believed to be only six bottles in existence. Three of them are the property of the Queen of

England. Two were reputedly purchased last year from a Japanese collector's estate by an intermediary said to be acting for Vladimir Putin. The last bottle was the sole and exclusive property of his most royal eminence, the Sultan of Amin, known to his friends as Sully.

I was also thinking about Elias Macchetta.

I suspect the financing for Matteo's next deal is coming from Sully, who has been rumored to be acquiring land in New York. Matteo has been quietly making moves, purchasing parcels to change the city skyline. It is big. This is why I am so interested in getting to know Elias. I have a hunch he can shed some light on the situation. After all, he is the most prominent real estate lawyer in the city.

I know I told Matteo that I wasn't interested in seeing Elias but that isn't the case at all. I'm playing the game. It can't seem as though I am interested in seeing Elias. Matteo could become suspicious. My pussy and I have worked too long and hard to blow it now. The truth is, however, that I very much want to see Elias, and the sooner, the better.

I hop into my Audi, grab my phone from my purse, and text Matteo.

> Zoe: On second thoughts…why not? You convinced me. Pass my digits to Elias.

I put the car in gear and head home thinking to myself, *not a bad morning's work,* and I still have the rest of the day ahead of me.

# CHAPTER TWO

IT'S 1:00 PM AND I'm attempting to speed through the streets of Manhattan. *Damn traffic.* I enjoy the flashes of brilliant sun that rhythmically peek through the clouds. I could have headed to my apartment for a quick shower but I'm enjoying the combined scent of Matteo and sex on my skin. Post-orgasm euphoria. I feel alive and energized. I have the afternoon to myself prior to an evening of business, but I'm in no rush to get home, so I drive aimlessly, collect my thoughts, and try to make sense of what Matteo has just revealed. But before I go too much further with my tale, perhaps I should introduce myself.

I'm Zoe Winstein. On television they say: "Some of the names and places have been changed to protect the innocent." In this story all of the names and places have been changed to protect me and I'm far from innocent.

I was born and grew up in the Bronx. Not the Bronx of today where you can find a Michelin rated restaurant next to the methadone clinic, but the Bronx where being in the wrong place at the wrong time got you killed. Where you always had to keep an eye open, especially the eye in the back of your head. If you let your guard down one of the locals would help themselves to your money and sometimes your life. You had to know what streets to stay away from and which corners were trouble. I knew. I learned about life there and, despite the odds, I studied hard, worked evenings, and succeeded. I also knew that there was only so far you could go before the augmented gravity of the Bronx pulled you down. I couldn't stay there. What did I do? Fifteen years ago, I left.

I knew what I wanted, but first I needed to renew and purify my soul. My surroundings were a ball and chain. I had to leave so I could come back changed, armed and prepared to do battle. So I left, and promised myself that I wouldn't return until the new me was ready to take on the world.

My destination was Stanford University. With just under two thousand dollars in my bank account, a scholarship and a single suitcase, I bought a one-way ticket to California.

Thirteen years later, I returned to New York City with a PhD in Behavioral Psychology. My schooling and my research taught me a lot, including how to win, how to be a cold, emotionless woman whose core belief is functionality, and how to remain untouched as I navigate my way through the seamy sewers of the world's greatest city.

I am calculating, deliberate and always measure my risk before taking the plunge. I have learned and perfected how to persuade and control people – in other words, how to be the puppeteer – and I excel at it. I am so good that when I completed my PhD, job offers were flying in from multiple colleges and marketing firms due to my published work and lectures on the Psychology of Sales. I accepted a research offer from Manhattan College and made my way home. I also found work in a clinic with a limited number of patients. But study and practice couldn't take all my time. I had big plans. I was in a great place which I would use as a springboard to achieve my dreams. I was ready to be back.

I rented an apartment in Greenwich Village with a spectacular view. I didn't tell family or friends that I had returned, with the exception of Blair. Blair is my oldest friend. One day I would let everyone know, but for now I needed to start anew. My routine was simple – gym, work, research then home. I enjoyed the independence and freedom. I needed structure and calm in my life. I was planning and looking for opportunities. I am and always will be an opportunist. If you work hard and keep your wits about you the opportunities will come to you.

And that was when I met Stefano…over a scoop of ice cream. Little did I know how significant the repercussions of accepting such a seemingly innocent gesture would be. Only later did I realize how helpful my skills would be in exploiting the opportunity. Stefano became my mentor and my muse, and I became his. He quickly intuited that I was very much like him with some important physical differences, chiefly a pretty face and a body that could get me with people and into places Stefano could only dream about. Stefano is smart and devious, and had finally met someone who understood him. We made quite a team.

Intellectually we were equals, and with my looks and charm and his hard-earned knowledge we were unstoppable. We would have dinner together, and I would, on occasion, suck his cock. We weren't lovers, but I loved teasing him and feeling his cock throb and swell in my mouth. He wanted me sexually and I wanted him in my own way. I needed him to enjoy my company, our conversations, our plans and our one-way sex. Why? Because I knew. I don't know how I knew, but I knew that Stefano was the one, the one who would get me to the next level…long term. I wasn't sure yet what opportunity Stefano was offering, but I was certain we would figure it out together. I liked Stefano and I'm a patient woman.

On our outings, Stefano would watch me work the room. All the men would gravitate toward me and open their hearts, while trying to open my shirt and slip their sweaty hands into my elegant, lacy bra. He sat back and smiled, confident that I would be leaving with him, enjoying and understanding the power I had over these men. He knew I was good at reading people. He knew that I could be his Mata Hari, so why not let Mata Hari get to work?

And put me to work he did.

Stefano Souzas is a real estate developer. He was a smallish developer then, but he was smart and hungry, was growing quickly. Interest rates were falling, asset values were rising, and Stefano was riding the wave. Stefano saw a niche for my talents. What talents? Did I mention that I love sex? Sex is definitely one of my best talents. Actually, although it has become a talent, it is more a gift, a blessing. I can't get enough sex. I have never met a man that can keep up with me. And because I love sex, I have practised it a lot and become very good at it. Very, very good. And it has become part of my arsenal. My arsenal for getting information.

Information is key in the development industry. What areas are becoming sought after? What deals are happening? What deals are falling apart? Extracting information in the development world can be challenging. You never know if what you're hearing on the streets is truth, lies, or deliberate misinformation. Misinformation is a big part of the game in development. Point competitors one way so you can quietly go about your work elsewhere. I don't know the development business but I know Sun Tzu and *The Art of War*. Distract the enemy by giving false information. Always create multiple stories so that they can never be sure of what's real and what's not.

I was good at connecting the dots. If something didn't add up I would question its validity and discount it. I was very good at getting information for Stefano. I'm not going to lie and tell you that I did it using only my brains, because that couldn't be farther from the truth and, more importantly, what would be the fun in that? Sex plays a central story in my life and in this story. Don't judge me and please don't feel bad for me. My brain and my pussy have found this job very stimulating and my net worth has swelled like Stefano's cock in my mouth. I think you get the idea. But I'm getting ahead of myself.

My current job for Stefano is to get information about Matteo's latest development. It's not easy, but if it were I couldn't charge Stefano what I'm charging. This isn't a few lots in Queens or some brownstone retrofit in Harlem that we're talking about. This is the big time and it is taking longer than anticipated, but the payoff will also be larger. New challenges need new strategies, but more about that later. For now, it's time to race back to my apartment. I'm ready for that shower, ready to meet my muse.

# CHAPTER THREE

HE ARRIVES AT 9:00 PM sharp, as promised, driving a Ferrari. Red, of course. A 488 Spider for the aficionados. The scent of his mid-life crisis oozes from his every pore. Stefano is a paradox. When in a crowd, he is the one doing all the talking, the only 'mother-fucker' in the room who has the balls to call a spade a spade. He doesn't give a fuck what others think of him, you either adore him or loathe him. His business associates would outright call him a selfish SOB who they would never do business with again, but I knew Stefano as a lonely mother-fucker incapable of loving anyone, including himself. He is my 'so-called' employer, or so he would like to believe, and when you work for Stefano, he treats you like one of his possessions.

He isn't attractive. But he is rich. VERY RICH.

"Great waist to ass ratio babe," he calls to me as he makes his way out of the driver's seat.

My hips sway seductively with each step as I head towards the passenger door. I am rehearsing for the night.

"Wow, Stefano, you're a mathematician too?"

Stefano laughs sarcastically and holds the passenger door open for me. Just as I am about to get in, he snatches my right wrist and draws my lips to his.

"What a beautiful dress." Stefano kisses me and looks deeply into my eyes. "I hope it doesn't come with underwear."

My body shivers. I'm not sure if I'm repulsed or stimulated. It's usually both.

I sit silently as he drives. I know that one of the characteristics Stefano appreciates about my company is my ability to be seen but not heard.

"Be on your best behavior tonight," he says, listening to *Luck Be a Lady Tonight*, which he plays for me. He knows me well.

He doesn't need a response. I sit there and enjoy the blurred city lights reflecting on the passenger window. At 43rd he makes a sharp right turn, the tires gripping tightly to the rain slicked pavement as he whips around the corner.

Stefano slows down and veers into a dark, narrow alleyway. An alleyway that is all too familiar. As we got closer to the far end, the lights from George's came into view. George's is your average greasy spoon - and that's being generous - empty except for maybe a couple of hundred cockroaches. But George's, as I know, offers one thing that a greasy spoon would not regularly offer - valet parking.

Stefano gets out of the car. A very large man appears out of the shadows, nods to Stefano like they know each other, and takes his keys.

Stefano turns around and says, "Get out, babe."

"Don't you think I'm a little over dressed for a burger joint?" I stay in my seat and contemplate locking the doors, for pure amusement and entertainment. I have this desire to put on a show for Stefano. "It's up to you who has the keys to your fancy car, but I really need to get home at some point tonight, and I think your chances of ever hearing the lovely purr of this engine again are slim." I know exactly what lies behind George's façade, but I play stupid.

"Just get out of the fuckin car."

We make our way to the entrance. Stefano reaches for me. I instinctively move towards him and allow him to take my arm. I enjoy being controlled. It turns me on to be forced to do things I would never otherwise do. How can I be blamed for the bad things I do if someone else is forcing me to do them?

We walk into George's and my pumps click on the checkered tile flooring typical of a 'back in the day' diner. At the tail end of the place there is a white phone camouflaged against the pale white walls. I walk towards it and count the eighteen steps to get from the front entrance to the phone hanging on the wall.

"Pick up the receiver," says Stefano in his authoritative tone.

I hesitate. "Why?"

"Just do it."

I pick up the receiver and hear a deep voice say, "How many people in your party?"

"Two." I should be winning an Oscar for my performance tonight.

To my right, the hidden doorway clicks open, revealing a dark, narrow opening.

"What are you waiting for? We don't have all fuckin night." His fingertips press up against my lower back, nudge me forward into the darkness.

I take my first step into the tunnel, with Stefano right behind me. I can feel his exhalations on the back of my neck.

The entrance is the best part of Plato. Everything else is anti-climactic. Once my eyes adjust to the darkness I notice handsome, naked men and voluptuous women to both my left and right, chained to the walls, their eyes inviting you to touch them, to feel them. These men and women are gorgeous and serve a purpose, they are demons ready to extract your soul in exchange for a night of sin. It is a good offer and, on another night, or perhaps in another life, I would have considered it, but tonight my plan is to keep my soul intact and my wits about me. As I continue to walk through the narrow corridor, the demons reach out as far as their chains permit, brush me with their fingertips. Their touch is electric, providing instant gratification. I feel desired and I want more. The distraction causes me to forget all about Stefano, temporarily.

I feel guilt, but guilt is foreplay for me.

Stefano nudges me forward, leaving the delicious demons behind in the dark tunnel. We enter a cavernous room with black ultra-violet lighting, in the center of which is a perfectly square white marble bar with mirrored walls which allow guests to glimpse their own reflection at any moment, at every turn. Overhead, glittering crystal chandeliers hang from the thirty-foot ceiling, dangling just inches above the heads of the perfectly sculpted mannequins, standing on podiums in awkward poses, their mirrored mosaic tiles throwing back disorienting reflections, blinding those daring enough to take a peek.

Stefano brings me back to reality. "Wait here."

Before I can utter a word, he disappears into the crowd. I am left standing in the middle of the mob. My eyes gaze in every direction. Stefano may have asked for me to 'wait here', but I'm not one to obey.

I make my way to the bar, looking to make eye contact with the bartender.

Instead my eyes land on the tall, lean man at the far end of the bar. He has greasy slicked-back hair, oversized green eyes, chiseled facial features with high cheek bones. He is obviously in pursuit of his next lay. His eyes wander the crowd - lingering in all directions - appreciating the bevy of enticing women surrounding him. I imagine his cock throbs as his eyes reach out to those women, who stand in pairs, waiting for the moment where his eyes will lock with theirs, to speak to one another through the art of body language. His tactic is to use empathy to get laid.

I glance to my right, to the slender red-head sitting perched on an ottoman. She leans forward, her back slightly arched to expose her smooth, firm breasts. She is looking for her next sugar daddy, selling the dream of a sexy, fiery red-head, with long, flexible legs. She is experienced, knows to speak only when asked a question, how to bat her eyelashes in order to receive those materialistic rewards that bring her temporary happiness.

In the center of the room I notice a gentleman wearing a cowboy hat, carrying a black Tumi leather-bound briefcase. He is unrolling his wad of cash, showing the world he has made it. *Look at ME!* – his attire screams. He is a true cowboy from Texas.

I won't allow myself to be fooled. I see things for what they are. It is an occupational hazard for me to be out in the wild observing these creatures, their behavior so predictable as animals in the wild.

I feel a hand rest against my waist. "Let's go."

Before I reply, Stefano grabs my wrist and drags me to the other side of the club. The strobe lights flash to the bass, bringing awe to the facial features of those in the crowd. We arrive at a corner booth where a small group lounge on the deep velvet cushions.

"Zoe, I would like to introduce you to Paul, John, Samantha and Elias. Gentlemen, and lady, this is Zoe."

My heart begins to pound, my body motionless. It's Elias! *Shit!* How do I react? Do I pretend as though I don't know him? Has Matteo spoken with him already? Does he know Matteo told me about his interest in me? My heart begins to race. *Fuck me!* Does he think I know anything? My mind rapidly calculates the possibilities. I'm totally off my game. *SHIT!*

"Good evening," I say with a feigned confidence.

"Please have a seat." John shifts over in the booth, offering me the seat next to him.

I glance at Stefano and he gives me the nod. It's John I have to charm this evening.

"So," John pauses for a moment, "how do you know that guy over there?" He points to Stefano.

Paul and Samantha are distracted with one another at the end of the booth and Elias is intentionally zoning in on our conversation.

Elias leans forward. "Yes, how do you know one another?"

Typically, when I'm used as bait on a night out, I receive a list of clients who will be in attendance. I do my due diligence and research them, learning their interests and where they fit into the game plan. I am always well prepared and complete my homework; but tonight, I've had no prep time. I have to be on my 'A' game.

"He used to babysit me back in the Bronx and now that he is old and infirm I feel compelled to babysit him," as I point in Stefano's direction.

Stefano quickly responds, "Infirm, that's bullshit. I can still get firm...ish."

John and Elias chuckle, and I join in.

I look over at Stefano for his approval. Once again, he gives me an almost imperceptible nod. Elias notices.

"Full disclosure, we met at the gym."

John's eyes widen as he interrupts me with laughter. "Stefano works out!?"

"Now you're putting words in my mouth."

"My apologies. I assume it wasn't last week." John continues his subtle interrogation.

"I was a regular at the gym, and took notice of this loud and obnoxious fellow who would train with this guy that resembled The Rock, you know, the actor. One day, in the middle of my workout, Stefano walks in and I overhear him yelling at his personal trainer 'I'm late. Fuck this. Let's go for a ride.' Just as I was leaving the gym, Stefano and his trainer arrived back at the gym each with an ice cream in hand. For the sake of amusement, I asked him where mine was, to which he replied, 'Let's go!'. And that was the beginning of our friendship. That was just over two years ago."

John raises his eyebrows. "You became friends over a scoop of ice cream?"

"Two scoops," I reply with forced excitement.

"Let's ditch this joint and grab an ice cream." John winks at me.

Is he flirting with me? "Not before you tell me how you know Stefano."

"We go way back. I have known this guy for over twenty years."

"My condolences." I glance over towards Elias's direction and smile. His eyes are on me, quietly observing me.

"Stefano is a nut-ball," continues John. "We did a fifty-million-dollar deal on a napkin after knowing one another for three hours."

"I think it was more like three minutes," Stefano interrupts.

"And how did that work out?" I was curious as to how transparent John would be.

"Project was completed on time and on budget. That property was in Soho. Stefano managed the construction of the high-rise building. We all made money. Our first business deal."

"And why was Stefano the lucky partner?"

"Because he was the only potential partner who wasn't kissing my ass to make a deal. And because he taught me about FSL - fucking, sucking and licking." John can't keep a straight face.

Stefano bursts out laughing.

It's all true, except that this time Stefano isn't looking for a business partner - he is looking for me to get information from John. Now that John is in politics, he is a valuable player in Stefano's game. But I also know how valuable John is in my game.

I notice Elias staring at me. "Would you like a drink?"

"Why not? Let's go to the bar so these two can catch up."

Elias takes me by the hand as we negotiate the crowd. We finally arrive at the bar, surrounded by beautiful people.

Elias smiles and pulls a stool out, "Please take a seat." He takes a seat next to me and leans towards me, "What would you like to drink?"

*Do I mention anything about last week? Do I play it cool?*
"Vodka soda, please." I don't know where to look. I don't know what to say. So, I just sit there in silence.

It takes Elias a few minutes to get the bartender's attention. When he does, he leans in towards the bartender and orders our drinks. Elias doesn't say a word, nor I.

Our drinks arrive and he hands over my glass. Our eyes lock as he raises his glass to mine.

I clink my glass with his and down it within seconds.

Elias places his hand on my waist and leans towards me. "Who are you, Zoe? I can't figure you out."

I almost spit out my drink. I wasn't expecting that. My eyes still locked on his, I reply, "Anything else you want to share?"

He leans back and sits there in silence for a moment, then smiles. "Yes, there is something else I would like to tell you...actually ask you. When can we have dinner, just you and I?" His hand gently caresses my upper thigh.

I allow it, intrigued to see how this unfolds. Does he know I am pantiless?

I take his wandering hand and squeeze it in mine. I pause, to glance at our booth. "I'd better get back. Thanks for the drink." How am I attracted to this unattractive man? I release his hand and return to our booth without looking back. I can feel his eyes on my back. The hairs on my neck stand on end.

When I arrive at the booth, I glance back nonchalantly. Elias has disappeared.

Stefano and John are in business mode. I take my seat next to John, catch a fragment of the conversation.

"...we have an issue in block C. Our people in the rate payers group say that there is resistance to the plan among certain groups."

"Fuck them. I'm going to make them all rich," yells Stefano from across the booth.

I don't approve of Stefano's tactic, but it works...most of the time.

"I agree, but you have to get to those guys. One way or another." John turns to me, "Zoe, where did you disappear to?"

Elias has yet to return to the table, which is probably for the best.

"I wanted to give you and Stefano some alone time."

"That is very considerate of you. But enough with the business. Let's dance." John stands and holds out his hand to me.

I reach out and allow him to pull me onto the dance floor. Looking back, I see that Stefano has a smirk on his face. He doesn't know how to express his admiration for my approach with businessmen, and I would never ask him for affirmation. I don't need it from him. We both just know.

John escorts me to the dance floor, where we can't be seen by our present friends. He places both hands on my waist and pulls me in. I inhale and hold my breath for a few seconds. His body wraps around mine. Although John is in his mid-forties, he is solid. Six feet tall with broad shoulders, he is a man who has control, but he also has a sense of calm that I'm drawn to.

"You smell yummy," he says.

I move closer to him.

Game on.

I allow him to move my body closer to his. My arms wrap tightly around his shoulders. My body expresses trust, as I allow him to control my movements. My face presses against his chest. The music hypnotizes me.

John looks down at me. "You are too nice of a girl to be hanging out with Stefano."

I agree with him. Stefano is vulgar, rude and inconsiderate, none of which I am, but in other ways we are the same. "I have known Stefano for what feels like forever. He was there for me when I needed a good friend and I will never forget that. I'm loyal to my friends and accept them for who they are."

"For some reason I think you bring out a different side of people."

"What would make you say that?"

"Being in politics, I have to have my game face on 24/7. But with you, I don't need to pretend to be something I'm not."

*Who is fucking who here?* Great politicians are great actors. Can I believe a word he is saying? Probably not. "I have a simple answer for you. I have no expectations of you and am probably one of the very few people who isn't going to ask for a favor after knowing you for three minutes."

He laughs.

"I would hate to be in your position," I continue. "You never sincerely know if someone is genuinely friendly with you because they value your friendship, or if they want something from you. Similar to a man worth millions who is in search of true love. Are women with him because of his heart or his cash? If I was rich, I wouldn't let anyone know it."

"Smart woman."

*Remember what Matteo said, Zoe...'vulnerable.' Think fast.* "I get it from my father. He always insisted on me driving his Corolla when going on a date, in lieu of my Audi. He thought I'd frighten them off...I'm expensive and a lot of maintenance."

"Your father is a smart man."

*Vulnerable Zoe!* "Was a smart man. And yes." I am going to hell for this.

John squeezes me tighter. "My condolences, Zoe."

"Thank you, John. You ready for a drink?"

"Ready when you are."

Once we arrive to our booth, I turn to John and whisper in his ear, "Time to put on your poker face."

The rest of the evening consists of Stefano being the class clown while the drinks flow. I take on the role of Mata Hari, hoping to avoid the execution part. There was nothing for me to do, as John and Stefano talked for hours. I kept having drink after drink. I am careful not to overindulge in situations such as these, but my goal for the evening had been accomplished, so I took some liberties.

AFTER A FEW HOURS of this, Stefano finally gets up to leave, knowing that John is pleased. I stand up and I am unsteady on my feet. We say our good-byes and head back to my place.

Stopped at a red light, Stefano reaches out his right hand and caresses my inner thigh with his fingertips. "You did good tonight."

I nod and take a deep breath. My head is spinning and my stomach is not in good shape. I want so desperately to say, *no fuckin kidding*. I'm more than a little drunk, but I hold my tongue. Instead, I reply, "Your," *my*, "plan is well on its way."

"It better be," Stefano replies.

"Your previous relationship with him is beneficial to me." After a year of befriending Matteo, I needed a plan 'B' in case I got nowhere with him. So, I've done a little research myself. The construction industry, like a chess board, is simple to navigate once you know your key players and you can anticipate their moves. John is a key player. He is, after all, the Mayor of New York. I was clever enough to have Stefano introduce me to him. And with Elias just inches away, I now have two powerful men that are going to assist me in gaining the information I need. It is time to work my magic.

"Are you going to invite me upstairs?" he asks.

"I'm not feeling so well." I reply.

"That was a rhetorical question," he says in his possessive tone.

Stefano parks his car underground. The elevator ride is silent. We arrive to the Penthouse level and he follows me. As I turn the key to my door he touches my lower back with his fingertips. I cringe, but he most likely interprets that as interest in him.

I open the door and walk directly into my bedroom, while Stefano tails me. I have no interest in offering him a night cap or having a discourse about our outing. I've already had too much to drink. I don't want to prolong the evening any longer than I have to.

Without hesitation Stefano undoes the button on his pants and with some difficulty hunches down to remove them. I remain fully dressed and remind myself that sucking slow will bring him to a quicker climax. He lies on the bed and I crawl between his spread legs as he holds his penis up against his round belly. Knowing what he likes well enough, I start licking his balls while moving my tongue in a circular motion. Keeping my tongue soft is the trick, too much pressure too soon will only prolong this. I move from his balls to the shaft of his cock. His cock isn't erect, so I squeeze the base of it with my left hand and stroke it with my right. I intentionally avoid any eye contact as I lower my mouth onto his cock and begin going up and down...slowly. This lasts for what feels like an eternity. His penis slowly grows in my mouth. At this point he reaches into the pocket of his pants and pulls out a cock ring and hands it to me. I know the routine. I spread the cock ring and place it on the base of his cock. It's tight. I slowly suck and intentionally don't speed up. This drives him crazy and he eventually starts thrusting his cock into my throat all the while pinching and massaging his nipples. If he doesn't finish soon I will throw-up. Luckily, he is out of breath so I pause for a few moments, for him to re-focus. When he's ready again I begin to suck the tip of his cock while rolling my tongue around it. I pick up the tempo, sucking harder and faster until he finally comes. *Thank God.* There is no come. It all remains in him, until he removes his cock ring. How do I know he has come? His shriveled balls are telling. The whole procedure has lasted five minutes. I get off the bed unsteadily and straighten my clothes and prepare to leave while he dresses and cleans himself up. I wait at the door and kiss him on the cheek and say good night. I run to the bathroom and throw-up.

I used to enjoy pleasing Stefano, but that has faded. Our one-way love making was a turn-on but lately it had become mechanical and routine. Could it be a reflection of our professional relationship? Am I outgrowing Stefano? Is it time for Zoe to leave the nest?

I will think about that later. For now, I have homework. I have to make a new friend – John.

# CHAPTER FOUR

I SLOWLY OPEN MY EYELIDS as I roll onto my side to avoid the sunlight shining in through the blinds. I don't remember it ever being so bright. In addition to the bright light, the room is spinning, my breath reeks of liquor, and my hair is sticking to my face. I am lying in bed with food particles in my hair. I definitely over indulged last night at Plato. I close my heavy eyelids in the hope that I will sleep through this hangover. I definitely have no interest in starting the day.

I have just started to drift back to sleep when a text comes in, startling me. I ignore it. For the next few hours I need to sleep. The annoying beep signals another incoming text, and then two more. Could this be urgent? Or is this someone without patience? Or both?

I roll over and glance at my phone. It's both. The ever-impatient Stefano for whom everything is urgent.

Stefano: Morning Sunshine
Stefano: 1 PM @ 3rd Ave and E 12th St.
Stefano: Confirm
Stefano: ASAP
Stefano: NOW

Shit! I notice the time…almost noon. Doesn't this man spend any time with his family? Wasn't last night enough for him? I reluctantly respond.

Zoe: Confirmed.

As he gets older, Stefano becomes more driven, and more impatient. A year ago, I had made him fifteen million dollars with information from Chad Greenberg, general counsel and minority partner for a medium size developer, Lion Corp. Chad was a middle aged lothario with a need to impress his lover – that being me - with all the big deals he was doing. He enthusiastically enjoyed anal sex. Not giving…getting. The more fingers I used, the more details he blabbed. I guess you could say he had a big fucking mouth. On one of these deals the land assembly was far from complete. To make a rather long and involved story short, Chad and his partners had to pay Stefano fifteen million for the strategically located parcel Stefano acquired while the Lion partners were enjoying their vacation in the Turks and Caicos Islands. That was an expensive vacation and the last time Chad got screwed in the ass by me. My take: one million. That was what Stefano and I had agreed upon, a million dollar bonus but it came with strings attached – in this case, being at Stefano's beck and call, 24/7.

I spend half hour getting ready before I rush out the door. The crisp air is like a slap in the face and I welcome it. I feel a little peculiar today. Vulnerable, yet strangely, fearless. I feel like an ancient warrior, although slightly hungover, living in the moment, pumped and ready for battle. I am ready to take on the world!

I hail a cab and make my way to 3rd Avenue and East 12th Street. In the cab I entertain myself by people watching, observing strangers speed walking on the streets of Manhattan. The driver brings me back to reality.

"North or south side sweetie?" he asks.

"Right here is fine. Thank you."

I swing the door open and slowly get out of the cab, waiting for Stefano's arrival.

I look down at my watch. 12:54 PM. As I raise my head and look straight ahead, Stefano has materialized right in front of me.

"Walk with me," he says.

We walk east on 12th Street. I don't say a word and fall in step with him. We walk half a block and he stops, looks to his left before turning right down a narrow alley. I follow. Stefano loves his alleys.

I catch up to him at the end of the alley and notice a sign that was out of sight from 12th Street. It reads 'Revue Theatre'. Stefano enters through a purple metal door and I trail behind him. The sign is misleading – this may have been a theatre once, but now it is more like a post-apocalyptic bar. Everything is from a bygone era, with the exception of the up-dated bar. A hidden gem, it has the look and feel of a 70's porn set. Stefano loves vintage porn and he subjects me to watching it with him now and then. The walls are emerald green, with candle chandeliers hanging throughout the space. We are the only ones present, excluding the bartender. Vintage tables and random style chairs are scattered throughout the space, a florescent pink couch with white cording boa trim in the corner. Stefano walks over to a corner table and takes a seat. He has a clear view of the entrance and I have a clear view of him. The Revue Theatre is not one of Stefano's usual haunts. He is usually very predictable, a man of habit. *Why is he here* and, from my perspective, more importantly, *why has he brought me here?*

The bartender/waiter – and for all I know headliner in the porn film – makes his way to our table with drink menus in hand. Stefano stops him before he makes it to our table, "Give us a few minutes, kid."

I turn my head and watch the bartender retreat to the bar.

"You are extremely quiet, Zoe."

I am. I typically take charge in situations like this, but my thoughts are in over-drive. "Just a little distracted."

"With?"

"Calculating, extrapolating, fornicating," I reply.

"Well that better change." His eyes look directly into mine and then he cracks a smile, "The first two anyway."

I don't look away. I smile back.

Stefano and I have a connection. Stefano shares his deepest and darkest secrets with me. For someone like him to talk about his feelings and weaknesses is challenging, yet he hints them to me on occasion. All I have to do is read between the lines. I know more about Stefano than his wife. Stefano's past is a haunted one that to this day has affected his ability to love. His coldness derives from his childhood. When he spoke to a professional a few years ago, Stefano told the psychologist to 'fuck off'. The thought of speaking about his past angered him. He was abused, and no one was there to protect him.

Perhaps we are more similar then I would like to admit. Stefano was, scratch that, IS a very smart guy. I know how to make him happy. I also know how to get under his skin and make his blood boil. I am loyal to him in my own way but I am feeling restless. It is time to move on, but not just yet. I always do what I promise to do. I gained his confidence immediately when I began working with him, gave him information which was later verified, let him know who his friends were and who were not. Stefano opened up a crack and started to let me in.

Stefano is also an impetuous and sometimes reckless man. His big mouth has landed him in some very dangerous situations, like the time he called his friend's mistress a 'stupid cunt'. His 'friend', a forming contractor with silent partners in the Sicilian mafia, caught up with

Stefano in Miami and gave him a beating he will never forget. Stefano has been paying for that mistake ever since, paying in the literal sense.

I scrutinize Stefano's facial expression and say in an even tone, "Matteo is useless."

Stefano places his hand under his chin, pauses for an instant and says, "Sometimes I think you are a useless fucking bitch."

Immune to his vulgar language I ignore his outburst, respond without hesitation. "Calm down and listen," *you repulsive piece of shit.* If only I could blurt out the latter.

"I think I will decide what is necessary. And why the fuck should I calm down?"

This is the Stefano I know. He isn't upset. He knows what is going on. He just loves the banter.

And so do I.

"I know this is taking longer than anticipated. However, your new strategy," *my strategy*, "is more effective. Introducing me to John is a great starting point."

He pauses for a moment. "You better know what you are fuckin doing."

I smile.

"What have you found out about this 'big deal' Matteo is working on?"

I didn't ask for the back story between him and Matteo. I didn't need to. Besides, I have plans of my own. "Do you play chess?" I ask Stefano with a smile on my face.

"Who the fuck gives a shit about Chess. Answer the fuckin question."

"Life is like a game of chess, Stefano. I'm playing the Queen's Dance."

"What the fuck are you talking about?"

"The Queen's Dance is when the Queen checkmates her opponent with the assistance of her King. Are you my King Stefano?" I raise my eyebrows and smile at him.

He rolls his eyes and mumbles something under his breath and then very clearly says, "I think it's time for a drink." He makes eye contact with the bartender and flags him over to our table.

"What will the lady be drinking?"

"Vodka soda please."

Stefano interjects, "I'll have the same, except double."

The bartender nods.

I'm not sure what Stefano is thinking or how he is going to respond. He looks around the room. "What an interesting place. Portrait paintings surrounding the room, and then you have this one-off panda painting. What do you think that's about?"

What a random thought, but so true. "Carelessness? Intentional? Who will ever know?"

"Why don't you ask the owner?" He smirks.

I think about it for a moment. "What's the deal with the panda Stefano? I must say, totally unexpected and out of character for you."

"Never reveal all, Zoe. Keep them guessing."

"So why the panda?" I ask.

"It wasn't carelessness."

My eyebrows rise, we are having fun.

"It's the anomaly. We meet characters, many characters, and we lose interest quickly, but every once in long while, we meet a character we want to get to know…someone we actually want to spend time with. Someone who makes us re-evaluate ourselves. You know, look at the world in a different way." He pauses. "You are my panda, Zoe."

Our drinks arrive. We both raise our glasses and look into one another's eyes.

He toasts, "To Pandas."

I reply, "To Pandas."

Our eyes are still locked as we take our first sip. I know he is in love with me. He knows he is in love with me, but Stefano can't really love, he loves the only way he knows how, and that is not the love I want.

"You, Zoe, are like no other woman I know."

"Really?"

"Yeah. The smartest and stupidest woman I know all rolled into one."

I laugh, "Thanks…I think." I pause a moment. "Remember our first dinner together?"

"How could I forget."

"You picked me up and took me to that lobby bar."

"The Chelsea."

"Yes, the Chelsea. Crystal chandeliers and renaissance paintings. I was wearing that yellow Dior dress that flowed to the floor. It matched my blonde hair. I miss being a blonde." My eyes look away. I'm transported back to that night. Lost in the moment, I continue. "My back was to the bar, sitting on a stool, amusing myself by people watching."

"You know how to spot talent."

"The only talent in the room that night that had even slight potential were the three in the corner booth, so I decided to have a bit of fun with them. I pulled out a prop from my purse, handed it to the bartender and asked him to deliver it to the man in the blue suit. At first, he laughed, then he had that puzzled look on his face. He hesitated, but in end agreed to deliver it."

"Handcuffs. I knew then and there we were meant for each other."

"And that is my plan with John."

"What, to handcuff him?"

"To have him trust me enough to be handcuffed."

"You think you can manage that in a reasonable time frame?"

"I am confident I will."

"Good."

It was time to make my exit. "Am I dismissed?"

"You didn't finish your drink."

I grab my glass and guzzle the rest of it. "Now am I dismissed?"

"Lunch this week?"

"Sure. In the meantime I will get in touch with John."

"Get it done, Zoe," Stefano replies in a firm tone. He may love me but he's all business. He loves the game and he loves to win. But then again, so do I.

"I was going to visit him at his office."

"Want his number?" He reaches for his phone attached to his belt strap.

I roll my eyes. "Don't worry about it. I'm bringing him a gift."

"It had better not be your pussy."

"Can't say it's better than that, but a distant second."

"Not your mouth either."

I laugh. "Creative response. Not those gifts, a book."

"A book?" he laughs.

"A book every politician should have."

"Whatever you say, Zoe."

I stand up and give Stefano a hug. "Now go home."

"Where are you going in such a rush, why don't you stick around?"

"You're becoming almost human in your old age Stefano. If I didn't know you better I'd say you were missing me."

"Don't get carried away, Zoe. Let's just say I have a soft spot in my heart for those who make something hard in my pants."

"Bye, Stefano."

"No pussy or mouth! Those are for me and me alone!" he shouts as I walk away.

"Yes, boss," I reply from a distance.

I step outside. The day has turned grey and a cool breeze is blowing. I have had enough excitement for the day and am ready to embrace the evening. I hail a cab.

"Where to?"

"Hudson and 11th please." It was time to rest...I had earned it.

## CHAPTER FIVE

WHEN I ARRIVE HOME, I remove my heels and head straight into the kitchen to pour myself a glass of wine. I make my way to the couch, turn on the television and surf aimlessly. I am preoccupied. My mind is full of thoughts that I try to push off for another time, but they seem to have caught up with me. Am I free from my past? I have what I always wanted, at least in the material sense, so why is there this feeling of dread, this fear? Fear of what? Uncertainty? What am I doing it for? Before I can take my first sip of wine, my eye lids shut tight, and I'm gone.

I wake a few hours later, once again to an incoming text. I glance at it for mere amusement.

Unknown: Hungry?

I am. But who could this be? I choose to respond nonetheless.

Zoe: Always.
Unknown: Pick you up in an hour.
Zoe: And with whom will I have the pleasure of dining this evening?

Unknown: Surprise.

I'm intrigued. Dinner with a mystery diner at an unknown location? I don't respond immediately. I take a moment to think. Is it John? I don't think so. Not his style at all, this feels much too playful for him. I am curious. I like this game, but then I guess I like all games – they give me the chance to win, and I love winning.

Zoe: Need an address?
Unknown Name: See you soon!

With an hour to spare and prepare myself for my evening of mystery, I decide that conservative attire will be appropriate for the 'unknown individual'. A white blouse, navy blazer, blue jeans, pumps, a hint of make-up, hair up, with thick framed glasses. Very demure.

IT'S 7:00 PM AND I don't receive another text from the mystery date, so I head downstairs and wait in the lobby. Within minutes an orange Lamborghini pulls into the roundabout. *Who do I know that drives an orange Lamborghini?* It stops, and a woman gets out and runs into the building, straight past me, without a second glance. An instant later a white Civic pulls up and stops at the lobby doors. I see the driver's door open and Elias gets out.

"I'm glad you were hungry, I'm feeling a bit peckish myself."

I can't believe my eyes. Elias in a Civic. I'm speechless. After what feels like half a minute I say, "A girl's got to eat."

He embraces me. He is strong.

Attempting to breathe, I say, "Just so you know, the way to my heart is through my stomach."

"Shouldn't that be my line?" he responds as he releases me from his arms.

"If that's the route I will never make it to your heart. I don't cook, not at all, zero, nada, niente," I snigger.

"If you really cared about me you would learn," he says laughing. He opens the passenger door and I take my seat. He makes his way around the car, gets in and drives north.

As much of a control freak as I am, I decide to not ask where we are headed for dinner and just allow the night to unfold the way Elias intends it.

Elias looks over at me for much too long and says, "You look great…actually maybe better than that."

"Thanks," I say, "but what's better than great?" I smile in kind.

"Super great of course. Zoe Winstein you look Super Great!"

I laugh, tentatively, uncertain how to take him. Is he serious or is he making fun of me? I'm usually confident and self-assured, but right off the bat I'm caught off-balance with Elias. I have to regain the high ground. I could take a guess as to how he desires me to respond, but I refuse to give him what he wants. At least, for now. "I feel as though you know a lot about me, but I know nothing about you."

"Really?" he responds in an ambivalent tone. "What do I know? I know the company you keep, I know you disappeared for fifteen minutes the other night. I know that you are a psychologist. But other than that, I know very little about you."

"I guess that gives us a lot to talk about over dinner."

"Indeed, it does."

We reach the meat-packing district, he parks the Civic and we walk arm-in-arm, stop in front of a place called Paradox.

The hostess notices Elias and quickly comes to him. "Good evening, Elias."

"Sandra. How are you?"

*Great. A regular.*

"Good. Table for two?"

"Yes please."

We follow her to a table in the back corner and we take our seats.

"Can we please have that Cabernet from Napa I had last time." Elias is keen to get the night started. He looks at me and asks, "Is that okay with you?"

"Of course."

"Let's get this party going. For appetizers we'll have the octopus and the chanterelles. Maybe the cod croquette as well. I will let Michael decide what we should have for our mains. Whatever he pleases. Unless of course the lovely Zoe has a specific wish."

"Nope." *But you can ask me again after dinner.*

I watch Elias as he commandeers the evening. He is a breath of fresh air, the exact opposite of the men I typically keep company with. Most men allow me to take control of the situation, but not Elias.

"What do you have in store for me tonight, Mr. Mysterious?" I pretend to be cool, calm and collected but I'm not at all. I'm nervous. I can't peg him, and it frightens me a little. I feel vulnerable.

"I met you a week ago with Matteo. Last night you were with Stefano and John. You are a popular woman."

"Is that a question?" I smile, challenging.

"You know a lot of important people."

"I have friends, yes. As do you, since you are friends, or at least acquainted, with the very same people."

"Yes, but they're just friends."

"Why are your friends 'just friends' and my friends are somehow more than friends?"

"Like all good lawyers, I think you already know the answer. I'm a little jealous."

I am off kilter. He is the lawyer, not me. What an odd conversation. Here is a man I have just met and barely know telling me he is jealous.

"Stefano is a smart man who started with nothing and took risks," I tell him. "That's my kind of man. He is a mentor. He motivates me, and I enjoy spending time with people that motivate me. However, we're just friends, no more. Matteo and I met a year ago. He was out with some friends and I joined them for a few drinks. I think he thought I was fun to hang around with. So, I'm part of the entourage, as you witnessed last week." I won't tell him that I had planted myself at that bar to meet Matteo. That I had done my homework, knowing his usual spots and the company he keeps. I knew exactly how to lock myself in with Matteo at our first official meet-and-greet.

He takes a moment before responding. "You are fun to hang around with, Zoe."

"I know I am, but you're completely indifferent towards me."

"You've fractured my ego. It doesn't happen often – or more truthfully, it happens with disturbing regularity but I don't usually care. With you I do and I'm not happy."

I pretended not to notice him last week. I allowed Blair to entertain him that night, knowing full well that he would come after me. But I won't tell him that either. I just smile. "As I remember it, Elias, you were the one who wasn't paying attention. You didn't even notice my best dance moves."

He smiles. "Maybe initially. You aren't exactly my type. How would I know you are special? You didn't say a word."

"Is this when I stand up and leave?" I laugh. "Why did you invite me to dinner if you thought I was a bimbo, not to put words in your mouth?"

"I was the bimbo. I was bored. I'd had too many drinks. Your friend was talking too much. I wasn't really paying attention. I am typically right, but in this case, I was completely wrong. You tricked me. I had written off the evening and couldn't wait for the cab to take me home when all of a sudden on my way out of your apartment I saw your degrees in your home office. I have a few degrees myself, but not five, Zoe. What can I say, I made a mistake."

"Is that why I get dinner?"

"I'm very attracted to you, Zoe, but as you probably know, I'm married."

Elias is a man in his late forties, not much in the looks department. Medium height, thin and particularly handsome. He is completely not my type. I have no interest in him physically. Professionally, however, I know he can be of service. "Happily married I assume?"

"I love my wife and have no intention of ever leaving her."

"I'm happy you're happy and I have no interest in you leaving your wife." *And I'm not kidding.*

"I had someone very dear to me in my life for ten years."

"I'm trying to connect the dots but need some context here."

"Her name was Lennox. It ended over a year ago..."

I interject, "And you are looking for a replacement."

"Easy there, Zoe. I just want to know who the real Zoe is: Bimbo, brain surgeon, or something in between?"

"Maybe a bit of a, b and c, and by my own admission, a big dash of d, crazy. Zoe may be hazardous for your health."

"I always wanted to be with a woman who comes with warning from the surgeon general."

I laugh. At least he is funny. "Let me rephrase." I look him straight in the eyes and slowly utter, "I am dangerous."

"I wouldn't expect anything less. I hate safe and normal," he replies.

"My definition of normal is a temperature between hot and cold."

Elias smiles. "I like."

"Don't be stealing my material."

"Damn." He laughs.

The wine arrives along with the appetizers. I feel defenceless and weak with Elias and I'm coming under his strange spell. What is going on? When you least expect it something strange happens. Why am I telling him about myself? Why am I just blabbing away? Why am I so comfortable around him? I sense I can be myself and he won't pass judgement. I feel that in many ways we are the same. Maybe he's crazy like me, a little bit dangerous too. He isn't normal, that's for sure. I take a sip of wine. For once I consider being just me, then my logical brain reminds me that would be a stupid idea.

"What is it that you are looking for, Zoe?"

I almost choke on my wine and begin to cough. "My life is complicated."

"Are you married? Seeing someone?"

I laugh out loud. "Never married, one hundred percent single, and always seeing someone or two."

"Good answer. But what are you looking for?"

"I'm not one to disclose my intentions." I take a deep breath before continuing. "I will say that I have never had a desire to be tied down with someone." I'm not acting this time. I'm being genuine. "I can't imagine walking down the aisle in a white dress, living an unfulfilled life. I'm not judging – Lord knows I can't sit in the judgment seat – but personally I just couldn't do it." I take a sip of wine. "I actually feel sorry for married people living a lie." My gut is telling me that Elias is different, but my brain is telling me otherwise.

"Here is what I think you're saying: You want to love and be loved but you don't trust yourself or anyone else and therefore you decided to take yourself out of the game."

I burst out laughing once again. "Is that it, Doctor Mystery?" I reply in a sarcastic tone.

"Why are you so cold and calculating, Zoe?"

"When you have a past like mine it tempers you."

"What do you mean by a past like yours."

"I don't want to get into it with you now, Elias, but my childhood was mostly about me being a codependent." Elias is attentive. And I can't stop talking. "I endured a lot of pain from loved ones growing up."

"I'm sorry to hear that." Elias brings his chair next to mine and holds my hand. "And now?"

I don't know what it is, but Elias brings out a different side of me. His energy seems genuine and sincere. This man is getting to me. I can't stop. "My entire life, all I have wanted to do was take pain away from others. I thought I was strong enough to take on the pain of the world." A tear rolls down my cheek.

"OK, Zoe. Let's get out of here."

"But what about dinner?" I pause. "I'm sorry."

"Sorry? For what?"

"For ruining our night."

"Zoe, you didn't ruin it. I hope we become friends, good friends. I think we will."

He stands up and takes me by the hand and walks me to the car. I have the urge to kiss him, but I just hold his hand on the ride home. Sometimes that's all we need, a little human touch, right? Except this is me we're talking about.

# CHAPTER SIX

I INVITE ELIAS in for a night-cap. I'm not the least bit attracted to him, but I am curious, and this is business. I lead him into the bedroom. Uncertain as to how I was going to begin, I place my arms around his shoulders, close my eyes as I nibble on his lower lip. His frame feels different, he is all bones, his body feels frail compared to the typical New York businessman body I am used to. It doesn't feel right. I most definitely am not enjoying this experience, but I soldier on and continue, focusing on the job at hand.

I open my eyes and he is leaning on one arm, staring deeply into my eyes. It doesn't intimidate me, on the contrary, I feel a tingle in my belly. I move my hands down his back and bring his body closer to mine. He wraps his arms around me and squeezes me tight. He is surprisingly strong. I return the gesture and tighten my arms around him. His touch is delicate and passionate, he knows how to touch a woman, and I begin to react. I still feel that there is something missing, but I choose to ignore the feeling. I begin to apply more pressure onto his lips. Our tongues are intertwined and my hands move away from his back to his face. I am beginning to enjoy him and I become more engaged.

Before I know it, passion fills me. It's a cliché but it's like an electric current, energy running through my body. My body just starts to suck in energy and winds me up until I'm ready to explode. I push him onto the bed and undo the top button of his jeans, tilt my head, as I look up at him and gaze into his eyes as I slowly unzip his fly with my teeth. He is loving it, gently thrusting his hips up and down, anticipating the moment when my mouth will envelop his cock. I tug on his pants to remove them, only for him to sit up and once again kiss me on my lips, moving to my neck and biting it. I like his moves. He is not at all passive. I move away and completely remove his pants. My hands grip his shoulders and push him onto his back. He raises his neck to have full view as I lick his inner thigh and gently caress his torso with my fingertips. I have yet to remove his briefs.

I want so desperately to sink my nails into his skin and leave a permanent mark on his body, to brand him, to let the world know that this is Zoe's and she has bent him to her will, but he is married.

I place my right hand into his briefs and grab his surprisingly long cock. This guy keeps surprising me. Deep throat isn't going to be as easy as I thought. Thankfully, however, his cock is long but not too girthy. I can handle it. I remove his briefs and lick the tip of his cock as I tickle his balls with my fingertips. I'm not ready for him to explode in my mouth just yet, I want him to wait. I want to tease him. I want to feel his cock at the back of my throat. He grabs my hair and pushes it down forcefully on his cock.

"Suck it baby. Take it all," he says.

He isn't one-bit shy. Somehow, he anticipates my desires. I want him to take control of me. To use me.

"Call me your dirty whore," I urge him. "Do it." I know a thing or two myself and I know how to push him to get what I want. I love this dance.

"Suck my cock, you slut. I'm going to come in your mouth and you're going to swallow it all like the dirty little whore you are."

I move my mouth to the base of his shaft and deliberately lick his cock to the tip, move my tongue around the head. His body tells me he is ready. His hips thrust six inches off the bed. He again grabs a handful of hair and slowly pushes my head down as he thrusts his hips up forcing his long cock deep into my throat. He is pacing himself and me, he is controlling me while I please him. I open my warm mouth and willingly accept his cock. I resist his pressure. After many strokes and a lot of sucking and gagging, my lips finally contact his tight abs as his cock pushes against the back of my throat. I gag again, but he doesn't allow that to stop him, nor me for that matter. He thrusts deeper into my throat, and his eyes widen. "Oh God, that's good," he moans.

I change tactics and begin to tease him once again. The tip of my tongue barely touches his ridged shaft as it travels up from the base of his balls, gently moving upwards while my eyes stare right at him through my glasses, my mischievous grin firmly fixed in place. I edge upwards to the tip of his head, and I taste his pre-come just as I reach the tip.

He is ready. I can see it in his eyes. I take a long, gentle stroke upward on his ridged cock and at the same time I lick the bulging tip free of its white droplets. This isn't a job anymore. I'm loving this. I'm loving it a lot. I thoroughly enjoy pleasing him, his forcefulness, his dominance, his certainty. And I love how he moves, and how he is making me squirm. I want to please him. I continue teasing and being just as mischievous with him before it's too late, and he explodes all over me.

Before I complete another stroke, he quickly grabs me from the floor and tosses me over his lap. I undo my pants and he rips them off. My ass is fully exposed, up in the air. I look over my shoulder daring him to take me in whatever way he wishes. He begins to stroke my ass cheeks getting ever so close to the crevice between my cheeks and the glistening clean-shaven lips of my steamy, damp pussy.

With a burst of completely unexpected strength, he curls my petite frame off of his lap, and rotates me to face him, the skin of our chests touching. I come to rest atop him, my smooth delicate lips ready to open up and take his ridged cock inside me. His long cock reaches deep inside me and touches new places as I begin to gently grind on him. His hands grab my ass cheeks, he gently separates them and moves his index finger closer to my anus as I grind a little harder to reach it. I love the way my body is reacting. As he moves away I slow my movement. As he gets closer I grind a little more, inch by inch.

He looks down to see that I have now spread my legs wider, exposing my very wet labia, his glistening cock below my juice coated pussy. He can feel it! I move forward far enough for my clitoris to rub against the head and shaft of his cock. Bad move. If I keep this up, he's going to explode. He knows this, so he firmly grabs my waist to restrict my movement. I try to move but he is strong and is holding so I am completely immobile. I am going crazy, I need to freely grind my pussy until it comes but he knows it and stops me. Restricting me from grinding means he must be enjoying this or perhaps he is enjoying watching me go crazy.

His fingers travel across my body to my pussy. I rock my wet clitoris back into his cock...this time he gently spanks my ass.

"Stay still, or I will spank you again, much harder this time."

I immediately stop moving.

He gently starts to caress my cheeks. I anticipate another slap, but he brings his hand to his mouth and spits on his fingers. His hand returns to the crack of my ass. He knows his stuff and he is completely confident, intuits what I like and what I don't like. I don't so much as move. There is a little tremor in my body as he gets closer to my anus...he ever so slowly moves closer and closer in small circles. His touch is delicate and light like a feather. I start to grind again and he gives me a hard smack. I stop moving again and he continues with small circular motions until he is able to caress my anus with his finger without me moving. My ass cheeks feel hot when he touches them and I'm sure they have a rosy glow. He looks down – my labia are extremely puffy and very wet. His cock responds by getting even harder and in doing so pushes up against me and my very slippery clit.

Once again, he lets the tip of his cock slide inside my wet pussy. He only lets the head penetrate me and I love it. The more he teases me the wetter I become. I have felt the entire length of his cock in my mouth and throat and I want it all inside my pussy, but he continues to tease me mercilessly.

"Do you want more?" he asks.

"Yes, give me all of it," I say.

"Say it! Tell me what you want."

"I want your cock. I want you to fuck me harder. Make me come. Fuck me hard and make me come. I need to come now!"

He thrusts his long cock inside me hard. I scream. He continues to pound me hard. The smell of our sex is intoxicating. He likes it. No – he loves it. We are both beyond ready to explode. I begin flicking my clit with my fingertips. My eyes roll back and I scream, "Oh fuck, oh fuck, oh fuck!"

"Come for me baby," he commands.

My body tightens and pulsates. "I'm coming!"

He doesn't stop fucking me, but he slows down. His voice softens. "I'm coming too." He pulls his cock out of my pussy and climbs on top of me and forces his cock into my mouth. He strokes his cock as his fluids fly to the back of my throat and I swallow it all. I almost pass out. He flops down on the bed beside me with his eyes closed catching his breath.

After sometime I come back to reality and ask, "How was it?" My signature question after each sexual encounter.

"Not bad," he replies.

"Not bad?"

"Okay Zoe, it was good. Not bad at all actually."

I don't respond. I just lie there in silence. Once more he has taken me by surprise.

"I'm joking," he laughs. "That was amazing!"

"How do I make it better?"

"Better? That was the bestest ever!"

"Really?" I say, not knowing if he is finally being serious.

"Really." Our eyes lock. "Tell me your fantasy," he says suddenly.

I laugh. "My fantasy?" I roll my eyes. I have figured out that he wants to be the dominant one in this relationship, while I will be the submissive. I know what I have to say. "Being kidnapped and then used for sexual pleasure." *Totally not my fantasy.*

"Tell me more," he asks.

"I need the adrenaline rush. The unknown excites me. It makes me wet."

"You are a very naughty girl, Zoe Winstein. Now come here so I can hold you." He opens his arms and I snuggle my way in.

There are a few things I don't do, snuggling being one of them, but I want to make him happy, so I give him what he wants.

That's just the way I am, I don't want a man touching me after I come. *Let's get down to business and then get on your way. Or, just get the fuck out.* Perhaps this is my way of protecting myself emotionally. And they definitely don't spend the night. Fortunately for me, Elias has family obligations.

He holds me for a long time. Perhaps it is guilt, but I don't think so. He is not rushed, he is calm and he makes me feel calm and at peace. After the nuclear explosion that just occurred in my bed this is a welcome and refreshing change.

I fall asleep in his arms.

He wakes me. "I have to head out. I had a wonderful evening. When can I see you again?"

"Ditto."

"Tuesday night?"

"I believe I can."

"Great. I will come over straight from work. Say 6:00 PM?"

"Great."

"Sleep well, Zoe. I'll lock up."

"Good night, Elias."

And within moments, I hear the front door close and I pass out.

# CHAPTER SEVEN

THE NEXT MORNING the air is extra crisp. Early autumn has brought rain. After my morning run and coffee, I make my way to the office to finish up some research.

My phone rings. It's Blair calling. I need a break so I answer her call. "Hello?"

"Girlfriend, what's going on? I haven't heard from you all weekend."

Blair is my polar opposite. She is empathetic, with a great heart. Perhaps she's the mother figure in my life.

"Sorry Blair. I was a little distracted."

"With what? Is it raining men again on your street?"

"Hilarious." Blair doesn't know the extent of my 'other life'. To her, I'm just as sweet as her. "What are you doing tonight?"

"I was going to catch up on some work."

"No plans. Good. Meet me at The Riverside for drinks at 5:00 PM."

"Isn't that a little early?" I wonder.

"It isn't if I'm planning on taking you to the hockey game."

Excellent. I love hockey. My night is looking up. I need some R & R. "Sounds like a plan."

"Dress sexy. Love ya. See you later."


MY OFFICE HAS WHITE walls and white furniture with no clutter. I work best with no distractions. I open my computer and type in my key words, *Sultan of Amin*. His recent social media posts show him in Los Angeles, Toronto and Montreal. Nothing in New York City. And then I remember…Matteo was in Montreal a few weeks ago. He'd said that he was looking at Canadian opportunities, he suspected that the Montreal market would be more lucrative than Manhattan. Many overseas investors are beginning to shun the U.S. and looking to buy in Canada, Montreal and Toronto in particular.

It is pretty obvious to me that Matteo is getting funding from Sully, that John is in his back pocket greasing the regulatory wheels, and Elias is papering deals and doing whatever it is that lawyers do. And hopefully it isn't too obvious that Zoe is the little fly on the wall.

This is big and I'm perfectly positioned to do what I've become very good at doing: putting two and two together to figure out where the deal was. I have to be patient. Until the time is right, it's good that my three friends don't suspect anything and continue to underestimate me.


BLAIR SITS AT THE bar with her over-sized smile, sipping her glass of wine.

I take the empty seat next to her. "You look way too happy."

She turns her head and looks at me. "I'm in love, Zoe."

"What?" I mimic her giant smile.

Blair is very excited. Her face lights up. "His name is Michael."

"I'm so happy for you." And I truly am. Blair has been in her fair share of unhealthy relationships. It's about time she found a little happiness.

"What's been going on with you?" She's a curious little one.

"Absolutely nothing. Tell me more about Michael." I attempt to keep my focus on her.

"He works in the construction industry. Divorced with two kids. And he is amazing. This weekend he brought over groceries and cooked dinner for us."

Blair lives a sheltered life compared to mine. She is naïve, but always smiling. I envy her. She always sees the good in people.

"He is a keeper if he's making you this happy. And he can cook? Can he clean too?" I reply.

She smirks. "I'm sure he can, and yes he is. And he has friends." Blair winks.

I have no interest in adding additional men into the mix at the moment. "Never mind his friends, tell me more about him. What does he look like?"

"Well, he is tall, a brunette, with blue eyes."

"That sounds pretty close to tall, dark and handsome."

A man interrupts us by placing his hand on Blair's shoulder. "Sorry to interrupt ladies. Are you ready?"

"Yes, we are. Zoe, this is Richard, Michael's driver. He is taking us to the game."

Interesting. Michael has a driver for a ten-minute walk? I appease Blair by showing excitement. "Okay, let's do it!"

We are dropped off at the executive suites entrance of the stadium. Michael is standing by the door, ready to welcome Blair. He's a business man. He seems sophisticated and poised. I have some good clues: his watch is a Patek Phillippe, his shoes are hand-made as is his suit. He isn't the slightest bit pretentious. He doesn't have to be, he is fine with being himself. Good work Blair!

Michael opens his arms in anticipation of Blair running to him. "Baby! Did Richard treat you ladies well?"

"He certainly did. I would like to introduce you to my bestie, Zoe."

"A pleasure meeting you, Zoe. I've heard a lot about you."

So far so good. Michael is no crude construction idiot. I have dealt with too many and know to stay away. "I appreciate the invitation."

"Anything for Blair." He looks down at Blair and smiles.

Michael and Blair lock arms and I follow them inside.

Blair turns to me as we enter the box suites. "So, what do you think?"

"This is amazing Blair." *I have been in this scene way too many times.* "It seems Michael knows how lucky he is to have you." And I certainly hope that Michael isn't like many of the men in the construction industry – barely one step above whistling at you on the streets as you walk by. "Are you going to tell me how you two met?"

"It's actually a funny story. I was walking along 5th Avenue and dropped my phone. Before I could reach down to pick it up, Michael picked it up and handed it back to me. We locked eyes and that was it." Blair is glowing.

I smile. "I need to drop my phone more often."

We both laugh.

Michael walks over and stands between us. "Dare I ask what's so funny?"

"I was just telling Zoe how we met," Blair beams, looking up at Michael.

"Don't be telling everyone how soft I am. I have a reputation to maintain." He winks at Blair. "Let me introduce you to our hostess, Lisa. Can she get you ladies something to drink?"

"A glass of red wine please."

"Make that two," I add.

"Coming right up," says Lisa.

We are the first to arrive, and slowly the box begins to fill, a mix of men and a few women. I am an observer tonight, yet I can't turn off my attention to detail. An occupational hazard.

I sit away from all the action and enjoy the game. It is a pleasant change. I turn around and notice Blair and Michael smiling and laughing with one another. Is this temporary or long term, I wonder? Do people even care anymore?

During the second intermission, I walk over to the happy couple only to notice out of the corner of my eye Matteo walking through the hallway of the executive suites with two men and two women, all dressed to the nines. All I can hear is Matteo's laughter. I don't want to be seen, so I avoid doing a double-take. I do however, notice that John is with him.

Blair turns to me. "Zoe, are you okay?"

She's noticed the quick change in my mood. When I'm not completely on, my facial expressions can give me away, and this is one of those times. "All good," I say smiling.

Michael looks over at me. "Looks like someone needs a refill."

Before I can say a word, Blair jumps in, turns to Michael and says, "Absolutely. Can you please grab us another glass of wine, sweetie?"

Michael follows Blair's order and goes to the bar to get us more wine.

I turn to Blair. "Michael seems like a nice caring guy."

"He's is gem. And as an added bonus, he is hot as hell."

Just when I think Blair and I will have a few minutes to ourselves, we are interrupted by a short guy wearing thick flats to add an extra inch to his height. He does, however, have a nice head of blonde hair. "Ladies! How are you this evening? Enjoying the game?" His voice is raspy.

Blair rolls her eyes and smiles. "Do people actually watch the game here?"

"Where are you ladies from?" He grins.

"Both of us live in the city," Blair replies.

"Nice to meet you." He extends his hand, "I'm Dan."

"Nice to meet you. I'm Blair and this is Zoe."

Michael makes his way back and hands us our wine glasses.

"Michael, why didn't you tell me you were inviting these beautiful women to the game tonight?" Dan grins.

I am not flattered in the least, nor is Blair, but being Michael's guest, I don't flat out tell him to get lost as I would have otherwise very quickly done. I can play nice when required. "That is so sweet of you, Dan."

"What is it that you do, Zoe?"

"I'm a psychologist."

Dan leans in towards me and whispers in my ear, "Can you play with my mind?"

"I prefer a bit of a challenge," I joke.

"Ouch. You don't like Prada or Gucci?"

I once again close the space between Dan and I and whisper into his ear, "Perhaps you failed to notice that I'm wearing Gucci and I have a closet full of Prada. I don't have room for any more." I stand straight and smile at Dan.

"You're a frisky one, Zoe."

"Thanks, Dan. You're frisky too, but I've gotta run. There is a man I have to frisk." I leave my wine on the table and make a quick exit waving goodbye to Blair and Michael.

Another night out, and I can't say I enjoyed myself. I wonder about Michael and his intentions toward Blair. If Michael associates with the likes of Dan, how different to, or similar is he from Dan? Still, he seemed to be okay, so maybe it will be fine. I choose to stay as far away from Blair's love life.

I hop into a cab and pull out my cell phone. I have two missed messages.

Matteo: Free later tonight?

Blair: Thanks for coming out. Text me once you get home.

Rather than be alone tonight, I message Matteo.

Zoe: Be home in 20.
Matteo: See you soon!

I have a plan for Matteo tonight. The metronome.


WITH ONLY MINUTES TO SPARE, I glance at myself in the bathroom mirror to ensure nothing is out of place. I hear a knock at the door and quickly answer it. I open the door wide to fully expose myself to Matteo. His eyes devour me. He has never looked at me that way, as I have never looked this good for him.

"Umm, good evening. I am here to see Zoe. Is she home?"

I smile. "Zoe is indisposed. She asked me to take care of you this evening."

He seems intrigued. He casually walks in and is about to make his way into the living room, to enjoy the goose-down sofa, when I grab him by the wrist and drag him into my bedroom. "I thought I would give you a music lesson. Do you like the sound of 'tick, tick'?" I ask him.

He is confused. "Is there a bomb in your apartment?" he asks.

I instruct him to remove his pants, and he does. He is commando. Typical. I push him onto the bed, and he lies there, legs spread. I open my side table drawer, pull out my metronome and hand it to Matteo.

"What am I supposed to do with this?" he asks.

"Let' try something different. It's a metronome. Musicians use it to keep time. I am giving you control of me…of my tempo. I call it the climax counter."

The look on his face is priceless.

"Let's start the device at its slowest time. Twenty beats per minute." I turn on the device and it starts to 'tick, tick, tick'. "When you want me to speed up, you increase the speed by turning the dial."

He laughs. "You've got to be kidding me?"

"Humor me, will you?"

His cock is erect, awaiting my mouth. I turn the metronome on to twenty beats per minute and hand Matteo the device.

My wet mouth begins to devour his cock, going up with a single tick and down with the next. I enjoy each and every movement of sucking his cock. Time passes and Matteo has yet to change the tempo. Either he isn't interested – unlikely – or he is enjoying the moment without any distractions. Then, without warning, the ticks begin to speed up. My eyes look up at him. He returns my gaze through half closed eyes. His mouth is partially open and his breathing is heavy, enjoying the increasing tempo. My mouth and tongue pick up speed, faster, and faster, until a large shot of come is released into my mouth, a little spilling out and onto my breasts.

I only have one more thing to do…keep swallowing. And I do.

# CHAPTER EIGHT

I WAKE UP EARLY this Tuesday morning for my morning run and coffee, then return to my apartment and prepare myself for my unannounced visit to John. His gift is neatly wrapped in light blue paper and a red bow and I hold it close to my heart – literally. The elevator is full of distracted people in their business attire, heads down as they play with their devices.

This encounter isn't about being sexy. It is about being real. No make-up, no heels...just unadorned Zoe. I patiently wait to arrive at the fourth floor of the New York City Hall Building. When I finally arrive, I am stopped in my tracks. "May I help you?" A red head attendant enquires from behind the marble desk.

*It is true what they say about red heads? You know...wild in bed?* "Good morning. I'm looking for John Kolka."

She glances down at her computer screen. "Do you have an appointment?"

"No, I just wanted to…"

"I'm sorry," she responds without letting me finish. "You will need to make an appointment through his office and complete a security check and be issued a badge."

I laugh in my head. "Perhaps you could call his assistant…," and just as I'm finishing my sentence John walks up from behind me.

"Zoe?"

"John, I apologize for coming unannounced."

"No need to apologize. It's great to see you. To what do I owe the pleasure of this visit?"

I know better than to hand him his wrapped gift in front of an audience. "I was in the area and thought I would stop by and say hello."

"Perfect, let's chat in my office."

The receptionist doesn't even look up as I follow John into his office.

John has a corner office, flooded with enough natural lighting to fill a greenhouse. It needs it with all the bulky furniture in the room.

"Make yourself comfortable."

I hand him his gift, then take my seat.

"What's this all about? What a lovely surprise." He looks genuinely touched. "That's very nice of you, Zoe. Should I open it now, or should shall we go for an ice cream first?"

I smile. "Go ahead and open it."

He makes sure the door is closed, then begins to slowly unwrap his gift, first removing the red bow. As he sees my gift he looks surprised. Perhaps a box of condoms would have been more appropriate, but I'm going for the mind fuck.

He leafed through the pages. "The Prince, by Machiavelli. Am I your prince, Zoe?"

"I hope not. Lorenzo de' Medici was reputed to be very unattractive."

He chuckles.

"A man who has been successful in business and politics? I wasn't sure if this was something you'd have already read and maybe memorized, but I took a chance."

"Hmmm. I must say, Zoe, I am truly intrigued by you. You have many layers. And you reveal yourself one layer at a time."

"I'm not a showy person and I love to learn. Especially from smart people." And that I do.

"Are you learning anything, Zoe?"

I stand up and give John a kiss. "Yes I am. You have very positive energy. I like that...a lot." I pick up my purse and prepare to make my exit.

"Leaving so soon?"

"I'm sure you have things to do. I will let you get to them. I'm lucky I made it through security."

"Can we see each other soon?"

"Of course. Someone owes me an ice cream."

"Just ice cream?"

"For now." *But I do have plans for you.*

"How do I get a hold of you?"

"Be resourceful."

"You will be hearing from me soon."

"Can't wait." I walk out of his office and close the door behind me. A feeling of excitement runs through my body. That was easier than I expected.


ELIAS IS ARRIVING SHORTLY. It's different with Elias. He is different. I want him for a purpose, but there is a certain excitement I feel when I'm with him or when my thoughts drift to him. I find myself thinking about him more and more these days. The sex is animalistic, the orgasms are intense, and all I can think about is his cock moving oh so slowly, teasing me, in and out of my wet pussy, again and again.

I yearn for Elias. I crave the heat that envelopes me when I'm with him. I crave his long cock, a perfect match for his slim frame. The body of a runner. I find myself getting wet just thinking of his cock entering me, slowly but firmly, inch by inch. The tempo of his thrusts makes my body writhe, and there are many inches to anticipate.

I slither into my sexiest cocktail dress. It feels so sexy against my bare skin, no cleavage, a conservative length, but glued to my curves. At a glance I appear naked. Tonight isn't about me being vulnerable – it's about him being exposed.

I slip on my shoes and walk out of my building, where Elias waits. He leans against the passenger door with an appreciative look, then walks towards me, embraces me. "Baby, I missed you."

His soft lips connect with mine and I immediately begin to squirm. He doesn't allow it. He just squeezes me harder, not too hard, just right, constraining my movement. I have never felt more desired and loved by a person who is, let's be honest, almost a stranger.

"What did you miss?" I breath softly into his ear.

"All of you, although I do miss certain parts of you more than others."

"Which ones?"

"Your brain, my love."

"Do we have to go out?" I inquire.

"Unfortunately, yes," he replies apologetically.

He takes my hand and opens the passenger door. We don't say a word to one another. I know what I have to do, his eyes are telling me. *Be submissive Zoe.* I was going to ask where we are going, but decide to let him revel in my complete submission. It's what he wants.

"So, tell me about your day?" he asks.

"It was very productive."

"Productive? Do tell."

"I started the day with my morning run before grabbing a coffee at my usual spot. I grabbed the paper, read my daily horoscope, which did mention luck coming my way in the near future. I completed the Sudoku puzzle before making my way to visit your good friend John."

He looks puzzled. "John?" He turns his head towards me and raises his eye brow.

"Really?" I reply in my sarcastic tone.

"Yes Zoe, really." He pauses a moment. "Kolka?"

"Yes John Kolka. Isn't he a friend of yours?"

"John and I go way back. He is a friend." He comes to a rolling stop at a red light and turns to me. "Why the visit to John? Are you planning on trading me in already?"

"Wow! Jealously?"

"Baby, I want you all to myself."

"But you're married." I laugh.

The light turns green and he accelerates. "I may be married, but I still want you all to myself."

*Some men want it all.* I laugh and say, "If I were to trade you in, it would be for a newer model."

"Well, can you at least hold off on that for a while?" He smiles.

We arrive at our destination, and before getting out of the car, he turns to me and says, "Are you ready?"

I demonstrate my readiness through my actions – I exit the vehicle. Elias catches up to me. He has to. I have no idea where I'm going.

We stop in front of a twelve-foot rose glass door with concrete trim. It is the most beautiful piece of art I have seen in a long time. From industrial to sassy, modern architecture contradicted its counterparts on that street.

"Where are we?" I ask.

"Just another restaurant. I hope you like it."

"I'm intrigued."

"I hope you don't mind, I invited my friend Wagi to join us."

*Wagi? Does he wag his tail when he's excited?*

We are greeted by another hostess that Elias knows – this guy gets around. Wagi is waiting for us at the table.

"Wagi!" Elias cries out from across the restaurant.

Wagi seems fairly reserved compared to Elias and chooses to hold his greeting till we arrive to the table. Once we make our way over, Wagi stands up and gives Elias a masculine squeeze. "Brother, how are you doing?"

"I'm great." Elias turns to me. "I would like to introduce you to my friend, Zoe."

His eyes move up and down. His facial expression is

very telling. He likes what he sees. He extends his arm. "A pleasure to meet you, Zoe."

"Likewise."

"Please have a seat." Elias pulls out a chair for me.

Wagi is an older gentleman with a pronounced nose and intelligent eyes. His white hair, with the slightest hint of blond, is perfectly coiffed. It gives him a look of sophistication. His appearance resembles that of a foreign film director.

The two of them immerse themselves in conversation and I just sit there and smile. But I spot something, notice that while Elias is apparently in deep conversation with Wagi, he isn't in the moment. He is absent-minded, his eyes wandering the room. Wagi is sharing the status of his relationship, a woman many years younger. Headliner – 'Rich Man with Younger Woman'. Cliché, I know. Wagi has never been married and has no kids of his own. His ex has recently married another man and Wagi is absolutely heart-broken. Someone has to tell him which way was up and who better than me?

"I can't believe she is married," moans Wagi.

I turn to Wagi, remove my filter and blurt out, "Let me summarize this for you in a couple of sentences," I say. "If you truly want love I would strongly recommend: a) don't let them know you have cash and b) don't give them cash. When a woman sticks around without a and b, you know she genuinely cares for you."

This conversation could have gone one of two ways. He could have disregarded my opinion, thinking 'who the fuck is this bitch?' Or he could realize that he has met someone who didn't give a fuck about his feelings and would tell him the ugly truth. I didn't care either way.

Wagi turns to Elias. "Where did you find this one? I like her. She is smarter than the others." He winks at me.

I glimpse at Elias and spot him gawking the waitress. My blood begins to boil, and my hand rolls into a fist. I'm angry. I'm hurt. *I'm fuckin jealous. What the fuck?* Not wanting to draw attention to my freaked-out emotions, I turn to Wagi. "Other ones, eh?" I'm not interested to know about the other women...or at least I think I'm not. I convince myself that I'm just looking for a distraction.

"What should I tell you? The tearful 2:00 AM phone call I got from his old girlfriend accusing Elias of seeing other women? Or the other old girlfriend who wanted him to leave his wife?"

I giggle. "You are a hoot, Wagi. Love that name. So, how Wagi is Wagi?"

"Wagi enough, but I'm not here to impress, I'm here to entertain." He glances at Elias and focuses his attention back to me. He takes note of Elias' lack of social skills. From one socially awkward individual to another. *I'm at the fuckin circus tonight.*

I contemplate leaving, but choose to ignore Elias' distracted behavior.

"You're gorgeous, smart and fun Zoe, and I have only known you for a few minutes. Where do I find a woman like you?" asks Wagi.

"Like me?" I reply.

"Calm...with substance."

*Not to mention upset.* But I don't let on as to how agitated I truly am. I squint my eyes. "Hmm. As I already said, stop dating women half your age who want you for your cash, but I hear that's a hard habit to break."

"Simple, but not easy."

"That's half of it. The other half is to stop meeting women at TryBeck, Schivel, Rare...you know, places where women are hungry."

Wagi smiles. He knows exactly what I'm talking about. And he doesn't disagree.

Elias puts his arm around me. "Baby, I knew you and Wagi would hit it off."

"Welcome back," I grin.

Elias gives me a funny look. "Welcome back? Where have I been?"

Wagi interjects, "What are we eating for dinner?"

"I got this, guys." Elias waves down the waitress.

Wagi turns to me. "So, what is it that you do that makes you an expert on how to find the right woman?"

The waitress arrives and Elias places our order, while I continue my conversation with Wagi. "Actually, I'm an escort." I chuckle.

Wagi looks at me with a vacant gaze, smiles and responds. "Yes. And I'm a gigolo. We should exchange trade secrets."

"Actually Wagi," Elias interrupts, "Zoe is a Psychologist."

Wagi responds. "Then I better think twice before I say something. You may figure me out."

Elias is quick to say, "she already has. That's why she is blushing. You're such a pig Wagi."

The truth is Wagi isn't someone who is going to change. Being in his late forties, never married, wealthy and without responsibility, he is set in his ways and has no motivation to do anything differently. I am fully aware that all my efforts in giving him advice will go in one ear and out the other.

As for Elias, his behavior this evening is telling. He makes me feel uneasy. I carry on the evening with an open mind and remind myself of its purpose.

The rest of the dinner conversation is Wagi and Elias reminiscing about their past adventures. Wagi doesn't have any friends. I'm certain that Elias and Wagi aren't as close as they think they are. Although their friendship goes way back, it's a relationship based on convenience.

We finish our meal and I'm ready to remove myself from the dinner table. Elias pays the bill and we say our farewell to Wagi.

Elias takes my hand and leads me to the building across the street. Once again I choose to not say a word. He buzzes into the building and takes me into the elevator to the top floor. He pushes me against the back wall of the elevator and stands directly in front of me, inches away, gently caresses my face, touches my lips with his fingertips.

He brings his body closer to mine and kisses my eyelids. "You are so beautiful."

I don't reply. The elevator doors open to the fifty-seventh floor and I follow him into the stairwell. He walks up a set of stairs and I glue my feet to the floor.

He turns around. "What are you waiting for?"

"Should I follow you?"

"Umm, yes."

"Up there?"

"Give me your hand."

I reach my hand out and he drags me to the top of the stairs and opens a door that says *Do Not Enter* in large letters. I am curious as to where he is taking me. For a moment I feel unnerved, until he opens the door and I see a beautiful rooftop garden. String lights illuminate the garden and I immediately feel warm and cozy inside. There's a cabana in the center of the garden and we head toward it. The cabana is open on three sides. In the cabana there is nothing except a bed with deep red rose petals strewn around it.

"Surprise, baby."

It is a surprise. I'm speechless...for once.

"I hope you like it."

"Wow, how did you manage this?"

"The owner and I are tight."

"And let me guess...you own the building?"

He chuckles. "Am I that transparent?"

"You are that and more."

He escorts me to the bed. "I can't resist you, Zoe. Let me?" His hands caress my shoulders and arms, barely touching me. His hands begin to travel down to my hips and thighs, and finally to my knees as he kneels down. His eyes follow his hands to my feet, where he stays still and tilts his head. His dark eyes are hungry. He places his hands at the bottom of my dress at my knees, yanks my dress over my body, exposing my naked body to all of Manhattan. I close my eyes and take a deep breath. The cool October breeze brings numbness to my body. My nipples harden and blood flows to my clit. He has conditioned my body to anticipate his touch, his lick, his penetration. He twists his body as he tosses my dress onto the floor and turns back to me while he takes a step back.

His eyes move up and down my body. "You are beyond beautiful. You are a dream."

I am shy and insecure all of a sudden. I don't want him to examine every inch of my body and notice my imperfections. "Are you going to kiss me?"

"Let me admire you a minute longer."

He makes me feel like a woman; wanted and desired. I stand there paralyzed even though I want to cover my body with the silk bed sheets.

He takes a step towards me and touches my naked body, my face, my hair. Making a mess with his hands. Primal passion. All I do is close my eyes and feel his rough and jagged touch all over my body. He kisses my rigid lips, his saliva dampening and softening them. He bites my lower lip, not hard, but hard enough. He places his hands on my hips and twirls me around. His hand changes direction as he begins to caress my ass cheeks and hips, slowly moving his hands up and down. I tilt my head back and turn my head to kiss him. I am panting while he moans. I love a man who moans. He pushes me onto the bed and I land on my hands and knees. He continues to caress my ass with his left hand, as he unzips his pants with his right and pulls out his cock. He rests his hard cock on my ass and I begin to squirm. He loves this. He smacks my right cheek.

He spreads my cheeks and spits onto his fingers and lathers his cock with his saliva. He puts the tip of his cock inside and I instinctively arch my lower back even further. His unhurried movements are what drive me mad. Slowly, deliberately, he gently fucks me, controlling the tempo, not giving me the satisfaction of his entire cock. I begin to rock my body back and forth, attempting to get more of his cock inside me.

"Don't be greedy," he tells me.

"Don't make me beg. Give me all of it."

"You have to really want it, Zoe," he replies.

Elias's cock has endurance. He is fully erect with self-control. He wants to please my body, and I am open to allowing him to.

Finally, after what seemed a lifetime, he thrusts his entire penis inside of me, hitting my back wall. I scream from the pleasure and pain simultaneously coursing through my body. He begins to pound my pussy, takes my right hand and licks my fingers. He already knows my passion. I begin to rub my clit. I want to please him too, so I drop onto my shoulders and with my left hand under our body I fondle his balls in a circular motion. Within seconds, my body commences to vibrate pre-orgasm. I want to stay in this state for a little longer before he makes me explode.

"Fuck me baby! Fuck this pussy! It belongs to you!" I began to flick my clit even harder in an oval motion. "Baby, I'm going to come," I scream to him. And just as I am about to release a piercing scream, I hear what sound like gun shots. I look up and notice the sky light up with fireworks. My body collapses, but Elias doesn't stop.

He begins to thrust even harder as I scream in ecstasy, "Oh my God! Oh my God! Keep fucking me baby. Come for me."

And come he does. He pulls out his cock and comes all over my ass, his body spasming, his eyes closed and mouth open in ecstasy. It is one of the most beautiful things I have ever seen.

He throws himself onto the bed, grabs me around the waist and says, "Let me hold you baby."

I snuggle with him. A perfect fit. I have never felt to close to someone I barely know.

How did I let this happen?

We lie there in silence for a long time. He doesn't rush. After the smoke from the fireworks dissipate, he takes me home and puts me to bed and everything becomes clear.

# CHAPTER NINE

I HAVE TO REGAIN FOCUS. I put on my headphones and begin to run, and don't allow the music's tempo to slow me down. I'm running as fast as the thoughts racing through my head. I see fireworks, burst after burst, taking me back to last night, to Elias. One foot in front of the other, I run. To where? He's consuming my thoughts. This is an unnecessary distraction. I needed to re-evaluate. How am I going to use this emotion to my advantage? *Think Zoe. Think.*

And then it comes to me. Who said my game only had one king? In an about-face, I race back home to prepare myself for my lecture. There are two types of confidantes – the ones that tell you what you want to hear, and those that tell you the truth. I had always been the latter. Was it time to switch it up and try being the former?

After my morning lecture, I make my way to my usual spot for a late lunch. Walking into Monika's, I do a double-take as I see Stefano sitting in the corner. I shouldn't be surprised, he is, after all, an impatient employer. Our eyes meet as I make my way to his table.

"We need to talk," Stefano says to me with dead eyes.

*When don't we need to talk?* I don't question how he

knows where to find me, it doesn't surprise me at all. Stefano is smart and resourceful.

"Take a seat. I already ordered for us."

I take the seat across from him.

"How is your day so far?" Stefano asks.

"I know you didn't come here for the food," I reply. "So let's skip the chit chat, we both hate it. Tell me why you're here."

I can see by Stefano's face that this isn't a response he expected, but I need him to know that he can't do this without me.

"How did your visit with John go?" he asks.

"Let's just say that he owes me an ice cream," I reply.

Stefano's frowns. "I don't give a fuck about your ice cream. Did he tell you anything about the deal?" he asks.

I grin and lock eyes with him, saying nothing.

"Well?" he demands.

"He will after I fuck him," I reply. "And stop hounding me and showing up unexpectedly, trying to throw me off. Trust isn't gained in a single day. I need time."

"You've had months, Zoe," Stefano bellows, drawing attention to our corner table. "Time is something I'm running out of. Maybe you've lost your touch for this business?"

"Winter is fast approaching, and construction will begin to slow down. Perhaps this is a great opportunity for you and your wife to head out of town for a few weeks and enjoy time with one another?"

"Are you fucked in the head?" he shouts. "If I wanted to go on vacation with a pain in the ass, I'd go with my fuckin proctologist."

"You may want to lower your voice," I suggest.

"I don't give a flying fuck about lowering my voice," he replies, raising his voice to new levels, defiantly.

Stefano is a very loyal customer. He frequents the same restaurants and spends enough money each month to pay their rent in full. Stefano knows he can buy people. Known for being vulgar and often using inappropriate language, Stefano uses his money and his anger as a weapon. And yes, he doesn't give a fuck! If he wants to, he would pay for everyone's meal just to shut them all up. This I've seen him do more than once.

Stefano is not an easy person to spend time with, but we understand each other. I'm one of the few people that can tolerate his insulting, loud and loutish conduct. I don't need him, but I won't stop seeing him. We are friends. Perhaps it will end...eventually, but for now, we will continue.

"Go somewhere on your own," I suggest, knowing Stefano never travels alone. If he isn't with his wife, he is with some other companion.

"Yeah, okay. Anything else?" he asks. "Any more useless advice?"

"I think that's it." I reply.

His grin returns. "Good. Now, the reason I'm sitting in this shitty restaurant with you is because I want to ask you a question in person."

"In person. Why?"

"Because I want to look into your eyes and see if you are telling me the truth," he replies.

"Fine. But then you will have to stop looking at my cleavage for a moment," I joke. Stefano, though, is in no mood to joke.

"Did you fuck Matteo?" he asks forcefully. It's rare for him to show vulnerability in public. That catches my attention.

I know how to keep him happy. He has been disappointed by many people in his life. The one thing that I give him is comfort. The comfort he needs to feel safe. His vulnerability is a weakness, but, I always keep my word with him.

"Aren't I? Figuratively speaking of course," I ask.

"You know what I mean. Are you working for him?

Something is not right, Zoe. This is taking way too fuckin long."

"Everything is going according to plan," *My plan that is,* I respond without hesitation. But the questions keep coming.

"Are you fucking him and working for him? Should I trust you?" he asks in a belligerent tone that I don't recognize.

"Are you deflecting?" I reply.

"I'm asking the questions here," he bellows.

"I have known you for two years, have made you tons of money, have saved your ass and have defended you countless times, and you are accusing me of not being loyal to you now?" I reply. Perhaps he is more vulnerable than even I'm aware.

"I know you like to fuck, Zoe, and I'm worried that you've turned on me. I don't know why, and I don't really know how, but I know you. I can read you."

Am I that transparent? I am willing to sell my soul to the devil? *But I certainly wasn't going to share that.* "Yes you do, Stefano. And you should also know that I don't bite the hand that feeds me."

"Smart girl," is his response, but I can tell that he is not satisfied. "Now, back to John. What can you tell me about him?"

"What would you like to know?" I ask.

"Should I trust him?" he replies.

"He's a business man, working in politics. The answer should be obvious."

"Enough said. Enjoy lunch," he says as he stands up from the table.

"You aren't staying for lunch?"

He hesitates for a moment, "I wouldn't be caught dead eating in a shithole like this. But you already knew that."

I remain seated and watch him leave. Stefano and I don't need chit chat. No bull shit, or not much anyway. It's refreshing, the intellectual stimulation I was in search of, but had a difficult time finding. It's easy to find beautiful people in New York City, the challenge is finding someone who doesn't need to be seen or heard in New York City.

LATER THAT NIGHT, relaxing at home, I pour myself a glass of wine and reflect on the day. That was a side of Stefano that I haven't seen before; a wounded animal lashing out at the world. *Am I in too deep? Have I lost control? Am I being paranoid?*

My phone buzzes. An incoming text. The timing couldn't have been more perfect. I'm bored, looking for stimulation.

Elias: What are you doing and when can I see you again?

I want so desperately to say 'right now', but hesitate. I don't want to come across as too eager, but at the same time, I don't want to push him away. I haven't yet decided what to do with Elias, but I am enjoying his company, as it serves my purpose.

Zoe: Tomorrow night?
Elias: How about tomorrow afternoon? I have a proposition for you.

A proposition? What could it be? I am more than a little curious.

Zoe: You got my attention.
Elias: Rouge Tower 58th Floor. 2:00 PM.

I take another sip of wine.

Elias: I can't wait to see you.

Zoe: Ditto, I reply

My meeting with Elias couldn't have come at a better time.
 I fall asleep with happy thoughts. *Thank you, wine.*

# CHAPTER TEN

EXITING THE ELEVATOR, I'm distracted by the glittering *Macchetta, Smith & Associates* sign on the wall behind reception. I'm in a fish bowl. Legions of people working away furiously in little cubicles. This is the fanciest sweat shop I've ever seen.

"Ms. Winstein?" a voice calls out.

I turn to see a woman in her forties. A brunette, fit, with short hair and a crisp blue suit stands in front of me. "Yes?"

"Mr. Macchetta is expecting you. Please follow me."

She escorts me to an office with transparent dividers and a stunning view of Central Park. I am reminded of Matteo's office…and, of course, sex. *Sex!*

"Please have a seat. Mr. Macchetta will be with you shortly. I don't anticipate him being more than a few minutes." She leaves the room.

I walk over to the window and just as I begin to take in the view, I hear Elias' footsteps behind me. "You sir, are late," I say to him in an authoritative tone.

"My apologies," he replies with a smile on his face. "Will you forgive me?" he asks as he locks the door behind him.

I laugh. "Hilarious. A lock on a door, but transparent walls. Do you cage animals in here and spectate from the outside for your amusement?"

"Do you think we should?" He stares at me for a moment before walking over to his desk and taking his seat. He touches something under his desk and the transparent glass becomes opaque.

I stand there silently, no facial expression, but I'm thinking *nice touch Elias*.

"Are you just going to stand there or are you going to get your beautiful ass over here and kiss me?" Elias asks. It's not really a question. It's a command.

I have this uncontrollable urge to jump on his desk and have him fuck me, but I restrain myself. "Is there a particular reason you wanted to meet me here – in your office? Wouldn't my place be more appropriate?"

"Look at you. All business and no pleasure," Elias chuckles.

"You got it all wrong. Business first…then pleasure," I smile.

"Who's making the rules here? Get your ass over here," he commands.

"You're used to getting your way aren't you." I lock eyes with him.

"You couldn't be more wrong about me. I get what I want because I'm always looking out for the best interest of others, therefore what I want and what they want are perfectly aligned. In this case, you," Elias responds.

I walk around his desk, lean onto his chest, passionately kiss him. "You are a beautiful man."

"I'm average on a good day, but you, on the other hand, are stunning, intellectually amazing, and as a bonus, pleasant to the touch. I can't stop thinking about you."

"Do you want to touch or talk? Shouldn't this 'thing' be a tad more discrete?"

"Thing? This isn't a 'thing'. I want you."

My eyes widen. *Why me?* I truly don't understand his motivations. I stand there expressionless.

He laughs. "You underestimate yourself, Zoe. You're special. One of a kind. The dimwits you associate with are too stupid to see it, but I know. They don't have the capacity or experience to understand and appreciate you. They focus on the physical, but there is so much more."

Now I'm really confused. *This isn't supposed to happen this way.* I stand up, walk around his desk to stand across from him.

He continues, "I can understand why this doesn't make any sense. I also understand that you may choose to say no. I am married, after all."

"Enlighten me." *Fucker! I can't say no. You haven't given me what I need yet.*

"I am attracted to you. It's gravitational. Resistance is futile. You are different. I can't put my finger on it. Let's just say you're not boring. Don't be offended – I've seen a lot, I get bored very quickly, always have. But you don't bore me, I don't think you ever will. And I am looking for something long term."

"I still don't understand where or how I fit in."

"I will never leave my wife, we are more like friends than husband and wife, but I want love and intimacy. I miss it. I may be selfish, but I'm being honest with you."

I say nothing. I know exactly where I fit in, I just want to hear him say it.

"You fit in perfectly." He clears his throat. "What I mean is, you and I could be amazing together. I just know that I am possessive, I don't like to share. Not sharing is caring in my book."

We have a problem. I am not a one-man type of woman. One man can't provide me with all the emotional needs and, moreover, the sexual needs I require. But he doesn't need to know that. I have experience. I know how people think. I know how not to get caught. I know how married men should conduct themselves so they won't get caught.... Never wear perfume, don't wear lipstick, don't call or text them after work hours, don't give them birthday cards, and most importantly, make sure that they never bring a new sex position home. Follow these rules and a few hundred more and you won't have to worry about giving half your assets away. I don't want these married men to leave their wives. It pleases me that they leave and return at my convenience. I know where I stand with them. It isn't a relationship. It IS companionship – and that is all I am prepared to give or accept. *The answer to your question Elias is it's me making the rules.*

And besides, my intuition tells me that Elias is not a one-woman type of man. He might attempt to play the part, he may even believe he is, but I know men like Elias all-to-well. I am not going to be his fool, or anyone's fool for that matter.

"Zoe, I see the way you interact with people. I see the way men look at you. They fall for you. You are an extremely desirable woman, but they want you for all the wrong reasons. To be specific, I appreciate and want you for more. There is a lot more to you than a pleasing physical appearance. I want you for many reasons and I want you all to myself."

"And what makes you so confident that this is something I want?"

"Because you know that I can love you."

Was he accurate in saying that? "I have one silly question."

"Go ahead."

"If I agree to this arrangement, what am I getting myself into?"

"I will love you and take care of you. I won't make any promises, but if my hunches are correct, you're a good person, my kind of person. I believe you are loyal and discreet. I will trust you, and when that happens, we will be great together."

"You can trust me Elias, but do your investigations or whatever you need to reassure yourself."

I stand up and walk to his side of his desk, roll his chair around, get down on my knees and began breathing on his cock through his pants. He is already erect. His cock wants to be inside my mouth. It's been conditioned; I have conditioned it. Having this power turns me on, it makes my mouth water and my pussy wet. I exhale warm breath onto his cock and moan slightly as I gaze up into his eyes. He looks down at me with his large brown eyes. They are beautiful, compassionate eyes but there is also something else there. It sends a chill up my spine. It doesn't last long. He begins to undo his belt and zipper. I pause while he pulls his pants down.

"Please continue," he requests politely.

And I do.

I look down at his cock, erect, staring back at me. I take my right hand and wrap it around the base of his cock. I begin by licking his balls, my tongue making its way up his shaft to the tip. I don't devour his cock yet. Instead I soften my tongue, returning to lick his balls again before moving up the length of his cock to its tip. I pause and look deeply into his eyes. His eyes are closed, he is enjoying every moment. I make sure he knows I am too, and moan softly.

I begin again, stroking his long, hard cock with my right hand. My saliva is all over his cock, but it's not enough, so I spit onto his cock and tug it as I rotate my wrist. I want my saliva to be dripping on the floor and flowing over my chin and down my neck onto my breasts. I lick my left hand, placing it on his balls, rubbing them slowly. What a sexy cock, I think, before opening my mouth and wrapping my lips around it. Its long and super hard. I take him into my mouth, inch by inch, his cock reaching the back of my throat. I gag and saliva spills from my throat all over his cock and me. Breathing, as best I can, through my nostrils, I deep throat him again. My eyes close as his deep moan fills the room. He is close. I'm extremely turned on and getting close myself. I start to rub my pussy under my dress.

"Oh, fuck. Oh, fuck. I'm going to come."

I rub my pussy hard, but slow the rhythm of my sucking, intensifying his orgasm. I feel his salty cum coat the back of my throat, and without hesitation I swallow. Every drop. And then I come hard and in waves that surprise me.

When I finally compose myself, I look up at him and wipe the remaining cum off my lips with my fingertips and suck them. "I'll need to sleep on it. Let me know the results of your investigations, when you finally 'trust me', and in the meantime I will think about this 'thing', or whatever we decide to call it."

"As you wish." He stands up and wipes himself before he pulls up his pants. "When am I…."

"Soon enough. Let me know when you are free," I say.

"I will," he says.

"Looking forward to it", I reply as I leave his office.

THE WEEKEND HAS PASSED and I can't stop thinking about Elias' proposition. My biggest obstacle is Stefano.

My phone rings. Unknown name. I figure, *What the hell,* and press accept. "Hello."

"Zoe? Hi. It's John…. Kolka."

"Look at you, being all resourceful."

He laughs on the other end of the receiver. "Well, I do owe someone an ice cream."

"And I was just beginning to think you had forgotten about me."

"Never. Are you free tomorrow night?"

"I can be."

"Great. Say, Il Laboratorio del Gelato 7:00 PM."

"Don't feel compelled to settle for an ice cream, John. With a little bit of work, you may be able to convince me to have a dinner with you."

"I have a sweet tooth Zoe. Let's start with dessert. Gelato for starters, then we'll play it by ear or stomach? You know what I mean…Can't wait. Enjoy your evening."

"You too, John. Good-night."

AN IDLE MIND IS the devil's playground, so I make a conscious effort to take a drive to clear my head. My mind is twisted in knots. I respect Matteo and trust him more than any other man in my life. That is frightening but telling. Then there is also John. Is he mere pawn in my game? He seems like a good enough man, but not the right man. Then there is Stefano. *I have to end things with Stefano.* And of course there is Elias and it is Elias who I can't get out of my mind. He is offering something I didn't know I wanted – attention. Not the kind of attention I'm used to, but I enjoy his attention. He makes me believe I am special. I return home to open another bottle of wine.

Is Elias providing me with something that I truly crave? Is it love I am in search of? Or is it admiration? Or security? Or all of the above? Perhaps, for once, I want someone to take care of me.

Just when you think you are in the clear, and that the sun is going to stay, the clouds return. That's how I feel. Which reminds me of my sister. Although she was ten years my senior, I was the one who took care of her. Growing up, we shared a bedroom, which wasn't fun. But things changed. One day, I went to go into our room and found the door was shut. I couldn't get in. At first, I thought it was locked, but we didn't have a lock on our bedroom door. I called for my sister, Angelica, and heard a whimper. I realized that she was sitting on the floor, with her back pressed up against the door. I asked her to open the door, which she finally agreed to after a bit of persuasion. I looked down at her with tears rolling down her cheeks, wondering what had happened to put her in such a state. Perhaps she had had an argument with dad? Or maybe she had broken up with her boyfriend? But it was neither. She just sat there crying for no reason, which totally messed me up. I didn't understand. Why the tears?

I was fourteen years old at the time, this was outside my sphere of understanding. I asked Angelica why she was crying.

Angelica's response? "I don't know."

I had always thought that tears were associated with pain and tragedy, but didn't understand the pain and sadness she was feeling. I sat on the floor next to Angelica and took her hand. I didn't want my sister to cry, wanted to transfer the sadness she felt to me. I thought I was strong enough to take that pain and sadness away from her. I closed my eyes and prayed to God that he would grant me my wish, asked him to transfer my sister's pain through our hands and into my body. I wanted to feel the pain.

Moments passed and Angelica continued to cry. I stayed with her, didn't let go of her hand. As time passed, I held her hand tighter and closer to my heart, until finally the tears subsided and Angelica began to smile once again.

The next day, Angelica didn't cry. Maybe God had heard my prayers?

Maybe Elias would hold my hand and take away all of my pain?

# CHAPTER ELEVEN

IL LABORATORIO DEL GELATO is crowded for a Tuesday night. I spot an available table at the back. It's perfect; it's discreet. I take a seat, glance at my watch. When I raise my head, our eyes lock. John wears a gorgeously tailored navy suit and a pink Hermes tie. He is very noticeable. His confidence makes him attractive – what woman isn't attracted to that?

I stand up to greet him with a hug. "Can I have dessert after we have dessert?" I whisper in his ear.

He tightens his embrace. "Another brilliant idea. I guess this is pre-dessert, dessert."

"I like the way you think," I grin.

He loosens his grip and looks into my eyes. "Machiavelli is teaching me a thing or two," he says, as we take our seats.

"Maybe I can help and teach you a third and fourth thing?"

He smiles. "One scoop or two?"

"One please."

"And what flavor would my princess like?"

"Princess?" I beam.

"I am your prince after all."

I giggle. "Vanilla please. Regular cone."

"I was mistaken. I took you for a pistachio girl."

"I'm full of surprises."

"Wait here. I will be right back." He heads to the counter to place our order.

I'm thinking strategy. The banter, the dialogue, the location, our immediate chemistry; everything is perfect so far. And then I see it. Right in front of me. And I know what I have to do. But first, I have to end the night with a bang.

John hands me my cone and takes a seat.

"So, what else is Machiavelli teaching you?" I'm a little curious to hear his response.

"To quote Machiavelli, *'Everyone sees what you appear to be, few experience what you really are.'* Am I seeing what I want to see in you?" He licks his cone.

"Perhaps. What do you see?" I lick my cone provocatively.

Is he going to give me the bullshit answer, or a truthful answer? Conversations such as the one we are having are integral to my understanding of the human cognitive thought process.

He takes another lick, "You are a unique individual who displays empathy for others."

Translation, he thinks I'm good. He isn't going to underestimate me. I have to be careful with this one. I try to look thoughtful. "I want to assist people to reach their full potential. I have seen too many people get hurt because of other people's lack of consideration. I always try to find a solution that is win-win." *Phew. I think that came across sincere.*

"So, what is your win-win strategy for Stefano and I?" he asks bluntly.

*Oh fuck!* "What are you really asking me, John?"

"I'm assuming you don't have any plans for the rest of the evening." His eyes twinkle.

"You assume correct," I reply.

"Let's go get dessert." He gracefully stands.

"Let's do it." *What is going on in that head of his?*

He looks down at me. "I would say trust me, but I know you are too smart to trust someone who tells you to trust them. Instead I'll say…let's go."

I'm not going to say no, at least not yet.

He takes the Robert F Kennedy Bridge to Astoria Park. The park has stunning buildings around its perimeter. He parks the car on 19th street.

"Do you like it?" he asks. "I built this community before running for Mayor."

"I have always loved this community. I know it well. I followed the construction. It won many awards and is now being copied all over the country." And it is.

"A subway line between 91st and Astoria is in the planning process. So, now we wait."

"That's not public information," I reply. Once the subway is constructed, property values will go sky high. But something feels off. Why is he telling me this? This is way too much way too soon. *What does his ego need? What emotional need is he craving?*

"Win-win Zoe."

John opens the driver's door and exits the vehicle. I stay put, not sure what to do. He opens the passenger door and holds out his hand and I reach for it. He escorts me into one of the buildings. We lock eyes and smile at one another as we walk into the elevator. He scans his fob and presses the PH button.

The elevator door opens directly into his suite, reveals a one-hundred and eighty-degree view of Manhattan. Wow! I am in pure awe. John releases my hand, and I continue to walk straight ahead to take in the view.

I stand still, enjoying the spectacular view. John comes up behind and wraps his arms around me. He begins to sway me back and forth, holding me. "Do you like?"

"Like? John, this is amazing!"

"I'm glad."

## QUEEN'S DANCE

"It's stunning."

He takes my hand and escorts me into the kitchen. He opens the fridge and pulls out of bottle of Dom Pérignon, pops it open and pours two glasses, places my glass in front of me. I look at the crystal glass, then him, and back at the glass before picking it up.

He looks at me and raises his glass. "To win-win."

"To win-win." We click our glasses, look into one another's eyes and take a liberal gulp.

"I must say, Zoe, you are very easy to be with."

"I'm flattered." *Not really. I know I'm easy to be with because at the end of the night you can drop me off and go home to your wife – aka the woman who isn't easy to be with.* "Why do you think that is?" I play along.

"I feel comfortable with you. I don't feel that you judge me."

"How could I judge you? Everything you have done, I have done – multiplied by ten."

He laughs. "Why are you with him?" he asks, as he takes another liberal gulp of champagne.

I'm a little unclear as to what he's really asking. "Him?"

"Stefano."

Now it's my turn to take a large gulp of champagne. "Stefano is great."

He lets out a short laugh. "Stefano is an untrustworthy, selfish, son-of-a-bitch. He is small minded and small time. You are wasting your superpowers by being with someone who really doesn't know how to treat you."

"And let me guess…you can do a better job?"

"Have you ever been with your equal? A man who stimulates and challenges you. A man you can have a meaningful conversation with."

"You assume he isn't and doesn't."

"C'mon, Zoe, we both know what Stefano is all about. You deserve the best, and Stefano reserves the best for himself."

"Great," I reply in a sarcastic tone.

"I just gave you your ticket out."

"Ticket?"

"Tell him about the subway line that hasn't been publicly announced and part ways with him. Make it clear your job is done. Do it soon. I will make a public announcement before the end of the month and word will get out before then."

John is clever enough to know that I'm on Stefano's payroll. I wasn't on my 'A' game the other night. John is a good actor. *But why is he helping me? What's his game? What does he want?* My head is spinning. "Is it that simple?"

"It is. You can also use the information for your personal gain. You don't need him."

With a small sip, I finish my champagne, take John by the hand and walk to the end of the hallway, where I assume there's a bedroom. I walk to the bed, turn around and look into John's eyes.

"I don't want to have sex with you, Zoe."

I shake my head. I'm at a loss of words. But my eyes can't lie. Not in a situation such as this one.

"I don't want anything from you. I like you. We can be great friends and colleagues."

I sit on the bed. "Come sit next to me."

He does.

Being a public figure, John spends the majority of the day putting on his poker face. Perhaps I'm allowing him the space to be vulnerable. Not passing judgement. Confidentiality and discretion. No expectations. No hidden agenda – that he is aware of. He is looking for a true confidante. And knowing the company I keep, he knows that I can offer him all that, and more. Perhaps that is why he is helping me? Because he wants to be vulnerable?

"No mics, no cameras. Tell me about yourself," I ask him.

"You first. What's in your purse for example?" He laughs.

"Photo identification, some cash, sex toys, the usual."

"Sex toys? Really? What have you got of interest?"

"There is my vibrator, handcuffs, lube, and a 'strap on' dildo," I say with a straight face.

His eyes widen. "I hope you don't plan to use that on me?"

"Not on a first date."

He smiles. "What would you like to know?" he asks.

"What makes you happy?" I inquire.

"You must be in work-mode."

"Actually, I'm in friendship-mode."

"I like that. To answer your question, I am happy when I am in the moment."

"Can you give me an example."

"Right now," he say quickly.

"Hmmm. Living in the moment without distractions."

"Yes."

"What else?"

"My family, ninety percent of the time."

"That's typical. Dig deeper," I demand.

"Public service. Helping others."

"And are you happy?"

"Should I be lying down for this Doctor?"

"That won't be necessary, unless that would make you feel more comfortable," I say with a straight face.

"I am happy now."

I smile.

"Being a public figure, you know that I have to conduct and carry myself a certain way. I don't feel like I am being true to myself. That's a burden."

"Life is too short to be unhappy. You need to change your cognitive process," I tell him.

"My what?"

"Your cognitive process. The way you think."

"Maybe I should lie down."

We both laugh.

"Change doesn't happen overnight," I tell him. "It's a process."

"Teach me."

"You have to teach yourself. I will, however, give you homework."

"Homework? Am I back in college?"

"You don't trust me?"

"I get it."

"Write down your definition of happiness. Make a list of what makes you happy. And start spending more time doing those things."

"You would be on my happy list, Zoe. At the top."

"Excellent, I like to be on top!" I wink and he laughs. Sometimes I just can't help myself.

"I assume we will be seeing more of one another?" I ask.

"There is one more thing I have to tell you."

"You really don't have to."

"Yes, I do." He pauses. "My wife is a Comanno."

The Comanno family is one of the five families in Manhattan. They control the unions, amongst other things. *What are you doing Zoe? You are now officially playing with fire. This is dangerous. Why am I wet?* I'm excited. Adrenaline is running through me.

In this moment I decide I have to have John. I look into his eyes and he into mine. I move closer to him and he does the same, until our lips meet. My hands are all over his face, moving to his back as I squeeze him closer. I adjust my position and mount him, as I continue to kiss him. Our soft tongues intertwine.

I stand and he can see the hunger in my eyes as I remove his jeans and underwear. His cock is rock hard. This time, I skip the tease and place his cock directly into my mouth and force it as far into my throat as it will go. My saliva coats his cock. It would be worth millions if I could mass produce it, bottle it and sell it. I rotate my tongue while I suck his cock up and down. He comes within minutes. He gasps for air.

"Why are you really here, Zoe?" are the first words out of his mouth after the orgasm.

*Strategy? Lust? Love?* I know what John has to offer. After all, he is a married man. But I feel a sense of calmness with him. "I don't really know."

"I need you to know. That's my homework for you. Perhaps you can let me know the next time we see one another?"

"I will."

He holds my hand the entire way on the drive home, without a single word being exchanged.

# CHAPTER TWELVE

I HEAR THE ICE CREAM truck from around the corner, run inside the house into the kitchen in search of some change, but can't find any. I know where my father keeps his emergency funds. I run into the basement and lift the ceiling tile. I reach in with my hand and pull out a DVD. I reach in further and find a five-dollar bill. I put the DVD back in its place and run outside. The ice cream truck is nowhere in sight.

I return to the basement and put the five-dollar bill back where I found it. My hand brushes up against the DVD. Intrigued, I retrieve it from the ceiling. My curiosity gets the better of me and I place the DVD in the player and press play. It's my father in a strange place, somewhere I have never seen before. A strange woman enters the frame and they begin to kiss. My jaw drops. *What am I watching?!* She unbuttons his shirt, then his pants, before dropping to her knees. I am embarrassed and shocked but I can't turn away. The strange woman's face is now buried between my father's legs, his head lifted skyward as he moans in pleasure. Placing his hand at the back of her head, he grabs a fistful of her hair and thrusts his hips. I can't believe what I am seeing. I quickly turn the DVD off, retrieve it from the player and put it back in its hiding place in the ceiling.

I want nothing more than to throw it away, to never to think of it again, but as with most things in life, it isn't that simple. He would return to his hiding place, find the DVD missing and come looking for me. Or worse, my mother. He is an abusive man – both verbally and physically – not the type of man to let things go. His justice would be swift and someone would get hurt. Even as a 12-year-old, I knew that it was better to look the other way. So that's what I do. Though I can't help but think: 'Does he still love my mother? Does he love me?' These are questions no child should have to consider. I can never forgive him for the way he treats us – as an inconvenient detour from his life's plan. My father is a proud man, but life has taken its toll on him, and he in turn takes a toll on his family.

I've carried this secret with me ever since. Maybe this is the root of my unhealthy relationships with men that have followed. How can I find trust within my heart, when my brain is aware of how men really behave – or misbehave? A person's true character is shown when no one is watching. Many speak of integrity, but very few demonstrate it. My heart craves to open up to love, yet I have been conditioned to believe that by doing so I leave myself vulnerable, open myself up to being disappointed and hurt. It's better to simply control my emotions.

This in turn makes me numb. I begin to separate pleasure from emotions, which later on in life attracts a certain type of man – the rich powerful man. It is a simple transaction. I meet the demands of those men and they give me what I want. Sex becomes a currency for me. The truth is I fear love, or believe that either it doesn't exist or that it can only cause pain in the end. Love comes with conditions…conditions I am not willing to accept. Stefano was my first encounter with sex as currency. It was easy…too easy.

I have become a calculating woman. Every word, action and response has become deliberate. I look at myself in the mirror. And yet I am finally happy…I think. I am in control of my life…I think.

I consider Elias' proposition. It couldn't have come at a better time. Although I have no intention of giving him all of me, he doesn't need to know that.

I make myself up and head to Stefano's office, texting him that I'm on my way.

Stefano is quick to acknowledge my text.

*Fantastic*. A quick in and out visit with information that will bring an end to our relationship. I hope.

I feel sorry for Stefano, and I don't want to disappoint him, but I don't want to be here. But duty calls and I make my way up to the twenty-third floor. His office isn't sleek, simple or clean. Open boxes and files are strewn everywhere. He neglects his office space. It was a mess.

I walk in, say hello to Jodi, the receptionist, and proceed to the boardroom where I find Stefano and Margaret, his accounting manager, finishing up a meeting. I take a seat across the table and wait my turn.

"Tell the fucker I am going to shred all of his invoices if he doesn't show up at the site tomorrow morning," Stefano yells at the top of his lungs, as he paces back and forth.

Stefano is not in the greatest of moods after talking numbers. I know I have to be careful with my choice of words.

"I think we are done here," Stefano says, finally calming down.

"Thanks, Stefano," Margaret responds.

Before Margaret leaves the room, she waves hello. I know she is thinking *good luck to you, Zoe*, but I don't need luck. I need an escape and now I have one.

"Well look who decided to show up." Stefano's tone is calm.

"Someone's in a great mood."

"I'm in a fuckin great mood? All work and no play, working fuckin eighteen-hour days. How is our friend John doing?" he inquires.

"John enjoyed his gift and is studying Machiavelli."

"Does it look like I give a flying fuck?"

"You will give a fuck when I tell you what I've heard." I pause. "A subway line is planned between 91st and Astoria."

He stands there silent for at least a minute, thinking, making his calculations. Finally, he says, "Very good to know. Is it for sure? What if it doesn't go through or takes another route?"

Was Stefano privy to information that John didn't have? There was only one other person who can answer that question…and it isn't John.

"You ask for info and I get you info. Would you like a money back guarantee?"

"And where is Matteo's parcel?"

"No idea," I respond without hesitation.

"Great, Zoe. Now go finish your fuckin job and find out!" He takes his seat and locks his eyes to mine. "Who informed you of this subway proposal, anyway?"

"A reliable source." I pause, knowing he is fully aware that John is my source. "We might be able to connect the dots with Matteo and the subway, but I don't have any hard evidence."

"Let's fuckin not play kids' games, Zoe. Get me concrete information."

Nothing is good enough for Stefano. Perhaps that is something that initially drew me to him.

"Go deeper," he demands.

"Bend over," I reply.

"Fuck yourself."

I laugh. A typical response from him. "With pleasure."

"Can I watch?" He smiles.

"Hmm. Let me think about that." I pick up my purse signaling my cue to leave.

"Something is missing, Zoe. Figure it out."

I turn around and say, "Yes boss," before I leave the room.

*Fuck me!* Although Stefano is a selfish son-of-a-bitch, I don't want to fail him. Perhaps that speaks more to my character. Having been let down as a child, I don't want to do the same to others. But to survive in this industry, I have to do what I have to do to win. My time with Stefano isn't up…just yet.

I walk purposefully along 5th Avenue. I enjoy the cool breeze that follows me, watch the tourists and locals walk from one hotspot to another. The hustle of Manhattan has always excited me. If there isn't a problem to solve, life is boring; and New York City isn't boring. There are always plenty of problems, new challenges around every corner.

As my mind wanders, I hear a raspy voice calling my name from behind. "Zoe?"

I turn around and Wagi is standing right in front of me. I put my arms around him. "What a lovely surprise," I say. "Are you playing tourist for the day, cruising 5th Ave?"

"You found me out," he replies.

"That's why I get paid the big bucks. How have you been?"

"Wonderful, with the exception of getting a 2:00 AM last night call from yet another of Elias' ex-girlfriends crying her little heart out. What is it with these women? Is he that good?"

I desperately want to know more, and am trying to hide the look on my face that screams *tell me everything*, as I recall my etiquette lesson from Matteo. Sometimes you are better off not knowing…and this is probably one of those times. I play naïve. *Could I be his next victim?* The truth is I know Elias is playing a game. But so am I. I just need to play better than he does.

"Someone's M.O., perhaps?" I reply, hoping humor will alleviate the tension.

"I must have a sign on my forehead that reads, 'I can solve your problem'," he complains. "Apparently, I have all the answers, with the exception of my own problems of course."

"Don't be so negative, Wagi." I pat him on the shoulder.

"My life is a mess, but apparently I give very good advice."

"Don't underestimate yourself," I tell him.

"Zoe, I am in my fifties, and just got dumped by a woman who was more interested in what was in the back of my pants, rather than the front...and I don't mean my ass."

"Perhaps you're right."

"Or maybe she did love me a little?"

"Does it matter anymore?"

"You're bruising my ego."

"I know your ego can handle it."

We both laugh.

"Say hello to our good friend Elias for me," Wagi smiles and embraces me.

"Will do. See you soon." Soon wasn't going to happen anytime soon. I'm just being polite.

And I continue to walk, with a purpose...or two.


I EXIT THE ELEVATOR, see Rebecca smiling. I have become a regular visitor to Matteo's office.

"Someone must have had a hot date last night?"

She smiles shyly. "I can't deny it."

"Good for you. Is Matteo around here somewhere?"

"Let me just give him a call." She picks up the receiver, says a few words and nods for me to go in.

"New glasses?" He stands with his head cocked to one side, his perfectly sculpted body silhouetted by the sun's rays.

"So nice of you to notice," I reply as I put my purse down.

"What's up?"

I drop myself onto his sofa, patting the cushion to my right.

His footsteps echo in the cavernous office as he makes his way to me, but he doesn't take a seat. He stands in front of me. Perfect height for a blow job. The ambiance is set – house music in the background, his cock erect, my mouth perfectly positioned. I respond by gazing upwards into his eyes.

I bite my lip, anticipating his next move. I mischievously did not close the door behind me. If he wants a performance from me, he is first going to be inconvenienced.

"Elias." Matteo knows me as a woman with few words.

He takes a seat. "How is our good friend doing?"

"He is doing great. But you know I want the goods." I am fully aware that the answer he is about to provide may have been scripted, but I have nothing to lose.

"He is a talented and well connected lawyer," he replies.

"I gathered that much. After all, you do utilize his services."

"What would you like to know?"

"What could he want from me?" I ask point-blank.

"To build his network?"

"Have you seen him with other new networks?" He knows exactly what I'm really asking him.

"I haven't."

"What can the handsome Matteo share with me about his good friend Elias?"

"He has this unusual gaze that would make others feel uncomfortable, perhaps?"

I blurt out, "Sociopathic?"

Matteo doesn't respond. He doesn't have to. His eyes are doing all the talking.

"So, what you are saying is have fun, however..."

He interrupts. "Zoe, I like you. I like him. Just be cautious."

And that is all I need to hear. Besides, I am an expert at distancing myself from men. I know the difference between love and lust. I know what I have to do.

And now, for my second purpose. "Astoria and 91st subway line."

"Hmmm. Someone has been doing their homework. That is, after all, very privileged information."

"Privileged enough for me to know? Then it's a bit of an open secret, isn't it?" I laugh. "So, who is trying to kibosh it?"

"You really are in the know." He laughs.

Stefano did know something. *Shit!*

"You are getting yourself into deep waters here, Zoe."

"But my hunch is correct."

"I didn't say that."

"You didn't have to."

He laughs. "We encountered some hiccups along the way. But they should be corrected very shortly."

"You, Matteo, are a good and knowledgeable man and you're not bad looking either."

"I don't know about the good looking part but I must admit you're not the first person to say so. My daughters tell me the same every now and then – when they want something. But I do know a few things. There are people in this industry that are greedy...and there are people who are honest. I like to think of myself as honest most of the time and greedy the rest."

"So, are there any other developments you can share with me? I'm always looking for an opportunity."

"You're in the know."

*Well, I guess that didn't work.* I kiss Matteo on the cheek. "Thanks. You know I appreciate knowing that you always have my back"

"I haven't had your back, your front, or any part of you in a long while, Zoe Winstein, and I miss it!"

"Soon…maybe." I smile as I walk out the door.

I must dance with the enemy, keep him close…perhaps too close? It is a dangerous dance. I begin to question my purpose. My opponent shows signs of weakness, yet I sense that he is vulnerable – but this could also be his strategy. I too am vulnerable. I know his softness, his fear – the husband and father who is defenseless to love – and I listen to the powerful voice. He is wounded by his family, so in lieu of love from them, he collects love letters from all of his women from around the world. How do I know this? He has shared them with me – his ego getting the better of him. After a few months of me opening up, he too begins to open up to me. He knows of my past, and I thus become vulnerable too. He asks me to read these letters aloud. They are poetic. It strokes his ego to know that strangers fall in love with him. He knows where he stands with his lovers.

But I have learned that he does love one. How do I know that she is different? Because he had no desire to know about her escapades, it hurts too much. Thus, I know how to destroy him…his weakness. I'm just not sure if I I'm ready to do so. The fucker – Matteo - is growing on me.

As I make my way out of the building my phone buzzes. It was him. Him who? The man who has my brain and my heart, Elias. But he won't be hearing from me today. The rest of my day is going to be dedicated to sleep. I need to shut off my brain…no sex this time.

I WAKE TO THE SOUND of my alarm. He is the first thing on my mind.

I glance at yesterday's message.

Elias: Miss me?

I know what he wants to hear, but I refuse to give in so easily. Hence, I wait to respond.

It is an *I love you* – *I hate you* relationship. Both masochists, we thrive on inconsistency. Perhaps that is what makes our love-making so intense. When our naked bodies are intertwined, nothing can break us apart.

My overactive mind is what will destroy us. And with him having characteristics of a sociopath, we are doomed.

I compartmentalize. I can detach myself from things – things being feelings. I am cold. Having sex with other men doesn't change my growing love for Elias. I am pragmatic and calculating. I know what to say, and how to say it.

Although I want desperately to respond, I have to wait a little longer before I can reply. I have to keep playing the game.


THERE IS A LOW DARK clouds over the city this morning. The sky is grey and the birds are silent...no chirping; no lullabies.

After meeting a few patients at the clinic, I pull out my cellphone. He/I have waited long enough.

Zoe: Maybe.

I wait a few moments before his response.

Elias: Really?
Zoe: Okay, maybe a little.
Elias: Really?

Zoe: Maybe a lot.
Elias: That's better. I'm thinking of you.

And I was thinking of him, but not in that romantic way. A plan is taking shape.

Zoe: Ditto.
Elias: Hope you are behaving.
Zoe: Yes boss.
Elias: I like the sounds of that! Sunday 8:00 PM.
Zoe: Yes Mr. boss, Sir.
Elias: I like that even more. I could get used to this.

I have a lot of work ahead of me this weekend and I'm not going to let anyone or anything distract me. Time to make my next move.

# CHAPTER THIRTEEN

THE WEEKEND IS OVER. I step out of the shower and look at myself in the mirror. *You are ready for this, Zoe. There is no turning back.* No guilt. No remorse. Every detail of my appearance this evening is planned. Slim, black tailored pants, black sneakers and a colorful blouse that accentuates my cleavage. And the final touch…neutral lipstick, glossy. *Yes, Zoe, you are ready for this.*

I need to win his trust, notwithstanding his assertions that I have already done so. I highly doubt that. I understand the difference between business and pleasure. I am beginning to take note of Elias' character flaws. He needs to be wanted. He needs to feel wanted. He wants attention. He wants to be loved. He is charming, yet he is unable to read body language. They – sociopaths – are unable to read people's discomfort. Sociopaths have no boundaries when it comes to personal space, they lie and believe their own lies. He is a sociopath and being attracted to a sociopath is dangerous…but at least I know what I am in for.

8:00 PM AND ELIAS PULLS into the roundabout. I walk over to the passenger door and let myself in.

I take a seat and politely say, "Good evening, Mr. Macchetta."

"So proper. Good evening, Ms. Winstein."

"Where to for dinner?"

"Only one way to find out."

Elias weaves in and out of traffic, not paying any attention to his surroundings and easily distracted by anything but the other cars on the road.

We pull up to a high rise building in the financial district.

"Been here before?" he asks with anticipation in his voice.

"Not sure, don't think so," I reply.

"You will love it. They've recently opened up here in Manhattan. The concept started in Italy and now they are expanding across the globe."

"And what concept is that?"

"A market with multiple restaurants."

"And what is this supermarket called?"

"Mangiamolto."

"How do you find all these amazing restaurants?"

"They are friends."

We walk into the building, then up a set of escalators that lead to the third floor. It's a happening place, a modern supermarket, with sleek shelving housing high-end products surrounded by dining tables packed with couples eating.

Elias takes me by the hand and follows the hostess past the fish market to a private room. He never makes reservations, but they always have room for him. What a strange and wonderful gift.

The room is large enough to seat a part of twenty, but there we are, just me and Elias, sitting adjacent to one another in this large space.

"Do you like?" he asks, seeking approval.

"I won't ask how you pulled it off," I reply, feeding his ego.

"I have nothing to hide, Zoe. You can ask me anything you like."

*Yes, Elias. I know I can ask you anything I like. But I am also fully aware that the response you feed me could be a full zip code away from the truth, maybe as far as the state line. Is that an indictable offence Mr. Lawyer? Transporting the truth across state lines.* "Why me?"

"Didn't I already answer that question?"

"Remind me, I have a short memory span." *And I'm curious if it will be the same answer that you gave the last time.* I smile.

He gazes into my eyes and caresses my hair with his right hand. "Because you are different, in the best possible way."

*Sure, sure.* "And how am I different, 'in the best possible way?'" Yes, there is a part of me that wants to be charmed.

"You are driven, charming, beautiful, intelligent, independent, strong minded and extra heavy duty sexy."

"Perhaps you are attracted to the challenge?"

"Without a doubt. You, Zoe Winstein, are a woman who is desired by men. It's not just the way you look. A blind man would feel your energy from a hundred yards."

The lawyer in Elias knows exactly what to say and how to say it. He is remarkable at times. He is a real estate lawyer but he would be great in a court room.

He continues, "I am fully aware that you know very little about me, so this evening is for you to ask me questions…any question your heart desires."

"Tell me about your ex." *What happened to your filter Zoe?*

"And here I am thinking you wanted to know about my marriage."

"I am content knowing very little about your marriage."

"Good to know."

"I have no interest in you leaving your wife. Actually, truth be told, I would leave you before you left your wife." *And I'm not kidding.* I'm not going to be the delusional women who believes a married man is going to leave his wife to be with me. And besides, if he is capable of leaving his wife for another woman, he is fully capable of leaving me for another woman. Why don't other women see that?

"Her name was Karen. She was divorced with kids. She had an ugly divorce and had no interest in re-marrying. Our relationship was convenient for both of us."

"Were you sleeping with other women?" I know the answer. I just want to know how honest he will be with himself.

"No I wasn't. I did, however, have other women companions."

Gotta love the lawyer response. Semantics. That's enough for me. "Did that make her feel uncomfortable?"

"She knew all of my friends. Any other questions?"

*He totally didn't answer the question.* "Yes. When can we eat?" I'm not interested in hearing his voice amuse me with lies and distractions.

"I have already spoken to the chef, and he is taking care of us...speaking of which..."

"Elias," I hear a male voice from across the room.

"Giacomo, come va." Elias stands up and gives him a hug.

"Benissimo caro, Wonderful to see you." A heavily bearded man looks down at me. "And you must be Zoe. So nice to meet you."

"Zoe, this is Giacomo, the chef."

I stand up and extend my hand, "A pleasure to meet you, Giacomo."

"What a beautiful lady, the pleasure is mine. Please, please sit down. I hope you enjoy what I have prepared for you tonight."

"I am confident it will be outstanding."

"Thank you. Let me get things started for you two."

"Thanks for saying hello," Elias replies.

Giacomo exits the room and the waiter walks in with a bottle of wine. Elias samples it and nods his approval. The waiter fills our glasses and Elias waits for him to leave the room before he picks up his wine glass. "A toast, to a beautiful friendship."

"To a beautiful friendship." I take a sip and fall in love with the oak aftertaste of the wine. "Mmmm."

"I'm glad you like it. It's a lovely undiscovered Barolo, oaky but not too oaky. Sorry, I'm getting carried away."

The food arrives shortly thereafter and Elias spends most of dinner with his eyes firmly glued on me, occasionally blurting out some key names in the development business. He knows everyone and isn't afraid to let me know. He has an interesting story to tell about each and every one of them. He couldn't be more charming and... insecure? Why does he have to let me know that he knows everyone? That is a sign of trouble.

"What are your expectations of me?" he asks as he finishes his pasta.

"Expectations ruin relationships." I know that from personal experience.

"Would the term rules be better suited for this arrangement?"

I laugh. "How about mutual respect, honesty and trust?" Now I'm talking nonsense.

"That sounds like a good foundation if you'll pardon the construction pun."

By the end of dinner, I have drunk way too much wine and feel very comfortable with my pet sociopath, but Elias isn't quite ready to take me home. "I have a surprise for you," he announces.

I'm intrigued.

"I hope you don't have a curfew tonight."

I am curious to know where our next stop will be. I am trying to compose my controlling nature. I hold off from inquiring and go along for the ride.

We get into the car and head to the Upper West Side of town. He pulls up in front of a beautiful building with valet parking and gets out of the car.

"Good evening Mr. Macchetta. Shall I park the car?"

"Yes, please. Thanks, Scott."

I remain silent as we walk into the lobby and into the elevator, where Elias enters a code. The thirty-eighth-floor button lights up.

He takes my hand in the elevator and turns to me. "Tell me this is what you want."

I turn to him. A sense of calm runs through my body. "This is what I want." And just as I finish my sentence, the elevator opens to a spectacular space with a sunken living room. "Holy shit."

"Do you like?"

"I love it! Is that an original Rothko? And a Kline?" My eyes widen. I'm in heaven.

"Yes and yes," he smiles.

I have to admit to myself that it's wonderful how nonchalant he is about the seriousness of his art collection.

"That you know and appreciate this art, as I do, is one of the things that draws me to you, Zoe. Follow me." He makes his way to the living room. We both sit down and he hands me a card.

"What is this?" I am more than a little curious.

"Open it and read it aloud."

And I do. "Precious deserves precious. Walk to the entrance where we leave our coats. There you will find a treasure of hope." I am a little confused. "What is this?"

"A scavenger-hunt," he replies.

"How adorable." I'm excited, but don't want to come across too eager.

"Go on. You know where to go."

I walk to the front door with Elias and open the closet. A teddy bear holding a heart with a note is on the top shelf. I turn to Elias. "Adorable."

He laughs. "Go on. Read the next note."

The note reads, "I give you my heart and a teddy bear. Your next hidden note is with the forks and knives of our future meals."

I hurry to the kitchen, open most the drawers before I find the forks and knives. A chocolate bar is in amongst the utensils, with another note, which reads, "I give to you a chocolate float. Your next hidden clue is with treasured love notes." I am puzzled. "Treasured love notes?"

"Where would someone keep their love notes?"

*His nightstand. A clever way of getting me into his bed.* "Your bedroom? I can see what you're up to, Elias."

He shows me the way and I follow.

"What side of the bed do you sleep on?"

He points to the left side.

I walk over to the nightstand and open the top drawer. There is a red box. I don't know what to expect. I sit on the bed and pause for a moment. I am anxious to open it but I don't want to be disappointed.

Elias sits next to me. "What are you waiting for?"

I take a deep breath and open the box. *Holy fuck! A diamond ring.*

"Zoe, I love you. I don't have to be your first love. Just your last."

My eyes began to tear. *What is wrong with you Zoe? Pull yourself together!* "I don't know what to say."

"I have one more surprise for you." He says as he hands me a note: *Your eyes are mixed up as is your mind. Don't pull your tears, I am not blind. No matter though, I love you so, steady and slow. My heart is filled. You are so special as feelings go. Your soft precious love still grows. So, stop your sorrow. Please don't throw it away. You'll see me tomorrow; our love won't stray.* He hands me an access card with a code on it. "Stay with me tonight. I want this to be our place. I love you, Zoe."

My mind is blank, maybe for the first time ever. I am caught up in the moment. I grab him and begin kissing him. He doesn't stop me. I feel safe. I don't feel like this is a game. What the hell is going on with me? I'm not myself. I go back and forth about this guy. My faultless intuition has completely abandoned me. I'm rudderless. No strategy. Just pure love and bliss. For the first time in a long time I feel as though I am about to make love to a man.


IT IS 7:00 AM AND HIS phone sings sweet lullabies, waking me from my deep sleep. The slender athletic man lying next to me gently rolls over and cups my bare breast with his left hand, kissing my shoulder. I have yet to open my eyes fully. The smell of sex is the first thing I notice.

"Turn around baby. Let me see that beautiful face."

I turn around and he holds me tightly in his arms. "Bacon and eggs for my baby?"

"Sounds yummy. Can I help?"

"No. Stay in bed. Like a good love slave."

Elias and I have breakfast in bed. He reads the newspaper, I sip on my coffee. "I could get used to this."

"I'm okay with that. I do recall a girl once telling me that the way to her heart is through her stomach. Don't give out too much information, Zoe. It will come back and bite you in the ass."

We both laugh.

"I must get ready for work, baby. Stay as long as you like."

And I do. I rest a little longer. I have completely forgotten my objective. Everything is a blur.

I eventually make my way back to my place and hide from the world. Stefano has finally given me some space. Matteo and I are getting closer. Elias is beginning to trust me the way I need his trust, and maybe I am falling in love. And John is in the background, waiting patiently for my next move. The pieces are all lined up. Now, I wait...I wait for one of them to let something slip, because eventually they all do. I just need to be patient and wait for the right opportunity to present itself.

# CHAPTER FOURTEEN

THE PHONE WAKES ME.

Elias: Good morning my love!

I look at the time. 9:15AM. I can't remember the last time I went to bed so early and slept in so late. I hear his voice in my head saying those words...*good morning my love*.

Zoe: Good morning.
Elias: I thoroughly enjoyed our time together the other night.
Zoe: Ditto!
Elias: Any exciting plans for the day?
Half in a daze, I have to think for a moment.
Zoe: Going to hit the gym, once I wake up, then spend the afternoon working from home.
Elias: Sounds like a productive day.
Zoe: That occasionally happens.
Elias: I have some clients in town from Italy this weekend. Care to join us Friday night for dinner?

I think to myself, why wouldn't his wife be going to this dinner, but I don't pry.

Zoe: I can make myself available.
Elias: Great. My Place for 7 PM. Now get that
      beautiful ass to the gym.

He definitely knows how to motivate me. I slowly get out of bed and mentally prepare myself for some weight training. I gulp down my morning coffee and head down to the underground parking garage.

I haven't taken my car out in a week, and it is in need of a wash. The dust that has accumulated over the past week has changed its color from black to grey. With my gym bag over one shoulder, and my purse over the other, I have to maneuver myself so that I can dig my car keys out of my over-sized purse.

Inches away from my driver's door and fishing for my keys, I hear foot steps behind me. Before I can turn around I am grabbed from behind in a vice like grip, a big hand clamped over my mouth. I can't move my arms at all. My assailant lifts me into the air and carries me off as if I'm a doll. I kick and attempt to scream but it's completely useless, I can only manage small gasps of air. A cloth is placed over my head and tightened around my neck, but I don't give up, I continue to kick while my hands are bound behind me with tape.

I'm dumped on a hard surface in complete darkness, a strong hand still over my mouth. I have exhausted all of my flight responses. I feel as though we are moving, but my body is inert, feels paralyzed by fear and shock.

I hear a man's deep voice that I don't recognize. "I am going to move my hand from your mouth, but you can't make a sound. Nod if you understand."

I nod instinctively.

"If you scream, I will stop you, and you won't like that. We are taking you somewhere and our instructions are not to hurt one hair on your pretty head – so long as you co-operate."

Once again, I nod. I can't breathe.

He releases his hand. I am unable to think clearly. *Do I scream? Do I shut up? What happens in the movies?* I knew I should have paid more attention.

I decide to stay silent for now, listen and recover. It sounds like there are two men, one driving the vehicle, the other sitting next to me.

I feel my heart jumping out of my chest as I struggle to breath. Where are they taking me? Who would do this to me? Stefano? But why? To what end? I know he would never hurt me…never. Matteo? Does he know that I am trying to interfere with his development? Unlikely.

I attempt to calm down and think clearly, but it's no good – plain, simple, naked fear takes over and I begin to scream. So much for calming down. I hope against hope that someone will hear me, save me. Within seconds, the man with the deep voice clamps his hand over my mouth, wraps tape around the hood, covering my mouth, asks me if I can breathe. I nod yes.

"I told you not to scream, lady. Why won't the bitch listen?"

My body is shaking and I begin to cry, my tears rolling down my face and soaking into the hood. After a minute or so he takes pity on me and says, "Relax, lady, you won't be hurt. The man made that very clear."

After ten minutes or so, the car stops for longer than a red-light duration and I hear the door open.

They lift me up, and I begin to kick and scream once again.

"Fuck, this chick is strong," says the one I haven't heard yet. He sounds young, like a boy.

They carry me into a place that sounds large and empty, sit me in a chair, tie my feet to the chair legs and secure my hands behind my back, then leave me alone.

There's a deep silence, broken finally by the sound of footsteps walking towards me. The steps come closer, eventually stop next to me.

I feel fingers on my neck, someone removing the tape from my mouth and untying the cloth over my head. The cloth is removed but I keep my eyes closed because of the brightness of the room.

"You can open your eyes now, Zoe."

I recognize the voice. I slowly open my eyes and see Elias standing next to me.

"What the fuck?" I scream gasping for air.

"Surprise," he says, a smile on his face.

"Can you untie me please."

He laughs. "Oh no. Not yet."

"This isn't funny, Elias."

"It's not meant to be funny, Zoe. It's meant to fulfill your fantasy. I've completed the kidnapping...it's now time for the sexual pleasure part."

"Can you please untie me?"

"Not yet."

"Where the fuck am I?" A black van is parked nearby in what looks like an abandoned warehouse.

He unzips his pants and takes out his semi erect cock. "Suck it."

"Make me," I reply in a harsh tone.

He laughs and slaps me across the face, hard. Then he grabs the back of my head and forces his cock into my mouth. I try to move my head and close my mouth. He moves away and slaps me again. He places his fingers on my cheeks and presses my mouth open, pushes his cock in until it reaches the back of my throat. I gag. "Yes," he says. "Suck it like that." He slowly starts to fuck my mouth, my saliva dribbling down my neck as he moves his cock in and out of my throat with long, slow, deep strokes.

"Good girl." He removes his cock from my mouth and gazes down at me. "Don't move." I watch as he pulls a Swiss army knife from his pocket and rips my blouse open, exposing my breasts. He puts the knife down but he doesn't stop there. He begins ripping my leggings apart exposing my pussy. He sits on me and begins kissing me, fondling my breasts and pinching my nipples. Involuntarily I begin to breath hard and my pussy tingles as I gasp for air.

He drops to his knees, pulls me forward to the front of my chair and begins licking my sex, his tongue parting my wet lips. I moan with pure pleasure. *Is anyone watching? Where did the two men disappear to?* He begins to finger me as his tongue swirls in a circular motion on my clit.

My head tilts back with my eyes closed and I am lost in the feeling as his tongue and his fingers move faster and faster. I don't want to be enjoying this but I'm helpless to stop it. Involuntarily I start to tremble. I gasp as a shudder tears through my body. I'm coming. An orgasm like never before. The juxtaposition of fear, terror, release and pleasure have mixed to give me the best orgasm I have ever had or may ever have. I almost pass out.

He licks every drop from my wet pussy, teasing his tongue round and round, up and down. "My turn," he says, standing up and gazing down at me. "I'm going to untie you. Promise me you are going to be a good girl, otherwise I am going to have to restrain you again and do what I want with you. Do you understand?"

I hesitate to give him the answer he wants, but give in. "I understand."

"Good girl." He unties me and demands that I, "Stand up and bend over."

I comply.

He rips off what's left of my leggings, roughly bends me over, inserts his cock into me in one powerful thrust. He holds still with his long cock deep inside me, then begins to pull my hair with one hand and squeeze my waist with the other. Holding me like that, trapped, he begins to fully thrust even further into me.

I scream.

"Scream baby! No one can hear you."

It is pleasure and pain all at once and it goes on and on, his cock buried deep inside me. After what seems like an hour but is probably no more than ten minutes, my body shivers as he comes, then collapses across my exhausted body.

"Fuck, that was a first," he says as he pulls his cock out of my dripping pussy. "Don't worry, I brought you a change of clothes."

I sit on the chair at a loss of words.

He walks to the van and brings back a bag. "Here, change into these. I'm taking you for lunch. Need to quickly stop by the office first."

I am still in shock, I can barely move. I slowly dress, trying to process what just happened. I can't deny that I am exhilarated, that there are butterflies in my stomach, I'm light headed and shivering, and yet...

"Are you going to say something?" he asks.

"Holy fuck!"

"That's more like it."

"Have you done this before?"

"No, can't say I have. This is a first. And you?"

"What the fuck happened?"

"I listen to what you said and gave it to you. This was your fantasy. My present to you."

"What are you talking about".

"You don't remember?" says Elias.

"Remember what?" I am perplexed.

"Our conversation in bed. Your kidnap fantasy?"

Oh shit. "OK Elias, but that was pretend. This scared me senseless."

"That's why it was so good, Zoe. If I dropped a hint, it wouldn't have been so good. Now come on, I have a meeting at my office."

His car is parked outside of the building and I hop in. The car ride is spent with him making or receiving calls while I sit there in silence, re-living the event, at once both terrifying and electrifying.

We pull up at his building. "Should I wait in the car?"

"No. Come up."

I follow him to the fifty-eighth floor and wait in the lobby. I take a peek at his office door but it's closed. I distract myself with the magazines in the lobby and notice a brunette walk past me into the elevator. Elias emerges with a smile on his face. Something doesn't feel right. My gut is in defensive mode, but I know better than to utter a sound.

Elias walks over to me and wraps his arm around my waist. "Ready, baby?"

"Ready."

We step into the elevator, and rather than going to the ground floor, he pushes the button for the sixty-seventh-floor. I have learned from experience not to ask too many questions. This man enjoys being in charge, enjoys being the alpha-male. The elevator doors open at a restaurant, La Belle.

Elias turns to me, "Have you eaten here before."

"No. Lots of firsts today."

"The food is spectacular."

We sit at the bar and he gets the bartender's attention. "Two dozen Thatch Island oysters, and two glasses of champagne please, you know the one I like, the pink one, I forget the name." He turns to me, "They say oysters are aphrodisiacs."

"I always enjoy oysters."

"Hope you're free for the rest of the afternoon. We aren't done yet. I'm a well-rounded criminal. I don't limit myself to kidnapping. Plus, I haven't received any ransom."

I haven't eaten lunch yet, but I have experienced the rollercoaster day of a lifetime, and it is barely noon. I'm not sure how much more I can handle in one day, but I'm willing to play along and find out. "Yes, sir," I say.

"Good girl." He takes my hand and notices I'm not wearing his ring. "Where is my ring?"

"I was going to the gym. Didn't want to wear it there."

"I want you to wear it at all time. I want people to know you are spoken for, Zoe. You know I don't share."

"I didn't realize it was that important to you. I thought my behavior is what counted and not something I wear."

"Don't monkey with a monkey, Zoe, wearing the ring is part of the behavior that counts. It would mean a lot to me if you wore it at all times."

"If it is that important, I will."

"Thank you."

*Wow. Is he really saying thank you? A man who always gets what he wants?*

Our oysters arrive. "Eat up, baby. You need all the energy you can get."

I sip my champagne and enjoy the oysters.

Today has opened my eyes, and now I've had a little time to process it all, I'm beginning to think that I can predict his behavior more accurately now. Like most humans, he has a set behavioral pattern he follows.

"Ready?" he inquires.

I don't ask for what. "Ready."

This time we go to the ground floor and get into his car. He drives south. I'm not asking where to, but it seems as though he is heading to my place. And that's exactly where we go.

HE PUSHES ME onto the bed and crawls on top of me, slowly inserts the tip of his cock inside me. This guy can keep up with me in bed – there are not many men that can. I enjoy the tease, begin to thrust my hips against his. "Zoe you're a greedy little slut. Stop squirming. Your pussy will get my cock when I'm ready." he says. "You can't have the whole thing…yet."

But I want the whole thing, and he knows it. He is exerting control. And although I am typically the dominant when fucking the so-called big-shot business men, Elias manages to bring out the submissive in me. He penetrates my pussy deeper and deeper, until his entire cock is buried deep inside me. He holds it deep inside me while pushing hard into me.

I thrust my hips up and down, while he remains still, fucking myself against his hard cock. He just stands there as I wildly and with complete abandon pleasure myself against his cock.

Suddenly he pulls out.

I open my eyes and before I can say 'what the Fuck!' He says, "That's enough for now."

I begin to protest, but just as unexpectedly he once again inserts the tip of his cock. I need to come, so I lick my middle and index finger and began rubbing my clit, while he moves in and out ever so slowly. I am very wet, my breath becoming deeper and longer. Attempting to hold my breath, he pinches my erect nipples and slaps my breasts, hard. I begin to rub my clit harder and harder. My breasts sting as he slaps them but even that feels good. Soon I start to come, a huge orgasm that has me screaming, "Fuck, fuck, fuck, fuck!!!!!" I come and come until I'm completely exhausted.

His cock stays inside me. He looks at me carefully. "How was it, baby?"

My eyes roll back. My body still tingles. "Fuck, I needed that."

"I'm glad I was able to please you."

"And how can I make you come?"

"What do you want to do for me, baby?"

I know exactly how he wants it. He enjoys it when I lie there submissively and allow him to use my pussy and other parts of my body for his pleasure. "Use me baby. Use my body. Do whatever your cock desires."

And that he does. He begins with quick thrusts in and out of my pussy with just the tip of his cock. He enjoys teasing himself too. As he gets closer to orgasm he thrusts harder and deeper. His final thrust is deep and long, and he quickly pulls out and goes onto his knees while he strokes his cock and spurts all over my breasts.

I moan with pleasure as he collapses on the bed beside me.

We lie in silence for a bit.

"Friday, meet me at the apartment at 8:00 PM."

"Yes, Mr. criminal boss man."

"I have a few deals closing this week, so I have a tight schedule."

"I understand."

"Good."

Elias gets out of bed and cleans up. I decide that it is time for an espresso and make my way to the kitchen.

Elias is now dressed and ready for his exit.

"I love you, Zoe. Thanks for a great day."

"I love you."

He kisses me good-bye and leaves.

I pull out my cell and find a message from John.

John: Did you forget about me already?
Zoe: I could never forget you.
John: Good. Free tomorrow?
Zoe: For you? Yes!

Just as I am formulating my text, I receive an incoming text from Blair.

Blair: Call me. ASAP!

# CHAPTER FIFTEEN

WITHOUT HESITATION, I pick up the phone and call Blair.

"Zoe girl!" the excitement in her voice immediately calms me and at the same time annoys me.

"Are you in prison? Are you dying?" I ask.

"Everything is great," Blair replies.

"You're chipper. What's up?"

"What are you doing tonight? Or better yet, what are you doing right now?"

"I was planning on giving myself a warm bubble bath, sipping something bubbly, and listening to Marvin Gaye while my playful and curious fingers remain submerged." I like to shock her, but I'm not lying.

Blair clears her throat. "Then you're in luck tonight! I'm saving you from possible blindness."

"Thank you. My vision is rapidly deteriorating. I should show some self-control when it comes to self-pleasuring. What's up?"

"Michael and I are going out for dinner tonight…and, well…he is bringing a friend from out of town…and…"

I interject, "Ah, just so we're clear, you're using me so that Michael's friend isn't the third wheel?"

"Who could do a better job?" She knows the right thing to say.

"And if I agree?"

"I owe you two," she responds promptly.

"When should I be ready?"

"We'll pick you up at 8:30."

I laugh. "I'd better start getting ready."

The truth is I have no interest in meeting, much less, entertaining a stranger, but I want to see Blair. I don't need to do anything more than smile and laugh at his jokes. I listen to "Sexual Healing" as I get dressed for the evening.

A WHITE BENTLEY PULLS UP to the lobby doors. Blair jumps, embraces me and whispers in my ear, "Important update Zoe: he is fuckin hot."

*Who cares?* I have never been drawn to what Blair considers 'hot men'. They have to be more than 'eye candy' for me to be even slightly interested. I have enough experience to know that hot men are horrible in bed, way too selfish.

Blair allows me to get in first. "Good evening, gentlemen."

"Zoe, so nice to see you again," says Michael. "Thanks for joining us on short notice. I would like for you to meet a really good friend of mine, Cy. Cy, this is Zoe."

"Pleasure to meet you, Zoe. Blair wouldn't stop talking about you on our way here."

I laugh. "Everything she said is true!"

"I can see that for myself," says Cy, smiling.

Michael hands me a glass of champagne. "Tonight, we celebrate friendship." We raise a glass to friendship and I sip my champagne.

Cy looks over at me from the corner of his eye. I'm not certain…is he impressed or curious? Probably both.

*Ready…set…go!* "So, I know you are not from New York," I ask Cy. "Where are you from?" Blair's description of Cy is accurate. Cy is a man who exudes sex, and within seconds I start to feel something. Sexual distraction is becoming a daily, maybe hourly, event for me, but I know that tonight's distraction will be just that. Knowing my place in the moment, in the world, is what has helped me get where I want to be.

"I'm from Montreal."

"What brings you to New York?" I ask Cy.

"I'm between jobs at the moment, and Michael invited me down for a few days. I haven't been to New York in over a year, so I thought this would be the perfect time to experience the city."

"Where are we heading tonight?" I inquire.

"Blair planned the evening for us." Michael says proudly.

"We are starting the night in Brooklyn at a restaurant called Luksus where the tasting menu is local, seasonal and fantastic, I am told, and then we are heading back to Manhattan to dance the night away at Cielo."

"Fantastic! Cy is getting the true New Yorker experience." I smile at him.

Cy turns to me and says. "Looking forward to the New Yorker experience," then leans over and whispers into my ear. "I have no desire to chaperone these two love birds tonight. I appreciate it."

Hot and smooth. I'm almost impressed. I lean into him, "I'm sure you will find ways to make it up to me."

We both laugh. Blair and Michael look at us, then back to one another. Michael whispers something into Blair's ear.

"You do realize that they are talking about us?"

I laugh. "Shall we give them something to really talk about?"

"I'll play along." He smiles.

I grab his hand and place it on my thigh. I enjoy the touch of his rough hands on my bare skin. It makes me shiver.

"How do you know Blair?" Cy asks.

"I found her in the lost and found at Bloomingdale's."

"Really?"

"No, we met in undergrad. Both from New York, first year at Stanford, we both enrolled in a marketing course and worked on a project together. We managed to get through the presentation without wanting to kill one another. She was ambitious and smart. I like that in a woman."

"And what was your presentation on?"

"Re-branding the New York Times to include more sex."

Cy almost chokes on his champagne as his eyes widen. "Intriguing. Like what, a Times Girl or a Times Boy topless in tight gym shorts tucked in on page 5?"

"Exactly," I laugh.

We arrive at Luksus and I notice Cy's eyes widen. I sense that he is uncomfortable in this setting, although he attempts to fit in. Cy takes my hand as we walk through the crowd and we follow Blair to the private room in the back of the restaurant. It is spectacular, a wine cellar with colorful Murano glass chandeliers. Blair and Michael sit across from Cy and I.

Blair quickly begins to interview Cy. "Michael tells me you are a consultant."

"I was a human resources consultant but have decided to change career paths. I'm re-inventing myself."

"And what are you planning on pursuing, what career? Are you moving to New York?"

He laughs. "Never crossed my mind."

Michael interjects. "Lots of career opportunities here."

"I am sure there are, however, I am planning on pursuing a passion of mine."

"Your passion?" I respect that. Too many people pursue money rather than passion, but do I tell him that only two percent of successful businesses are based on passion? "And what would that be?"

"Charity is maybe the closest way to describe it. I want to make lots of money and donate all of my wealth to charity."

Both Blair and I share the 'huh' look. So, this guy is either out to lunch or a little more interesting than meets the eye. In the end, it doesn't matter because I'm not going to be around to see his success (or failure). The good news is that he is a pleasing distraction, and, of course, that Blair now owes me two.

The wine begins to flow and the laughs continue through dinner. We are finishing up our coffee when I excuse myself to use the ladies room.

When I exit the bathroom, Cy is leaning up against the wall, waiting for me. Without hesitation, he puts his arms around my waist and places his lips on mine. I guess he never heard of #Metoo. There is a time and place for #Metoo, but it's not here and now. His hands move quickly to my body and time stands still. His lips are…soft. His touch is firm but tender at the same time. He holds me tight, but his soft lips and our tongues don't meet. It is a suspenseful, teasing, passionate, and I love it. How novel – I'm following his lead and enjoying it.

He grabs my arm and I don't resist, don't even ask any questions. With my coat in his hand, I'm assuming that he has informed Blair and Michael of our departure.

We make our exit. He snatches a cab and throws me in. "Gansevoort Hotel."

I interject. "No. Hudson and 11th, please."

Cy turns to me. "Who is in charge here?"

"You can take charge of me at my place," I smile.

He places his fingers over my mouth. I just want to bite them but relax my tongue and lick his fingertips.

*Zoe, are you really about to do this? A one-night stand without a precise business purpose? What is sex like when there is no ulterior motive, no agenda? I barely remember.* We don't say a word the entire cab ride, both intuitively knowing that talking could ruin the moment, and we are both in that moment.

We arrive at my apartment and he grabs me by the wrist and pulls the keys out of my hands to unlock the door. As soon as we step inside, he pushes me against the wall, grabs my wrists and raises my arms over my head. He is strong. While his left hand restrains my wrists, his right-hand roughly caresses my body. He moves slowly as he stares into my eyes, yet he won't kiss me. I squirm and slowly begin to rotate my hips. He releases my wrists and I touch his face. And finally, he allows his tongue to enter into my mouth. I breath heavily, inhaling and gasping for air as we kiss.

He takes off his jacket and I begin to unbutton his shirt while our lips are locked. His chest and abs are sculpted to perfection. I can't stop touching him, but he quickly puts an end to it, turns me around to face the wall and pulls off my jacket before turning me around once again. He does this so effortlessly that I can't help but think that he could pick me up and throw me on the bed. I secretly hope he will do just that.

He pauses for a moment and gazes into my eyes before resuming the kissing, his hands moving over every inch of my body. His touch drives me crazy. His hands squeeze my waist, and I moan with excitement as they move down my hips to my knees. He wraps his fingers around the bottom of my dress and in one quick move lifts it over my head and throws it onto the floor. I stand there naked and hungry. I want him badly. I look at him differently now, with a half-smile and half-closed eyes, say, "Fuck me! Do it now."

He stands there frozen for a moment as his eyes take in my body. I reach out and touch his chest. He grabs my wrists and effortlessly lifts me over his shoulder and carries me into to the bedroom, throws me down on the bed. *Wishes do come true.* He unbuckles his belt and quickly removes his pants. I lie there watching his every move and waiting anxiously for him to touch me again. He gently climbs on top of me and begins to kiss my neck, making his way to my breasts. My nipples are erect, enjoying his every nibble and lick. He stops for a moment and looks up at me, brings his lips to mine. I begin to squirm. He moves with me as our bodies lock in sync with one another. A total stranger being the perfect fit? *What the fuck is happening? Focus, Zoe, live in the moment. Enjoy this sensation, then get back to business.*

He moves his hand down to my pussy and begins to rub my clit. I'm wet...really wet. *You're doing this Zoe. Don't stop.* But my mind wanders. I'm with a man where I have nothing to gain and nothing to lose. I lie there naked, writhing, my body releasing dopamine. I feel it. His body becomes my drug and I am involuntarily becoming addicted to this release. *Zoe, wait, don't do it.*

I abruptly stop. "I'm sorry, I can't fuck you."

He opens the space between us and looks at me. "Why did you use the word fuck?" he asks, almost sarcastically, then continues, "I respect that."

I grab his hand and bring it to my face. "Your touch brings a sensation to my body that I have never experienced." *You're falling apart here Zoe. STOP!*

"I'm confused."

I gaze into his eyes and smile. "Every man I have been with has been for a purpose. But you...you don't serve a purpose. You have nothing to offer me. And I truly want nothing from you."

He facial expression changes. He looks perplexed. "I really don't understand."

"Of course you don't understand. How could you? I am not who I pretend to be. I'm not courteous and polite for that matter. If I am, it's because I'm manipulating the situation to achieve an outcome for personal gain. I am calculating and methodical." *Fuck, it feels good to finally let that out.*

"So what you are telling me is that you don't want to fuck me because I add no value to the exchange."

"What I'm saying is I have never done this before."

"And…?"

"I don't think we are supposed to feel this way sexually about someone. It just fucks you up."

He brings his lips closer to mine and once again I begin to writhe. Our breath is in sync, our tongues teasing one another.

He moves inches away. "Do you want me to stop?" he asks.

"No," I reply panting.

I lick my fingers, grab his cock and start stroking it. He is soft. *What the fuck? This never happens? Am I losing my touch?* He pulls my hand away and takes control, spreads my legs and throws his body on top of mine. *What the fuck is happening?* He grabs his shirt from the corner of the bed and ties both my wrists to the headboard.

I lie back, allow him to restrain me, whisper, "What are you doing?"

"What I know best," he smiles.

My hands restrained, he kisses my lips then slides his tongue down to my breasts, where he nibbles on first my left then my right breast, cupping them with both hands. But he doesn't stop there. He slowly makes his way down to my belly, then my inner thigh. He grabs both ankles and lifts my legs into the air opening me wide and exposing my clit. He looks up at me and smiles. I see it in his eyes, he enjoys teasing me and being in control. I smile at him, wrap my legs around his head, pull his face into my pussy. His tongue is soft on my clit, swirling at the perfect pressure and the exact speed, each motion calculated and deliberate. He reads my body, enjoys pleasing me. He restricts my body movement by placing his hands around my waist, controlling me.

My upper body is stiff and my pussy sensations are heightened as he swirls his tongue around, darts it in and out, softly sucks my pussy lips into his mouth.

"Come for me Zoe! I want to watch you come," he says, adding more pressure with his tongue to my clit, sucking and teasing faster and faster.

And with his permission, my body tightens, my pussy pulsates, and I come so hard that I scream to the Gods with pleasure, my legs clamping around his head to hold his wonderful mouth against my pussy as my juices flow.

When I finally release him, he unties my hands then holds me tight and kisses my forehead.

"Wow," I sigh. "You do realize that I can never see you again?" are the first words out of my mouth.

"You enjoyed the sex that much?"

"I have rules."

"Rules? Which would be?"

"No second date if we have sex on the first."

He raises his head and gives me a strange look. "Why is that? Besides, this wasn't a date, and that wasn't sex."

"Your behavior tonight tells me a lot about you."

He laughs. "But what if I want to see you again? If I actually like you? I'm not saying I do, but so far so good."

Now I laugh. "We have known one another for all of three hours. You don't know me at all." I'm not going to see this guy again, no matter how well he just satisfied me.

"Have you read *Blink* by Malcolm Gladwell?"

"It's been a while," I reply.

"His thesis is that the decision you think you have made may have actually been decided for you faster than the blink of an eye."

"Then I guess I have already made my decision," I reply.

"C'mon, Zoe, give me another chance," he begs.

"You may get off on a technicality," I tease. "I'll check with my lawyers and get back to you." I lift him off me and toss his clothes to him.

I stay in bed, staring at him as he prepares for his disappearing act. He walks over to the bed and gives me one last kiss. The goosebumps return immediately.

"Enjoy the rest of your time in New York." I look at him and smile.

"Can I at least give you my number?" he asks.

I hesitate at first but decide to appease him. I fish through my purse and throw my phone over to him. He rapidly types his number in.

"What's your last name?" I ask.

He pauses his fingertips and looks up at me. "Farrell."

"Cy Farrell."

"That's me." He hands back my phone.

He walks out of my apartment and I get back to work. But first, I have to do one thing. I grab my phone from the night table, find Farrell and press delete. *Farewell Farrell,* I say to myself.

# CHAPTER SIXTEEN

MY VISION IS BLURRED. I spend the morning reviewing my research on motivation. It involves the biological, social, cognitive and emotional energies that stimulate behavior. Motivation is the '*why*' to behavior. *Why did she have sex with him? Why did he have sex with her?* However, spending hours in front of a computer screen isn't an enjoyable task. I stare blankly at my computer screen and notice my phone light up from the corner of my eye. A missed call from Elias.

I want to detach myself from him a little, as is evident from my lack of immediate response. I need distance, otherwise I am uncertain of how I will react to him. I need to control my emotions. I'm happiest when alone. I live in my own head quite often – strange, I know, the woman who is so social is also so introverted.

Is it because I have always done everything alone? I have made it on my own. My entire life has been alone. I just don't know anything else. Would I even be open to having someone share things with me?

Growing up was done solo. I threw my own birthday parties with a few friends. I went to my musical performances, my graduations, everything, alone. My parents, being immigrants, didn't share any of my experiences with me, didn't understand their importance or were working and couldn't attend. I taught myself how to survive alone. I learned early in life that no one was reliable. My father was too busy either working or watching trash on television; my mother was not educated enough to know any better; my siblings too distracted and unwell to notice me.

I came to believe that most people lack substance. All the hot air, the wasted energy of words exploding out of people's mouths was useless noise. It was fuzz. Time is too valuable to participate in nonsense. For the most part, meaningful conversations have been removed from our interactions. Ninety-five percent fluff, five percent substance I always say.

I acknowledge that I am missing something in my life - real closeness. Someone who knows and understands me. No acting, no fluff, no fuzz. Someone who I can confide in and who is able to tolerate my messy, mixed up, often ambiguous thoughts. I'm not normal; actually, I am far from normal. It is too late to turn back even if I want to. The operative word, TRUST, is nowhere to be found. I am jaded. This isn't self-pity; this is self-awareness. I can't change now. I have no choice but to be independent and self-sufficient.

And then there are the married men I am manipulating. How am I to trust someone, when I have been exposed to the ugly mess of their lives, their living lies. How am I to trust them? Their lives are lies.

Observing human behavior and anticipating the next move is what I am trained to do, and I do it well. Life is very much a game. I compare it to a game of chess, and I always try to think five moves ahead, and five moves ahead of each of those five moves. I think so much that it hinders my ability to have a healthy relationship with anyone. I consider not only what is on the board but what could be on the board next, and so on. So, what's the next best thing? Being cold and detached. No tears will be running down my cheek because some fool emotionally scars me. Jackie Collins was right when she wrote "*any woman who relies on a man for an orgasm is either a fool or in love.*" I am no fool; and I will have never fallen in love.

I make my way to the kitchen and pour myself a glass of red wine. I take a sip while standing there, take a moment, swirl the wine in my glass and take another sip while I savor the taste.

I pace back and forth between the living room and kitchen, sipping my wine while contemplating the meaning of happiness. *Are you happy Zoe?* I am in a middle of a soliloquy in my head. *What is happiness?* I fetch my Oxford Dictionary.

**Happy** *adj.* **(happier, happiest) 1.** Feeling or showing pleasure. **2a** fortunate **b** appropriate, pleasing. **3** *informal* slightly drunk. **4** (in *comb.*) *informal* inclined to use excessively. **Happily** *adv.* **Happiness** *n.*

The wine is kicking in. Do I know what makes me happy? And not in the informal sense of the word. Does sex make me happy? Yes!

*Fucking!* Fucking makes me happy. Only two actions are capable of shutting off my brain – sleep and sex. So, I have sex – a lot of sex. It's my drug…my only drug, my version of sensation seeking. My psychological state changes, allowing my body to free itself from the world. I scream in my head…often. Usually screaming to myself. But I never share that with others. Doing so doesn't help me to get what I want. I prefer playing the part of the woman in despair, the woman who wants to please men for pleasure and personal gain. The art of manipulation, or as I like to call it, the psycho-fuck.

So you can forget about marriage. However, I do believe in arranged marriages. Why? Because they serve a function. Husbands and wives share their responsibilities and support one another. When marriage was introduced, our life expectancy was around thirty years, so you married at fifteen and stayed together for fifteen years. Now, however, our life expectancy has tripled; are we are expected to be monogamous for sixty years?

Temptation is everywhere. Marriage has changed. People are selfish, especially when they have so many options. Thanks internet. Everything now has an expiry date.

*Are you happy? Answer the Goddam question, Zoe.* I guess not.

*So, what makes you happy?* Apparently psycho-fucking men isn't on my *make me happy* list.


JOHN ARRIVES AND I CAN'T be more pleased to see him. John isn't the sort of guy that comes around the car to open the passenger door for me. He does, however, know how to give me a warm greeting, with a big hug and kiss. There is chemistry between us. We click. Maybe it's because we are so alike in many ways, with him being the full-time actor and me the full-time actress, however, my super keen senses tell me he is sincere with me. I feel my barriers slowly coming down as he kisses me with those devilish lips. I literally feel weak at the knees.

"I'm so glad you reached out to me," are the first words out of my mouth.

"I like to believe that I am smart at least ten percent of the time," he replies.

"Ten percent? That's pretty high, don't you think?" I say with a quizzical look.

"We both know that on any given day we could end up in the bottom of the Hudson with concrete blocks tied to our ankles."

The statement doesn't scare me. "So why are you putting our lives in danger? Does the adrenaline excite you?"

"Yes. Does that make me messed up?"

"Mega-mess-orama messed up John!" I reply without skipping a beat.

"Then I'm fucked up! Truth be told, I haven't been the same since I met you. I'm distracted at work and home. I enjoy being with you."

"Well, that's probably because there are no screaming kids running around the house." I laugh. "Your wife coming from the family she does, I assume they have influence." I know John is in the position he is not simply because of his talents but also because of his connections.

John laughs. "It's the big small secret that no one ever speaks of."

"I can only imagine." My brain wonders how deep-rooted the corruption in government and every other part of New York actually is.

"Zoe, I have a confession to make."

"Confess away."

"I'm driving in circles hoping to end up at your apartment, in your bed."

I laugh. "You should have joined me in bed earlier then."

"I also enjoy driving aimlessly with you." He takes my hand and holds it above the center console.

The interior of his Porsche Carrera GT is slick and sexy. This whole situation is making me excited. And I'm not afraid to show it. "Want to fuck?"

"What? Why?"

"Because it pleases me to please you. Fucking isn't meant to sophisticated. It's carnal. The act isn't meant to be done in suits and cocktail dresses. It's raw. It's passion. We have those things. This isn't love making, this is animalistic. Do you disagree?"

"You still haven't answered my question from the other night?"

"What question is that?" I know exactly what question he is referring to. I just need some time to stall, to formulate my response.

"What does Zoe Winstein want from me? A woman who is talented and sophisticated, who has the world at her feet. What does that woman want from a complex, messed up guy like me?"

*Information.* "All I can promise is trouble," I begin. "Perhaps we met to teach and learn from one another. To become better people." I do want him to find happiness. I feel pain emanating out of his every pore, and in our brief connection, which is always destined to be temporary, I want him to experience personal growth, so that when I do run he won't feel used. *Never burn bridges, Zoe.*

He pulls into the garage and parks, opens the trunk and pulls out a bottle of wine and some Chinese take-out.

I look into his eyes, and I feel as though everything will be okay. We make our way to his apartment and settle in on the couch, eating off the coffee table. It all feels very natural.

"How did you meeting with Stefano go? Do I have you all to myself now?" John smiles.

"Of course you have me all to yourself. Win-win," I reply with confidence, knowing full well I was feeding him a lie.

"That pleases me. This is new to me," John speaks with a bit of insecurity in his voice.

"You are doing a swell job at making me comfortable."

"I like to make you happy."

"Life is about moments. I anticipate making memorable moments and remembering how happy you made me feel in a specific moment in time."

He pours himself some more wine and takes a sip. "I wasn't looking for anything but sexual pleasure from other women. And then I met you, Zoe."

I have a puzzled look on my face as I sit there in silence.

"I wasn't in search of an emotional connection with a woman. I wanted instant gratification and release. And now, I have no desire to have those types of relationships any longer. You have given me a taste of something more and I want it."

*How am I going to end this? Fuck me!*

"Ms. Psychology major, or should I be calling you Doctor? I need your opinion on something."

*Change the subject! Perfect!* "How can I be of service," I reply as I take a sip of wine, listening attentively.

"It's a hypothetical."

*I'm sure it is.* "Go for it."

"Someone who has screwed you in business in the past has come to you because of a new position and is attempting to bribe you. Would you give them a second chance? I never have."

"I need some context."

He rolls his eyes, as he thinks of how he is going to provide me with some context. "What context do you need?"

"Tell me about this person asking for the favor. Does he or she have a history of exploiting people? Fucking them over?"

"Yes. However, they claim to have changed."

"And hypothetically, does this person have dirt on the person asking for a favor to use to their advantage."

"Yes, this person has dirt, but can't use it."

"So, they are powerless."

"Yes."

"My advice is to not accept the bribe unless they are in a position of power."

"And how does one do that?" he inquires.

"By not making yourself vulnerable. Think about their relationship long-term. Perhaps the best thing to do is not accept the bribe but provide them with their request without expecting anything in return. Once you build a new relationship of trust, then you can re-evaluate the relationship and make demands. Sometimes power isn't about having dirt on someone, but about making yourself invaluable to them."

"Do you believe that people can change, Zoe?"

I burst out laughing. "Yes, superficially people can change, but at the core they don't."

"You are so cynical."

"I'm a realist John," *who reads between the lines.* I smile.

"That you are."

"I think our time for business talk is up." I straddle John on the couch, and begin to move my body, biting his lower lip, wanting his body close to mine, skin to skin.

He places his hands around my waist and squeezes me tightly. I place my hands over his, wanting him to squeeze me even harder. I want him to leave marks on my body, to brand me as if I am his property. I show him how hard I want it. I move my hands to his shoulders and back, firmly caress him through his shirt, grab his skin with my fingertips, knowing I can't leave any evidence of him being with me. He, at the end of the night, must go home to his wife, pristine, without a scratch, without any marks.

I hold myself back for a moment and gaze into his eyes, inhale deeply, and as I exhale begin to unbutton his shirt. I move slowly while he sits there with his hands to his side, not wanting to interrupt my rhythm. I open his shirt and feel his chest. He pulls up my dress and asks me to lift my arms. I do so and he pulls the dress over my head and tosses it onto the floor. I get up, kick off my panties and slip off my bra. The only thing that I don't remove are my heels. His hands rub my entire body while he kisses me. I moan. My pussy is wet, his cock hard, still hidden under his pants. He puts his hands under my armpits and lifts me up. My natural instinct is to wrap my legs around him, which I do.

He carries me to the bedroom and throws me onto the corner of the bed. Without hesitation, he unzips his pants and they fall onto the floor. His thick hard cock stands at attention as he grabs my ankles and holds my legs back, raising my ass from the bed. His hard cock arches toward his belly as he pulls it down from the base to slide it into me. He knows what he is doing, hitting my G-spot, the experience a mixture of pleasure and pain. I try to hold back, but he doesn't allow it. His entire cock slowly slides all the way in. My pussy dilates. I stop holding back and give in to what he wants, my pussy juices covering his cock. I scream louder and louder, until oh my God, I squirt all over his cock and leave a puddle under me. He attempts to continue thrusting me, but my pussy just can't handle it anymore.

Wanting to please him, I asked him to lie on his back and lie between his legs to suck his cock. His cock is covered in my pussy juices, and I love the taste of my juices. I tightly wrap my right hand around his cock and begin twisting my wrist from left to right, up and down with my mouth in sync with my hand. I lift my head, not to get air, but to spit on my left fingers to caress his balls.

John moans and spreads his legs. I take that as a sign to lower my hand below his balls and to massage his asshole. I feel his asshole pulsate, inviting me to enter. He continues to thrust while my index finger tickles his anus like a clit. I spit on his cock, watch my saliva run down his shaft, below his balls to his ass crack. With the additional lubrication I insert my finger into the crevasse, slowly enter his anus and stimulate his prostate as I suck his cock. Within seconds he explodes into my mouth as his rectum contracts. I remove my fingers from his ass.

His body twitches post-orgasm. "I can't move," he groans.

I smile and say, "Don't worry. You don't have to."

## QUEEN'S DANCE

I get up and bring back tissues, but first I suck his cock clean, only using the tissue to dry him. He just lies there, arms and legs spread across the bed. He looks comfortable. I snuggle up to his chest and rest my head there, feeling and hearing his heartbeat.

We lie there in silence for a few moments, before he gets up and throws himself into the shower. I hear the water run as I lie in bed. He comes back into the room fully dressed and kisses me on my forehead. "This is for you," he says as he leaves a pile of hundreds on the sidetable.

"I don't want your money, John," I say with more than a hint of aggression in my voice.

"Don't be silly Zoe, I love you. Go and buy yourself something nice."

I have an odd look on my face. I don't need his money. It's very unexpected and maybe a bit insulting. Gifts I understand, but cash? "I can't accept this."

He walks over to me and holds both my hands. "I want you to have it, please."

I have never thought of myself as a whore. I enjoy sex. I enjoy controlling men without them knowing they are being controlled. That is my thrill. My adrenaline rush.

I don't want an issue of this, so I just grab it and throw it in my bag.

John drives me home, kisses me good night. I feel at peace, satiated and go straight to bed.

My eyelids are heavy and I fall asleep with the lights on.

# CHAPTER SEVENTEEN

LAST NIGHT I DREAMED I was running... running towards something. At one point I realize that I'm continuously running in the same spot, going nowhere. It was as though everything had become hopeless, and no matter how hard I tried to speed up I couldn't move. I was paralyzed. I wonder how Freud would have interpreted my dream. Sex, of course. I wake up in the middle of the night in a cold sweat. The next thing I see is the red glow of dawn peeking through my shutters.

I decide that today I'm going to grab my morning coffee and actually make my way to the gym. It's three miles from my apartment and I'm going to walk.

On the way I stop at Lola's cafe and impatiently wait in line. My gym bag is around my neck and my purse around my shoulder, I feel like I'm being weighed down physically and mentally. As I wait in line I notice a donation box labelled 'Mental Health'. It's a sign. I pull out the cash that John gave me and shove it all into the donation box. Someone needs it more than me. *Damn. It won't fit.* I separate the hundred-dollar bills and patiently place them in the donation box one at a time. As I do so, I notice there is a note amongst the hundred dollar bills. *What is this?* I unfold it and glance at it quickly.

"Welcome to Lola's. Can I take your order?"

"Sorry, gotta run, somethings come up." Without another word, I run out of the place. Change of plans. The gym can wait. I needed answers, right now!

I DASH THROUGH RECEPTION and knock on John's office door.

"Zoe? What is it. Is everything ok?" He walks around his desk and wraps his arms around me to calm me down.

I breath through my mouth. I am exhausted from the run. "I am so sorry to show up like this but I need to tell you something."

"No need to apologize. What is it?"

"I believe you accidently gave me something that I wasn't supposed to see." I shut the door and hand the piece of paper to John. "I hope I won't be seeing this name in the paper anytime soon," I joke, trying to make light of the situation. I am hoping my humor will lighten the mood. Or perhaps this is a test. *Did I pass?* Was this the fuck up I was waiting for?

"Do you recognize the name?" he asks.

"Can't say I do."

"Another hypothetical for you, Zoe."

"Okay. Don't forget the context this time," I smile.

"Someone is looking at purchasing a block of real estate, however, the owner refuses to sell their piece of that block. How do you persuade someone to sell their parcel?"

"How important is this parcel?" I inquire.

"No parcel, no development. It's crucial to the deal.

"Money....it all comes down to cash."

"Yes, most of the time it is money. Not in this case."

"What do you know about this individual who won't sell?"

"Other than the fact that he is stubborn and extremely unmotivated. Not much."

*Jackpot!* "How can I help?"

"This isn't something you can help with, unfortunately."

"Looks like you have some work ahead of you then."

"This job never ends."

"Why won't he sell?" I ask.

"Let's just say that sometimes the past comes back to haunt you. Some people have long memories."

"The right dollar amount, memories can dim. Dollars can usually be used to patch up old wounds."

"Some things money can't help. To use your analogy, sometimes old wounds fester."

"There is always a way. De-valuing the property by placing zoning restrictions?"

John gives me a strange look.

"Let me know if I can be of assistance."

"I will. When can I see you again?" he asks.

"I'll see you soon," I tell him - *once I figure out my game plan with you.* I give him a hug, head off to my missed appointment at the gym.


MY PHONE DINGS.

Elias: Playing hard-to-get?

I decide to respond.

Zoe: Can't a girl workout without distractions?
Elias: The only thing that should be distracting you is me.

He is high maintenance, always in need of my attention. A typical sociopath.

Zoe: Yes.

Elias: Meet me at our place tonight. I got a pass for the night and I feel like a work out myself.
Zoe: I thought I wasn't seeing you until Friday night?
Elias: Change of plans. I miss you! Be there for 8:00.
Zoe: Okay.


I USE THE FOB and access code Elias gave me to let myself in. It is just before eight and he hasn't arrived. I make myself at home and admire the artwork.

Thirty minutes later, Elias arrives and I welcome him at the door with a kiss.

"I missed you, baby," he whispers in my ear, as he put his arms around me and squeezes the air out of me.

"Baby, you are squeezing too hard."

"I can't help it. I missed you too much."

"I missed you too." The truth is I have missed him a little. There is something about him that is growing on me. Maybe it is his attentiveness when we are together. All he wants to do is lock eyes and admire me when we are alone. He wants to devour me, I can feel it in his eyes, and I enjoy the attention. I enjoy being admired, being wanted with such intensity.

"Come to the kitchen, Zoe. I picked up some food for us."

I'm famished. His timing couldn't have been better.

He places the bags onto the countertop and begins to take out the containers. "Hope you like Indian."

"I love Indian."

"Great." He begins serving me. "So what happened to you yesterday?"

*I was with John, you know, the Mayor…having sex with him.* Like that would go over well. "I was completing some research and didn't want to be distracted. When I'm in the zone, I'm in the zone."

"I get it. When I'm working on something, I block exterior noise out, including my phone."

"Why did you decide to see me tonight?"

"Did you have other plans?"

"Not at all, however I do recall someone telling me he had a busy week ahead of him."

"I couldn't be away from you. I needed to see you. I miss your touch, your lips, your curves."

"You missed sex." I smile.

"True, but not really."

"No?"

"I can get sex anywhere, maybe not great, but above average sex. That's not it. I enjoy spending time with you. You're fun, you're refreshing. I've never met anyone who sees things from your unique perspective. I'm not sure if I like it, but I'm drawn to it. I'm not sure if you are an open window to fly through or a flame that will consume me." He takes a bite of his samosa. "Tell me about your day. What did you get up to?"

"I'm trying to keep up with you, so I ran at the gym today. I thought that might help."

He laughs. "I try and get in my six-mile run every day."

I almost choke on my food. I clear my throat. "Remind me to never go running with you."

"Actually, that sounds like an excellent activity we can do together."

"Don't think I could keep up with you."

"I will slow down for you, as long as you promise to have sweaty, sticky sex when we finish. Preferably with me."

I laugh.

"I'm not kidding," he replied, a serious look on his face.

"Oh?"

"Let's finish up dinner, so I can take advantage of you."

We finish our last bites and he takes me by the wrist and pulls me to the bedroom.

I WAKE TO ELIAS' VOICE. I listen to him talking on the phone.

"The project is quite magnificent, a beautiful mix of business and residential. We just need Bergman's piece. He is the last piece of the puzzle and as usual he is the toughest piece."

*Holy shit! Holy fuck!*

Elias listens for a minute, then says, "Matteo, don't worry about Bergman. John tells me he has it under control. It's taking time but it's happening….I know it's not happening quickly enough and you don't like waiting….okay, I'm on it."

I hear his footsteps walking back into the bedroom. I quickly close my eyes and pretend to be sleeping.

"Rise and shine, baby."

*I am up. And you just gave me the information I need to exploit this opportunity.* "Good morning."

# CHAPTER EIGHTEEN

ELIAS DROPS ME OFF at my apartment. I open my computer, quickly draft the contract from a template I always use, change and head out the door. *What have I gotten myself into? Is this going to work? Am I going to survive?* I have nothing to lose and a lot to gain.

I storm into the boardroom. He is sitting at the head of the table, yelling into the receiver as usual. He doesn't seem eager to see me, nor is he in any rush to end his phone conversation. I take a seat and wait. He finally ends his call. "To what do I owe the privilege? You here for another check, Zoe?"

"Sign here, Stefano." I need to make him believe that he needs me when actually he doesn't need me. This time I need him…one last time. *I need an address.*

I pull out the contract and place it on his desk.

"What the fuck is this?"

"The usual contract, the same as always, just sign please," I say with my eyes glued to his.

"You think you can bat your eyelashes, wiggle your ass and I will sign whatever you put in front of me?"

"Pretty much. Yes."

QUEEN'S DANCE

He picks the contract up off his desk, quickly reads it over, signs it, hands it back to me. He isn't too happy.

"Anton Bergman," I tell him.

He scowls. "What the fuck is an Anton Bergman?"

"Anton Bergman is a property owner. An important property."

"Stop fucking talking in riddles, Zoe, and tell me what the fuck is going on."

"Anton Bergman is the owner of the missing piece Matteo is trying to purchase. Have your lawyer do a title search, but you can save time and money by trusting me on this."

"You'd better be right Zoe."

"Only one way to find out."

He picks up the phone and dials a number. "Joe. Anton Bergman. Start doing title and corporate searches on all his properties." He immediately hangs up. "Let's celebrate."

"You're going off prematurely again. You can get help for that, Stefano."

"Fuck you, Zoe. Let's have lunch."

That was code for his *I will buy you lunch, and you can suck my cock* prelude. "Unfortunately, I'm busy," I tell him. "Next time. Be in touch. I'll get out of your hair." I pause, smile and say, "Oh, that's right…you don't have any."

He says something under his breath. What is it? It doesn't matter. Our business and personal relationship are over. Literally and metaphorically. It is my turn to do what's best for Zoe and not what's best for Stefano.

BEFORE I KNOW IT, Friday has arrived. I'm not thrilled about my role for the evening – schmoozing. I am a chameleon but it's not my favorite part of the job. I hate feeding the egos of strangers, but I have a job to complete.

153

I arrive at Elias' at 7:00 PM. As promised I am wearing an emerald green dress that goes to just above my knees. It hugs my curves and shows off my hour-glass figure. Beige pumps give me extra height, elongating my already long legs.

"Wow, you look amazing," are the first words out of his mouth.

"Thank you, my love. You don't look too bad yourself."

He was wearing a crisp navy-blue linen suit with a white shirt, no tie. For forty-something, he looks great in a suit. He is really starting to grow on me.

We walk into the living room, where he has a bottle of champagne on ice and two tall crystal glasses waiting for us. He pops the cork and pours us each a glass. He hands me my glass and takes his.

"Here is to a night of making memories. To stolen glances across the room. And to me getting you home tonight."

"I'll drink to that."

He reaches over the couch, pulls out a black box and hands it to me. "Open it," he instructs.

I slowly open the box and peek inside. I'm expecting something nice, but I'm not prepared for this. The look on my face must be priceless.

"Do you like it?" he asks.

"You're fucking crazy. This is over the top. I can't accept this." I kiss him.

"You have to keep it. I bought it at the Van Cleef and Arpels' midnight madness sale. No refunds, no returns. Let me help you put it on."

"Are you sure you want me to wear this tonight in front of your clients? Aren't they going to think they are paying you way too much?"

We both laugh.

He takes the diamond necklace out of the box and I turn around and hold my hair up, giving him access to the back of my neck. Once it is in place I do a little twirl.

"Maybe you are right, Zoe," he says. "It's a bit much. Let's sell it on eBay."

"Too late." I give him another kiss.

I allow him to control the evening, assuming my trust, knowing full well that it is just an illusion I have created.

We make it to the Meatpacking District and I see a line snaking around a gorgeous old building with gothic architectural features. We get out of the limo and Elias takes my hand. We pass the crowd of beautiful people and head directly to the front door. The doorman and Elias nod at each other and we walk straight in and make our way to the elevator. *Where are we?*

The elevator smells of vanilla and cigars. The hostess presses the thirtieth floor button, and we stand there silently as he squeezes my hand. Just as the doors are about to open, Elias turns to me. "Are you ready?"

*Always.*

The elevator doors open to a beautiful oasis, a roof top patio covered with frosted glass. Crystals hang along the metal frames of an open roof. It's a clear night and the stars are twinkling. The room is divided by lime green bushes in white planters, the couches and seats blue-grey, the bar white marble with a red velvet bar-back. The DJ is on a stage adjacent from the bar, a perfectly planned symmetrical layout.

I am in complete awe.

Elias looks around the room notices his people in the distance. He isn't letting go of my hand.

We arrive at our table, there are two seats for us.

"Good evening everyone," Elias says, his arm around my waist.

"Well look who decided to show up fashionably late," says the man directly across from us. His green eyes contrast his black hair. He reminds me of an aging rockstar, still ruggedly handsome and a bit debauched.

"Greetings Tutti, I would like to introduce you to my friend Zoe. Zoe, this is Martha, Noah and that fine gentleman over there is Giovanni."

They stand up one at a time and shake my hand. I greet them in turn with a warm smile.

Elias and I take our seats and Giovanni pours Elias and I a glass of wine. With everyone's glass full, Giovanni raises his glass to make a toast and we all raise ours. "Gentlemen," he pauses, "And ladies, to all the loving and sex money can buy. Oh wait, what am I talking about, they are both the same thing." He laughs.

Did I just hear what I think I heard? From the corner of my eye I see a smile on Elias' face. I am not impressed, yet I have to play nice. The men laugh, and Martha and I give one another a look that says, *boys will be boys, but why are some boys so stupid?*

I bring the glass to my lips but do not take a sip. I recognize that if I'm going to get through the night, I will most likely have to drug myself with alcohol. I also think, if this is the mentality that Elias associates with, is he the kind of guy I want to associate with?

Giovanni yells across the table. "Elias, now that this deal is done, when are we going away to celebrate? Say, Tokyo?"

"Anytime you want," Elias replies.

"And should we ask these lovely ladies to join us?" Giovanni asks.

"Only if they promise to be good," Elias winks at me.

"Sand to the beach?" Giovanni replies. "Are you sure, Elias?

Martha interjects, "Remember Giovanni, when the cat is away the mice will play."

Giovanni is such a pig, and Martha knows how to respond. I like her. I need another big gulp of wine…and fast. I inhale it.

Elias places his hand on my thigh and turns to me. "Someone is thirsty." He refills my glass.

"I think that's her way of biting her tongue," Martha responds. "Keep that bottle in front of us please, we require sedation."

"Can someone please order another bottle?" I reply.

Everyone laughs, except for Giovanni.

Giovanni is the handsome Italian type with slicked back hair, sensuous lips and a swimmer's body, but not much upstairs. He knows how to add and subtract and how to make a lot of money, but beyond that he is stupid, ignorant, pompous. I could go on, but you get the picture. He wears a suit with a turquoise handkerchief in his breast pocket and cufflinks that you can't miss. His initials are sewn on his shirt at the end of his shirt sleeve and on his chest. He is a rock-star all right; an arrogant one and not nearly as handsome as he thinks he is.

I am uncertain if Martha is with Giovanni, or if she is just a business partner. She is a red-head with curls and a beautiful smile that would light up a room, and an intelligence to match. She has impeccable taste in clothing, wearing a classy suit that exaggerates her height and great curves.

Noah is more of the quiet type, sits there amused, or pretending to be amused, a constant smile on his face. He doesn't belong with this crowd. He is cerebral, a more sophisticated type.

Where does Elias fit in? I am still trying to figure that out. He can't be pigeonholed. He can carry on an intelligent conversation with Noah and joke with Giovanni.

I reach for my glass and take a few more sips to further numb my brain before it begins to race, an occupational hazard that I can't seem to escape.

"Slow down Zoe. The food hasn't even arrived yet," Elias says to me with concern.

"As you wish," I respond, certain that he will notice the twinkle in my eye. I bring myself closer to Elias and whisper in his ear, "I have to excuse myself to use the ladies room."

He nods.

I ask the waiter where I can find the ladies room, and he points to the entrance. I casually make my way in that direction, hoping I don't stumble. I realize too late that I've had too much to drink.

Just as I am about the push the bathroom door open, someone grabs my wrist with force and turns me around.

*Holy shit. Holy fucking shit.*

"Look at what the cat dragged in."

"Stefano." I stutter. "Hi."

"Fancy seeing you here, with our friend. I must say I'm a little jealous. Doesn't look like a business dinner."

"I'm a good actress." *Shit.* Stefano may be an asshole, but he is a smart asshole. My guess is he is putting two and two together. He knows my source.

"Are you?" he questions me.

"Yes." I laugh nervously.

He looks down at my neck. "Nice diamonds. I didn't realize I was paying you that much."

I laugh. "They are not real, stupid boy. Did you find an address yet?" I attempt to change the subject.

"Yes, but the mother-fucker won't sell. It looks like you might need to work your magic and figure out what he wants."

Stefano is also efficient. He has already approached Bergman? Thank God he didn't sell to Stefano. My plan might work after all. "I guess I have to do everything, don't I, Stefano."

"Just do what you promised to do and enjoy your business dinner." He lets go of my wrist. "My office, first thing Monday morning," and he walks away.

I rush into the ladies' room. At this point my head is spinning. When I arrive back at the table our food has arrived. Thank goodness.

Elias stands and pulls out my seat as he continues speak to Martha. "...I never understood those laws." They all laugh. "Buon appetito everyone."

I turn to Elias. "Was everyone waiting for me?"

"No, baby, it's okay."

I begin eating while the boys continue with their small talk. Martha and I give one another the look from time to time, and I continue to drink.

After our meal and a few bottles of wine, Elias is ready to call it a night.

"Gentlemen, I have to run. Busy day tomorrow." He stands, and I follow his lead.

"It was a pleasure meeting all of you," I say with a smile.

"Until Tokyo," Giovanni screams from across the table.

Elias, I can tell, is eager to take me home.

The limousine is waiting for us and we go straight back to his place.

I am on edge and anxious. The night's events have alerted me to inconsistencies and mysteries about Elias that I need to investigate. I will worry about Elias' personality quirks later. I know what can satisfy me - and him - right now.

We walk into his apartment and I slither out of my dress but keep my heels on. I wrap my arms around him as I softly, yet aggressively kiss his upper lip. He clings onto me with his arms around my neck. He doesn't want to let go. He begins to caress my face with his right hand. I roll my head back enjoying his every touch. He knows he has the power to make me melt. I've learned to long for his distinctive, very personal way of touching me. He uses the wall and presses up against me. I begin to bend at the knees, my mouth making its way down his chest and torso to his cock. It throbs through his pants as I unzip them, pull them off, place my warm mouth over his cock through his briefs and began to exhale my hot breath onto his hard cock. I want nothing more than for him to stuff his cock down my throat, but he hesitates, wants to tease me.

"Suck it," he says firmly.

I tilt my head up and roll my eyes back to look up into his eyes and say, "Make me."

I continue to exhale on his cock, slowly making my way to his balls and inner thighs. I moan and hum out of pure pleasure. I enjoy teasing him as much as he enjoys teasing me.

I roll down his underwear and take his cock firmly in my hand, squeeze the base while licking the tip. He places his hand behind my head, grabs my hair in a tight grip, forces his cock into my mouth.

With some difficulty I deep throat him. It's a very long cock to deep throat. The head reaches deep into my throat and I gag. I pull out his cock, and saliva flows all over me. I expose my soft tongue and begin licking his cock from the base to the tip, swirl my tongue around his cock, quickly change the pace and place his balls into my mouth.

"Fuck, baby, you have the warmest and wettest mouth," he groans.

I am drooling all over his cock. It's very messy and very sexy and I'm very turned on.

I pull off his underwear. He stands erect, takes me by the hand and escorts me into the bedroom. I don't fight him…yet.

Once we arrive in the bedroom, I tell him to lie on his back.

He obeys and stretches out on the bed. He is mine now.

I stand at the end of the bed and slowly begin to crawl up between his legs. I lie on my stomach and lick his inner thighs, making my way to his balls with my soft tongue, finally take his cock into my mouth.

"Suck it! Deeper!" he demands, thrusting his hips up towards my mouth.

I suck deeper and faster, my lips tightening around his shaft, my saliva making an even bigger mess.

His head tilts back as he comes quickly, deep in my throat. "Fuuuuuuuck."

He lies there with his eyes closed while I wash up. Upon my return, his eyes are open. "Your turn."

I don't want him touching me tonight, so I play my part. "I think I drank a little too much, baby. I need to sleep."

He gets up and returns with a bottle of water. "Drink this."

And I do, then he turns the lights out and joins me in the bed. He holds and I rest my head on his shoulder. Sleep comes quickly.

# CHAPTER NINETEEN

I OPEN MY EYES and Elias is nowhere to be seen or heard. A note is on the nightstand.

*Let's go away...Italy? I'm thinking 10 days. All I need from you are dates. I will take care of everything. Love Elias.*

How the hell does he get away with it? He keeps surprising me. I don't want to like him and I don't trust him but he keeps reeling me in. I decide to stay in bed a little longer, the pillows and sheets swallow me whole, and I fall into a light sleep, dreaming of my happiest moments.

Me alone, enjoying my travels in my twenties. Walking the streets of Rome, Athens and Paris without a care in the world, admiring the architecture and the art. Or on the race track in Las Vegas driving an Audi R8, stepping on the gas pedal and accelerating out of a turn. Or jumping out of a plane in San Francisco after a bad break-up – or so I thought at the time. Now I can't even remember who it was. And let's not forget the tongue and nipple piercings in Los Angeles. I was young and carefree, I wanted to do it all, and I did most of the things I set my mind on doing.

I continue to this day to be an adrenaline junkie, addicted to the highs. I want to feel fear and face it head on. Perhaps I'm more of a masochist than I would like to admit, always putting myself in situations where there is drama. I always say, I don't want drama, drama wants me. What can I do? If drama wants me so bad it can have me.

I roll out of bed and wander naked into the kitchen. Elias has prepared a fruit salad for me, with another note.

*Sorry I couldn't do breakfast in bed with you this morning. I will make it up to you.*

Underneath the note are two tickets to the opera, Dido and Aeneas at The Metropolitan, accompanied by a gift card from Saks.

*Buy yourself something nice for tonight. And no, you can't take another man with you. Girlfriends only.*

What fun! My day has gone from no plans to fully booked and I'm still not dressed.

I message Blair.

Zoe: If you have plans tonight, cancel them.
Blair: What's up?
Zoe: We are going to the opera.
Blair: Really?
Zoe: Meet you at the Met at 7:00 PM.
Blair: Michael isn't going to be too happy. I'm
       supposed to be his love slave lately.
Zoe: I'm sure he will understand.
Blair: See you at 7:00 PM.

One of the many things I adore about Blair is that she knows that I don't have any time or interest in small talk texting. She saves that for me in person.

I finish my breakfast and get dressed, ready to tackle the day...starting with finding that perfect outfit for tonight.


SAKS IS OVER-CROWDED AS USUAL, but I manage to negotiate the crowd and make my way to the third floor. I'm dressed in ripped jeans and a hoodie. The sales staff don't approach me, but I prefer it that way – I feel like Julia Roberts in *Pretty Woman*. Every woman should experience this moment. I am fortunate enough to say that this isn't my first rodeo, I have been here many times in many different situations, although each time, I feel like a virgin again. A born-again virgin. Stefano introduced me to this lifestyle, and now it is part of who I am.

Admiring all the beautiful gowns, one that shimmers in the light catches my eye. Embroidered with black lace and enough beads to cover all the sexy parts, it's gorgeous and no doubt fabulously expensive. I have to try it on. I find the sales associate and tell her which dress I would like to try.

"Give me a moment," she says. "I need to get the key."

While I wait, I decide to check the price tag. *What*. I do a double take. So, this is the dress I won't be buying. I still have to try it on though, and I'm not wasting the sales associate's time – I will be purchasing a dress, just not an $8,000.00 Valentino dress.

She returns with the key in hand, unlocks the security tag and gently carries the dress to the dressing room. "Let me get you some heels? I have a pair that go perfectly with this dress," she smiles.

"Perfect. Size seven please."

Within moments she returns with a pair of Jimmy Choo pumps. "Let me know if you need any further assistance. My name is Brenda."

"Thank you, Brenda." I close door and eagerly put on the dress.

I feel like a million bucks. The Valentino hugs my body, accentuating my curves. It's perfect. It's sexy. It's also eight thousand dollars!

I hear a knock at the door. "Everything good?"

"Yes. I'll be out in a sec." I open the door and do a twirl for her.

"Oh my God," she says, "that dress looks amazing on you." Brenda's mouth hangs open.

I know she is a sales associate who probably works on commission, and would say it anyway, but she actually likes it and likes my body in it. I often have that effect on sales people. It's the transformation that gets them. They see a girl in jeans and a loose hoodie walk in to the changing room, and a beautiful sophisticated woman appears moments later, like a butterfly emerging from the chrysalis.

I grab my purse, pull out the gift card and hand it to her. "Can you please let me know much is on this card?"

"Of course. Be right back."

*Soak it in as long as you can Zoe.* I smile, twirling around like Cinderella, admiring myself in the mirror, the way the dress clings and sparkles.

Brenda returns. "There's ten thousand dollars on this card, ma'am."

I smile at Brenda, trying to hide my surprise. "I'll take the dress," I tell her without hesitation, "and the shoes too."

"Great choice."

I walk back into the change room and do a little happy dance. Is this Elias' way of reeling me in? *Fuck, am I being reeled in?*


BLAIR IS WAITING FOR me on the steps. She doesn't recognize me at first.

"Blair."

"Zoe?" she says. "What have you done with my Zoe?"

I do a little twirl. "What do you think?"

"You look incredible!"

"Thanks. You don't look too bad yourself. You ready?"

"Do you know anything about this opera?" she asks.

"A little."

"Care to give me some background?"

"No. Let's go." I take her by the arm and escort her to our balcony seats.

"I'm not going to ask you who your patron is, but he has exquisite taste."

I smile. She knows not to ask too many questions.

The lights begin to flicker and I get comfortable in my seat. I love this opera and have seen it many times. Dido, the Queen of Carthage, meets the Trojan Prince Aeneas and they fall in love. *What a surprise.* The witches plot Dido's destruction and the sorceress brings about a storm while the men are hunting. The storm breaks and Aeneas returns to town, where the false Mercury tells him that he must leave Dido and sail to Italy. They prepare to leave and the witches are delighted. Aeneas leaves Dido, who kills herself once he is gone. *When I am Laid* is one of the most beautiful and heart-felt songs I have heard in a very long time. Tears roll down my cheeks. Purcell is a genius, as is Elias. Shivers run through my body, and all I can do is think about him. *What is happening to me? Am I falling in love with Elias?*

Blair reaches over and holds my hand. She is a great friend. I'm lucky to have her.

The curtains close, and I need a few moments to compose myself.

"You okay, Zoe?"

I look at her. "All good now. Thanks"

"Let's get that drink. We can't have that dress go to waste."

"I couldn't agree more."

"Michael is at Twenty-Two. Let's go and meet him there."

Club Twenty-Two is not one of my favorite bars, it's the local wannabee hangout. In less than ten minutes we are there.

"I see Michael by the bar." Blair leads the way. We reach the bar and Blair plants a big kiss on Michael. "Look who I brought. Doesn't she look gorgeous?"

"Yes, she does. What happened to you last week Zoe? You went M.I.A."

"Hi Michael. Sorry about that. Your friend Cy is a very bad influence."

"No need to say sorry to me, Zoe, but Blair was a little disappointed."

Blair turns to me, "I had to spend the night all alone with Michael. Do you know how difficult that is?"

We all laugh.

Michael turns to me, "What did you do to my friend Cy?"

"What do you mean?" I inquire, trying to maintain a look of innocence.

"He wouldn't stop talking about you. He's waiting for your phone call."

I laugh. "He may be waiting quite a while. I deleted his number."

Blair interjects, "Why would you do that? He is actually a sweet-heart of a guy."

"Sweet-hearts and I don't get along. I chew them up and spit them out."

Michael smiles. "You may want to re-consider this time Zoe. He really liked you, True Love and all that."

"Okay, enough about Cy. Let's order a drink," *so I can get out of here.*

And as promised, I have my one drink and go home, knowing that the week ahead is going to be a long one.

I WALK INTO STEFANO'S office. He is waiting for me. He is smart enough to know I will be at his office first thing Monday morning.

"Zoe, this is David Stern. David this is Zoe Winstein," Stefano says calmly. He is in a good mood, for a change.

I shake hands with David, not knowing why the formal introductions.

"David is trying to put this deal together, but no one on their side is being cooperative."

"So?" I can't come across too eager.

"I need you to talk to the owner. Fuck the lawyers. David, brief her on the property."

I see David's mouth moving, but I'm not listening. I'm day-dreaming of the day this will all come to an end and I can run away, without feeling paralyzed.

"…This is the address and this is how you can get a hold of Anton Bergman." David hands me a sheet with all the information that I need to know.

"Got it." I pick up my purse and am about to make my exit, when Stefano stops me.

"Where the fuck do you think you are going?" Stefano being his usual self.

"Is there more?" I look at David.

"No," is his response as he shrugs his shoulders.

"Fuck both of you. What's your strategy Zoe?"

"No clue," *yet*.

"So, let's figure it out." Stefano wants answers.

"I need time to think about it."

"We don't have time for you to think about it."

"When have I ever disappointed you?"

Stefano doesn't respond.

"Never! And that's because I think. Try it sometime Stefano. For now back off and let me work my magic."

I make my way out of his office to get some fresh air, but before I can take my first full breath, I see an incoming text.

Elias: I can't stay away from you any longer. I'm
    coming to see you...
Elias...NOW!

Apparently, everything is urgent today.

# CHAPTER TWENTY

I HUSTLE TO MAKE IT to my place before Elias, and luckily, I do. I do a quick run-through of the apartment, making sure my notes from the weekend are nowhere to be found. Just as I complete my sweep, Elias knocks on the door.

"Baby, I missed you," he says as he walks in and embraces me. He proceeds to put me in a bear hug so tight I can barely breathe.

"Easy there Elias, you don't know your own strength."

"Sorry, I can't help it. I want you close to me. Let's go and lie in bed. I want to hold you...naked." He says with his half smile.

"Okie dokie."

He leads me to the bedroom. "Don't move. I want to undress you."

I stand still while he crouches down and removes my jeans. It's a difficult task, they are snug. I assist him by wiggling my ass, and we both laugh. He stands erect, cocks his head, and puts his index finger to his lips.

"Hmmm, I think the shirt has to go also."

I extend my arms and allow him to do the rest.

"Wait." He unclips my bra. "Much better."

He shoves me onto the bed roughly and I lie flat on my back with my legs spread and dangling off the edge.

"Perfect." He crawls into bed, pulls me up so I'm completely on the bed, and lies down next to me. His arms and legs wrap around my body and I instantly begin to writhe.

He reaches between my legs and puts a finger in my pussy. It is wet and sensitive. He smiles. "Someone can't wait. Can I take my clothes off or should I just get right down to business my little whore?"

"Mmm. I am your little whore and I can't help it." I lightly bite his lower lip.

He pushes my lips away. "I enjoy spending time with you. You make me happy." He removes my glasses and stares into my eyes. "You are absolutely gorgeous."

I blush, staring into his large brown eyes. "I love you," I say, and maybe I even mean it.

"I want you to be independent." He has become very serious, all business. My wet pussy will have to wait. He sits up, leaning on his right arm. "What do you know about real estate?"

"They're not making any more of it?" I smile, lying there, tilting my head up and wishing he were fucking me right now.

"True enough. Do you know what ROI is?"

I decide to play dumb, humor him. "ROI?"

"Return on investment," he says. "I'll show you."

He gets out of bed, goes into the other room and returns with a pad of paper and a pen. He begins to write numbers on a piece of paper. "Let's make it easy. You buy a property for a million dollars, and, for the purpose of this example, you purchase it in cash. That is to say no mortgage. If you rent the property for $120,000.00 per year or $10,000 per month, and your total expenses for the property, such as taxes, maintenance, management costs and insurance are $12,000 per year, or $1,000 per month. Your return on investment is 10.8 percent. You do this by dividing your net annual income, in this case rental income minus expenses, $108,000 annually, by your total investment of $1,000,000. Got it?"

"Yes, teacher, but why are you showing me this?"

"You are smart, Zoe. This is a simple example and real things are much more complex, but I can teach you. You'll be better than me. The student will surpass the master. I want you to be self-sufficient and take care of yourself. I don't want you to have to rely on me or anyone else."

My life is becoming very interesting. Most men don't want me to be independent, they want me to rely on them. Elias is different. He acts like he sincerely wants what's best for me. He isn't worried that I might leave him, he believes that if I'm with him for his money that's not a good thing. I find his confidence alluring.

"I want to help you buy something," he says. "Let me help you? It will be fun." His expression changes. "But first let's have a different – and I believe a much more enjoyable – type of fun."

He leans over and bites my lower lip. I feel his body get rigid, his grip tightening around my shoulders. He kisses me deeply, our tongues dancing in perfect rhythm, the urgency increasing with each rotation. A moan escapes my open mouth as his hands move down my chest. He softly caresses the sides of my breasts with his fingertips. My hips rotate and my pussy inches closer to his cock, my body moving in time with his. I toss my head back, my cue to him to be a little more aggressive. He slaps my breast hard, the sharp pain shoots through my body, before settling into pleasure. He bites my neck and slaps the other breast, harder. I scream.

Reaching down, Elias forcefully grabs my ankles, pushes my knees to my chest and spreads me wide. "You'll enjoy this," he says, so sure of himself, as his head makes its way down between my legs. "Your smell turns me on," he says matter-of-factly.

I close my eyes and concentrate on his touch, his tongue first tracing circles up one inner thigh, then the other. I lose touch with time and space, surrendering completely to the pleasure. His tongue dances up my thigh before lightly grazing my now full lips. He looks up and gazes into my eyes.

I moan.

"What do you want?" Elias asks.

He is in no rush. He wants to satisfy me. Satisfying me, satisfies him.

I move my hands down to my clit and spread my lips open, in anticipation of his tongue.

He begins to slowly and softly lick my clit. "Is this what you want?"

"Mmm, yes," I reply.

"Say it, Zoe, tell me what you want."

"I want your tongue inside me. I want you to lick my pussy and make me come. Then I want you to use my body for your pleasure. Do whatever you want with. Use me however you want."

He begins lightly rotating his tongue on my clit, and I squirm, press my pussy into his face. His tongue slides in and out of me, meeting my thrusts, penetrating me, then he flattens his tongue against my clit, lets me apply the pressure of my choosing. Slowly his rhythm and pressure begin to accelerate. I can feel an orgasm building. Within seconds I'm ready to come and I can't hold it back.

"Oh, fuck, fuck, fuck." I scream.

He pauses. "You aren't allowed to come yet."

He continues to swirl his tongue, inserts a finger inside me slowly, inch by inch, then carefully withdraws it, just as slowly, before starting again. He does this for several minutes that seem like several hours while my orgasm edges ever closer.

My body begins to shake. I'm completely out of control. I was exhausted after the last orgasm and didn't think I could have another, but it is building, slowly but surely. "Oh fuck," I moan.

"Not yet," he scolds me. He controls me perfectly. Keeping me just at the edge, my body convulsing, but not letting me have my release.

He stands up, my eyes fixated on his hard cock.

"Are you ready to be fucked?" he asks.

"Mmmhmm," is the only reply I can manage.

"Beg, my dirty little slut."

"Please fuck me. I need your cock. I need to come. Fuck me now."

Lowering himself on top of me, he inserts the tip of his cock inside me, pauses before slowly thrusting in and out of me, never more than an inch at a time. I guess he wants me to beg some more. I reach my hand down and begin playing with my clit. "Fuck me harder, give me all of your cock," I whine.

He slaps me across my face. Hard. "Not yet, slut," he says, grabbing my hand, and moving it away from my pussy. He is in complete control. I don't fight him.

"And stop whimpering," he says before again slapping my breast.

*I'm so far gone that pain and pleasure have become one.*

"Do you like that?" he asks.

"Yes, do it again," I respond. "Please, slap me."

"Oh, you like it? That's my dirty girl." He grins before stuffing his entire cock inside me.

I moan loudly.

"Play with yourself now. Come for me," he instructs.

I don't need to be told twice. My hand releases itself from his strong grip, my fingers return to my clit, rubbing soft circles in time with his deep thrusts.

My other hand parts my lips so that I can caresses my clit. I apply more pressure, feel a tingle start in the base of my stomach.

"Come now for me," he instructs. He begins to fuck me fast and hard and I lift my hips to meet his thrusts. At the same time, he alternates slapping my nipples and pinching them.

My body begins to shake, the weight of him pinning me to the bed.

He slaps my face again. I'm not sure if that hurt or felt good, I am far from caring, I need just one thing: to come.

"Oh God! Fuck, fuck, fuck!" I scream as the orgasm washes over my body in big waves and just keeps going. Every nerve in my body is triggering, my body becoming very rigid, before collapsing into bliss after what seems an eternity of coming.

"Good girl. My turn."

He spins me around, still on my back, my head now dangling over the side of the bed. He stands up, one hand gripped tightly around his cock.

"Suck it baby. Taste your pussy," he instructs, sliding his cock into my mouth.

I look up at him, his eyes roll into the back if his head. He forces every inch of his hard cock into my waiting mouth. He is so deep in my throat that I gag a little, but he doesn't notice or doesn't care. I'm not sure how, but he continues to push deeper and harder into my throat.

"That's it," he says, "take it all."

I close my eyes and relax my throat, his thrusts providing the friction he so deeply desires, while my saliva provides the lubricant, streams out of my mouth over his cock and onto the floor.

Lifting his cock from my mouth, he grabs his shaft and lowers his balls into my mouth. "Mmmm," he moans, before moving his body forward. "Lick it, baby," he instructs, my tongue moving back-and-forth over his balls and down to his ass. He lowers himself onto my face, my tongue circling the outside of his ass, before entering it slowly. He moans deeply. "Fuck that feels good. Keep going. I'm about to come."

I do as I'm told, sliding my tongue in and out of his ass. Have I mentioned that I love eating ass? Or perhaps more accurately I love the effect it has on men. I feel his body tighten as he pulls away, now standing over me. Stroking his cock with one hand, he reaches the other over and holds my head in place.

He moans loudly as the orgasm takes over, shoots his semen all over my face. I open my mouth and manage to get some semen in my mouth and gulp it down. He stands over me, releases his cock, reaches down to wipe the come from my face, and puts his fingers in my mouth.

"Good girl."

*That was fucked up. That was amazing.*

He is fucked up. This isn't passion. This is dominance, and I play the submissive part perfectly.

He is completely spent. He lies down and holds me for a while, before rolling off the bed.

"What a grrrreat day," he says rolling the r in great. "Ready for dinner?"

"Yes, baby," I reply. If he wants me to play the role of the submissive, that's what I'll do.

Does this man want a serious relationship from me or am I delusional? My heart is telling me he is making a concerted effort to be with me. He lavishes me with gifts. He spends time with me. I have access to his Manhattan apartment. We have amazing, although slightly weird sex. He holds me like no other man has. He makes me feel important, for the most part. He wants me to be self-sufficient. And he wants me to be all his.

But is he all mine – minus the wife, of course?

My heart and pussy are trying to convince me that he really cares for me, but my brain, which makes a large part, if not the majority of my decisions, tells me to be careful. I hear Matteo's voice, "*He is a sociopath.*" Yes, he has some of the characteristic traits of a sociopath. He is socially awkward, he needs to be wanted, and perhaps love is a game to him. *Zoe, he is a married man.* Yes, he is married and supposedly loves his wife and kids. Yes, he will never give me the love I deserve. And yes, he will never give me kids. Does that matter?

*So, what am I doing? Focus Zoe.* He has a purpose in my life. Actually, he had a purpose. His purpose is over. So why continue this?

"How hungry are you?" he asks.

"Starving," I reply.

"Good. Get dressed. Let's go for a Bergman."

WE WALK INTO A RUSTIC bar. The smell of bourbon and beef dominates the dark space lit mostly by candles. Some would say it is charming and romantic, but it's not exactly my scene.

We find our own seats, and a waitress with black hair, tattoos on one arm and a nose ring, brings us our menus then turns and walks away. She's hot in a slutty, goth way, and I can't help but notice Elias' wandering eye blatantly following her. I have never seen anything like it before and it frightens me, makes me feel uncomfortable.

I try to get his attention, "Which Bergman do you recommend?"

No response.

I take a breath, thinking I really need a drink. "Baby?"

He turns to me. "Sorry, what did you ask?"

He isn't himself. I feel a shiver run through me, and not the good kind. "Which Bergman do you recommend?"

"They are all great."

He is preoccupied. I'm rapidly losing my appetite but don't want to disappoint him, so, I stay, but I'm definitely feeling uncomfortable.

The waitress returns for our order, and I notice Elias' gaze roaming over her body, taking in her firm breasts, her bare arms, her skin tight jeans. Am I jealous? Do I just find his wandering eye disrespectful? Or is it both?

"Hi. Can I get the veggie Bergman?" He turns to me. "What are you having?" And once again gawks at our waitress.

"I'll have the same, along with a double vodka on the rocks."

The waitress doesn't say a word, just turns and leaves, Elias's eyes on her gorgeous ass as she returns to the kitchen.

I think of distracting him. I'm hurt. Do they know one another, I wonder? Am I missing something? This night has taken a very negative turn. Why didn't I just turn off my phone, put on my pajamas and rest tonight? Why am I jealous? Why am I here? My job is done. I left his apartment this morning, ready to end it. Why do I stay?

I stay silent and Elias people watches. I notice the direction of his eyes in my peripheral vision, following every woman, measuring, assessing. How did I not see this behavior from him before?

He finally snaps out of it and turns to me, says, "did you have fun today, Zoe?"

Okay Zoe, play the part. Although you have finished your business, you can still use him and not let your heart get carried away. Close your eyes, spread your legs and open your mouth. You will be rewarded. "Sure did, I hope it's not over?"

"It's certainly not over yet. I've got a left a little in the tank. You're going to get fucked again."

"You're insatiable!" I try to sound enthusiastic, full of admiration.

"Or we could just go home and watch TV," he teases, "my poor exhausted lover."

Our food arrives. This time, Elias isn't distracted by the waitress. Maybe I'm being paranoid?

Elias smiles. "Look at that…saved by the food. Eat up. You can decide after you eat."

I take a bite of the Bergman. "Mmm. This is yummy."

"Told you it was good," he replies.

Just as I am about to take the last bite of my Bergman, Elias stands up, a big smile on his face, hugs a woman as she approaches our table. "Silvia, so good to see you." He gives her a big hug, holds her a little too long.

"Always a pleasure," the petite brunette responds with a smile.

"When are we going to go out for a drink?" asks Elias.

Am I invisible? Apparently so. I take the last bite of my Bergman, pretending to not pay attention.

"Later this week?"

"Perfect. I'll give you a call." He puts his arms around her and kisses her on the lips before she disappears.

*What the fuck?* The downward spiral continues?

Elias sits back at the table. "Ready? Let's get the bill."

I don't say a word as Elias pays the bill and we head to his apartment.

Doctor Winstein, how do you handle this situation? I wonder. With humor, I decide.

We walk into his apartment and he leads me into the bedroom. I'm biting my tongue.

*Think of something funny Zoe!* But nothing is coming to me. My emotions are getting the better of me. "Who was that woman at the bar?"

"Who, Silvia?"

"Yes, Silvia."

"Just a friend."

"A friend? Do you kiss all your friends on the lips?"

"What?" he stops and looks at me.

"Do you kiss all your friends on the lips?"

He stares at me with a puzzled look on his face. "What are you talking about?"

"You kissed Silvia on the lips."

"No, I didn't. I don't kiss friends on the lips and she is a friend, nothing more."

Is this really happening? "I will say it slower. You kissed Silvia on the lips."

"Are you cuckoo my love?"

"I know what I saw."

"Baby, I kissed her on the cheek."

*Oh my God. This guy is making me believe I'm crazy. Maybe I am crazy, but I know what I saw. Calm down Zoe, he is so not worth it.* I put on my actress face and give in. "I'm sorry. I don't like you kissing anybody in any way. I think I've had too much to drink."

"My poor jealous baby. Don't be that way. You're the only woman I love."

I know what he wants to hear. "Maybe I am a little jealous." *Fuck me! Am I falling in love with this sociopath? Zoe the professional is acting like an amateur.*

"Don't be jealous. You know that I love you."

He moves closer, grabs my hair, tilts my head back. "Ready to play?"

And so I became his submissive whore one more time, but this time I don't enjoy it at all. I close my eyes, count the thrusts, fake my orgasm and try and fail to fall asleep when it is all over.

I lie awake for what feels like hours, staring at the ceiling, listening to Elias' contented breathing, wondering how and when I'm going to extract myself from this before it turns too dark.

# CHAPTER TWENTY-ONE

SUPERFICIALLY AND AT FIRST blush Elias is charming. He is intelligent, but also delusional and irrational. He is never anxious or nervous. He is egocentric and incapable of love. These are my thoughts as I wake up, still groggy from the lack of sleep and the excess of sex. Good morning.

Elias has left for work. No matter how emotionally draining the day has been, sleep nourishes me, and I didn't get enough. It is my escape…that and sex. Elias has prepared the usual fruit salad for me in the kitchen, but I decide to leave, once again. *How did I let this happen? How did I fall in love with him? Why did I allow myself to fall in love with him? Was it because for the first time in a long time I felt taken care of?* I feel like a fool. I'm angry. Not at him, but at myself.

Perhaps Stefano is correct after all. I'm asking myself all these questions, but what I really need is someone to talk to, aloud.

Zoe: Can I stop by and chat?
Matteo: I will be at the office later this afternoon. Say

2:00 PM?
Zoe: Perfect! See you then!


"GOOD AFTERNOON," the blonde receptionist smiles.

Full Metal Capital's lobby is covered with the finest Italian white marble from floor to ceiling. "Good afternoon, I'm here to see Anton Bergman."

"Do you have an appointment?" she inquires.

"No, I'm sorry, I don't."

She looks me up and down, decides I'm probably not a threat. "And whom should I say is here to see him?"

"Zoe Winstein, from Manhattan College."

"Please have a seat Ms. Winstein. I will see if he is available."

I take a seat and she picks up the phone. I begin to peruse the magazines, until my phone vibrates. I glance at my screen.

Elias: Baby, I miss you already.

I don't need any distractions at this moment so I put the phone on silent and quickly place it back in my purse.

From the corner of my eye I see the receptionist stand and walk towards me. "Excuse me, Ms. Winstein, may I ask what business matter you wish to discuss with Mr. Bergman?"

"Sales and the Psychology of Sales." I don't want to give too much away, but I want it to sound alluring.

I return to perusing the magazines. After about ten minutes the secretary returns. "Mr. Bergman will see you now. Please follow me."

She escorts me through double metal doors to the office at the end of the hallway where she asks me to take a seat. Except, it isn't an office but a boardroom. I take a seat next to the head of the table, wait for him to arrive.

Anton arrives. He's in his forties with brown hair, the full-grown beard that all the celebrities are rocking, green eyes and a body to admire – which is exactly what I do. *Stay calm Zoe. This is extremely important.* He doesn't look this good on the Google images. Maybe this isn't Anton Bergman, but his brother? Or his assistant? Pawning me off to someone else on his behalf? He pulls out the seat next to mine, settles himself in, his eyes on me, giving me his full attention. "Good morning, Dr. Winstein. What can I do for you?"

I go for the direct approach: "1st and 74th." I'm nervous as hell, heart racing. This is the game right here.

"Well, I'm glad we could get straight to the point," he says as he leans forward, reducing the space between us to the point where it is mildly uncomfortable, his eyes locked on mine like an old fashioned staring contest. "I don't mean to be rude or dismissive, and you seem like a nice person but this may be the shortest meeting ever." He stands and walks to the door. "The property is not for sale, Dr. Winstien."

I turn towards him. "Please give me a minute, Mr. Bergman."

He stops, one hand on the door. "One minute."

"Why won't you sell?" I ask.

"That's not your business," he replies in a firm tone, still facing away from me.

"I know it's not my business, but you and I may have something in common," I reply.

He glances back at me. "Enlighten me, Doctor."

I lock eyes with him. "I want to fuck them over."

"You want to what?"

"Screw them, fuck them, get the better of them."

"Who is them? How do I know 'them' doesn't include 'me'?"

"Because I have no reason to hurt you."

"Who is them?"

"Matteo Rizzio."

"Ok, we may have that in common, but that's just one person. 'Them' implies more than one person. Once more, who is 'them'?"

"Does it matter?"

"It doesn't. But this meeting will be over if you don't tell me who the others are."

I don't stay a word.

"I guess we are done, Dr. Winstein." He opens the door.

*What do I have to lose?* "The other 'them' is Stefano Souzas."

His body language changes. I definitely have his attention. "Interesting. We do indeed have two things in common. But what's to say that you aren't going to buy my property and flip it to one or the other of them tomorrow?"

"I've got plans of my own, Mr. Bergman, and I'm working with another prospective purchaser."

He pauses. "I like the property. I have no plans to sell it at this time."

I walk over to him, shake hands with him and leave. "Thank you for seeing me Mr. Bergman." I've baited the trap. Nothing to do now but wait.

I'VE LOST MY APPETTITE AFTER my meeting with Bergman. I need to clear my head, so I decide to take a stroll to the Guggenheim. I still have two hours to spare before my appointment with Matteo.

Anton Burri's work is being exhibited. From doctor during the war to mixed media artist, his former profession is evident in his work. Stitches and blood. How frustrating to see something in front of you and not be able to do anything about it. That's how I feel about my current situation.

My phone vibrates.

Elias: Baby, is everything okay?

I ignore his text. Walking up the ramp I admire Burri's larger works. Simple, yet so full of emotions. By the time I reach the top, it's time for me to make my way to Matteo's office.

Before I even walk through his office door, Matteo is saying, "What did you do to our friend?"
I'm not sure what he is referring to. "Who?" I say.
"Elias. We had a pleasant lunch together and he couldn't stop talking about you. Has he experienced your many charms, Zoe?"
Oh God. What a question. All of a sudden I'm not so sure it was such a good idea to discuss Elias with Matteo, but I can't filter. "He is mixed up," are the first words that come out of my mouth.
Matteo tilts his head and laughs. "You were forewarned, Zoe."
My phone goes off again. I glance at the screen.

Elias: Baby, Baby, Baby?

I ignore the text again and put my phone away. "What should I do?"
"You know how the rodeo works, Zoe. Hold on tight and enjoy the ride. Jump off at the right time otherwise you'll get hurt."
Here I am thinking he was going to tell me to run, but no, he wants me to 'go along for the ride'. I don't like the analogy. "What does that even mean?" I ask.
"He has cash, connections, and he is fun. Enjoy it. Enjoy, but stay detached, and when you feel you're getting emotionally involved, jump off."
I know that's good advice and that I'm not going to get anything more out of our conversation, so I say. "Got it.

One more question, when are we going to party again? I miss you and your entourage."

"Assuming Elias gives you permission, soon Zoe...real soon."

"Great." At least my relationship with Matteo is evolving positively. I think he is becoming my confidante. I feel as though I can talk with him and rely on him for advice. I give Matteo a hug and leave. On the way back to my car I try to decide whether or not I should call it a day. I pull out my phone.

Zoe: Free tonight?
John: For you, absolutely.
Zoe: My place 8:00 PM.
John: What can I bring?
Zoe: Yourself.


I BUZZ JOHN IN, make my way to the front door and embrace him. "I'm sorry", I say.

He looks puzzled. "Sorry for what?"

"For not spending more time with you. Work has been hectic."

"Zoe, I understand. I am glad you reached out. I am here now, and that is the important thing."

*I just want to hurt Elias. He is playing with me and now it is my turn to play.*

I lead John to the bedroom and undress him. His cock is erect as he lies on my bed, legs spread. I crawl from the edge of the bed and gaze into his eyes. I grab a hair tie, put my hair into a ponytail, get down onto my elbows and begin breathing on his erect cock. His head tilts back, I begin to lick his balls with the tip of my tongue in a circular motion. I hear his breath quicken as I squeeze the base of his cock, my fingers forming a ring, keeping his erection strong.

*He deserves this, that bastard Elias. I don't believe anything he says. His actions are what I believe.*

I grasp the base of his cock with my left hand and stroke it with my right, lowering my open mouth over the tip. I close my mouth and flick my tongue back-and-forth, then take him deeper into my mouth and withdraw my hands completely, rotating and humming, his cock buried to the hilt in my throat. I gag a little, catch my breath, then start to move my head back and forth on his cock. I want him to feel powerful. He rolls his head back, exhaling and moaning, as I slide a finger slowly into his ass. He pushes back against my hand, craving deeper penetration. His body pulsates and his cock throbs. My rhythm slows down as I continue to suck his cock and slowly remove my finger.

"Don't stop," he pleads.

I have bigger plans for him. "Don't move." I gaze into his eyes. "Play with yourself for me."

He obeys, grabs his cock and begins to stroke it. "Mmmm," he moans.

I stand up, open my closet door and pull out my harness with a dildo attached.

His eyes widen. "This is for you," I tell him. "My guess is that you will like it more than my finger. Get on your hands and knees."

He doesn't respond immediately but he doesn't stop me either.

"You saw this in my purse that night," I smile. "I think subconsciously you might be a little curious."

Without uttering a word, he gets onto his hands and knees. "I am curious. Do it, but be gentle," he requests.

"Don't worry, this is about pleasure. Now, stroke your cock for me."

He begins to stroke his cock with his right hand and I spit on my palm and massage his ass with my saliva. I finger him with my thumb, preparing his ass for my dildo. His ass is hungry, asking for more. I pull out my thumb and insert my dildo, inch by inch, then begin to thrust ever so slowly. I do this for several minutes, until he begins to rock back onto me, wanting the dildo deeper. I massage his balls to heighten the sensation. I am deep inside him, thrusting harder and harder, until his body pulsates and comes.

He collapses onto his back and I lie down beside him.

He takes a few moments to catch his breath, before saying, "I want to show you something. Get my phone please."

I remove my harness, grab his phone as he takes me into his arms. He opens his browser and types in 'last pages'. He opens a profile and shows me erotic images of a woman. I'm not exactly sure what he is showing me.

I zoom into the images. "She is hot."

"She is a he," he responds.

"What?" I do a double take.

"I have never told anyone this before, but I have always been curious to be with a woman who has a penis."

This is a first for me. "Would you like to meet someone?" I ask him. "I can be there too if that would make you feel more comfortable."

"I can't believe I'm telling you this."

"Nothing surprises me. I have seen too much." I must admit, I am actually a tad surprised – the mayor likes it in the ass, fantasizes about lady-boys? Who would have guessed. How far does he want to go? "Do you want to have a cock in your mouth? I can arrange that too."

"I'm curious, but let's move slowly, Zoe."

"Have you ever been to a sex club."

He laughs. "When you are a married Mayor your life becomes an open book."

"How about out of the country? Have you ever been to the sex clubs in Berlin?"

He smiles. "I assume you have?"

"Yes."

"And how would you describe it?"

"It's like a pornographic movie playing 360 degrees around you that you can reach out and touch."

"That sounds unreal."

"With all the sexual adventures I have lived, my favorite is still missionary at a turtle's pace," I confess.

He laughs. "You are definitely different, Zoe."

He holds me for a few more minutes before he washes up and makes his exit.

My phone has been lighting up all night. I assume it's Elias, but I don't care. At least I tell myself that.

It's the end of the day, and I take score: I manipulated one, couldn't manipulate another and I am no longer in love…maybe. Just another day in my in the life of Zoe…

# CHAPTER TWENTY-TWO

I AM AWAKENED AT 8:00 AM by frantic knocking at the door. Naked, I make my way to the door, tripping over the clothes I left on the floor last night. Whoever it is, they are very persistent. The knocking continues as I make my way sleepily to the door. Impatient! How did they get by the concierge I wonder as I press my face against the door and stare through the peep hole. Elias! Who else?

I open the door. I guess I knew he would show up sooner or later if I kept ignoring him.

Elias just walks in. "Why haven't you returned my calls or texts? Why are you ignoring me?"

*Because I hate you right now.* "Work has been keeping me busy, then my phone ran out of battery last night."

As usual he puts his arms around me and squeezes me tight. "Baby, I love you."

I don't think he has any clue that I'm almost finished with him, although I do enjoy the attention and the sex, there are too many negatives.

"Why aren't your arms around me? Come on, let's lie in bed. I want to hold you." He grabs my wrist and drags me to my bedroom. I don't say a word. He pushes me onto the bed and lies next to me. I allow him to hold me. *Just lie here Zoe and let him do what he wants to you. Use him the way you want and give him what he wants.* The sex has no meaning. It never did. Never will. Enjoy it. Detach your heart from your pussy. It is a blessing and a curse. I remain silent.

He begins to kiss me and to caresses my face. "Let me look at you. You are gorgeous. I just can't get enough of you." He continues to kiss me gently and it doesn't take long for me to start to squirm. It's a natural reaction. He knows how to get that response out of me.

"Are you writhing for me?"

"I don't know. Am I?" I whisper in his ear.

"I think so, my excitable Zoe," is his immediate response as he begins to peel his clothes off.

With mock desire I say, "I want you to fuck me."

He rolls on top of me and I begin to arch my lower back and wrap my legs around his thighs. I may have plans to get rid of him, but my pussy still wants what it wants.

His cock is instantly hard. He licks his fingers and makes my pussy wet and inserts his head inside me. He slowly thrusts in and out, but only the tip. I begin to thrust my hips to get more of his cock into my pussy.

"Do you want more?" he asks.

"I want it all."

"Let me get back to you on that."

I begin to raise my hips higher.

"I need more time to think, Ms. Greedy."

He enjoys teasing me, and I enjoy every moment of being teased. He continues in this way for what feels like an eternity, then suddenly slams all of his cock into me. I scream his name. His thrusts began to quicken and become more aggressive. He sticks three fingers in my mouth until I gag.

"Tell me another fantasy of yours?" he asks.

I'm not shy. "Those fingers in my mouth are another man's cock. He is forcing his cock down my throat as you fuck me hard."

"Does that turn you on?" he asks as he continues to tease me with the tip of his cock.

I moan. "It does." *Perhaps I enjoy the acting.*

"And would you lick pussy for me?"

"I would devour a pussy if you were watching."

He groans, "You're such a slut, Zoe. Tell me more."

I tell him all the thoughts that I believe he wants to hear. "I want you to fuck me at the edge of the bed while another woman spreads her legs and sits on my face, forces me to lick her pussy. I want your cock to be hard and ready to explode as you watch me."

He begins to pull my hair with his left hand and grab my wrist with his right while his elbows support him. I scream from pleasure and pain.

He gets onto his knees and spreads my legs apart as he sticks his cock deep inside me. He allows me access to play with my clit. I lick my fingers and begin to rub my labia as he fucks me. He grabs my inner thighs and squeezes them while spreading my pussy. "Come for me."

My eyes roll back and I hold my breath as I orgasm. "Fuuuuuuck!"

He turns me to my side and takes me from behind. He slaps my ass cheek repeatedly. I scream with each slap.

"Oh yes, oh yes! I'm going to come. Ohhhhhhh Yesssssss!" His body weight collapses onto me. He stays still until our sweaty bodies begin to cool down.

"Not bad, Zoe. You're getting the hang of this," he smiles. "Let me make you some breakfast," he says as he climbs out the bed, watching me as I clean up the come that is all over my back and ass.

"A coffee sounds like a wonderful idea right about now. Some asshole got me out of bed early this morning."

"Don't you mean into bed?"

We both laugh. I hate him right now but it's hard to hate someone after an amazing orgasm.

"Coffee and oatmeal coming right up," he says and leaves the room.

I stay in bed, thinking. I represent the dark side of love, romance and relationships. Functionality is the operative word. I'm incapable of feeling and I acknowledge that. Fairy tales are just that, fairy tales that create unrealistic expectations.

Elias walks back into the room with coffee and oatmeal. He places the coffee on my nightstand and gets back into bed with the bowl of oatmeal. He feeds me while we lie together.

"It doesn't get any better than this." He smiles.

I look at him. "Do you enjoy feeding me?"

"I enjoy doing anything for you." He puts down the bowl and puts his arms around me. "I love you, Zoe."

"I love you, Elias," I tell him. In his own way I believe he does love me, but the reality is that the phrase *I love you* is thrown around just like *I'm sorry*. Are people truly sorry? Actions speak louder than words, and most of the time the behavior that leads people to say *I'm sorry* is repeated. People are who they are – at the core. A leopard doesn't change its spots, and people don't change their M.O. If you want to predict future behavior, just look at past behavior. That's why one of my strategies is to ask men questions about their past.

I sometimes wish I wasn't this way. I might actually be happy and think to myself that I have found true love.

"What does my baby want to do today?"

I try to hide the sadness in my face. "Don't you have to be at work?"

"I took the day off to be with you."

"Teach me more then."

He laughs. "I think it's the other way around."

"No, I mean teach me something else about real estate."

"What would you like to know?"

"How would one buy a property without any serious money."

"Well, you have options."

I interrupt. "A bank loan isn't an option."

"No banks. Investors?"

"Investors?"

"Yes. People know real estate is a smart investment. They know nothing about managing a property, so they invest funds and take less of a profit while someone else does the work."

"And what would an agreement like that look like?"

"Hold that thought." He gets out of bed and returns a few moments later. He brings paperwork with him. "Okay, so take a look at this document."

"Should you be showing me this?"

He looks at me in the eye acting all serious, "Can I trust you?"

*No.* "Yes."

He asks me to read the partnership agreement as he hands it to me. I take my time and scan the document.

Once I finish reviewing the document, I say, "It's a Co-Tenancy Agreement. Everyone's rights and obligations are set out. Some have financial obligations, some have development and construction obligations. It's all set out. The financial person is obligated to fund the venture while others do their part. He gets a preferred return and a portion of the equity. You don't do your part, you are in breech and there are remedies."

"That's correct. Any questions," he asks.

"Nope."

"That's my girl." He kisses me on my forehead. "What shall we do now? Discuss the benefits of oatmeal?"

We laugh.

He takes my hand and pushes it onto his cock. He is hard, yet again.

"You make me so excited. I think you have a voodoo doll with an erect penis, hidden in your drawer."

I laugh. "My secret is revealed. Who told you?"

He shuts me up by sticking his tongue deep into my throat.

He holds me close to him, until he is ready to go down on me. He pulls me to the edge of the bed, and tells me to spread my legs wide and hold them to my chest.

"I'm going to fuck you hard. Tell me what you want. How should I fuck you?" He waits for a response.

"I want you to control me."

This time he doesn't tease me. He just pushes his full cock into me with one long thrust. I scream. My hands hold onto my bed sheets, trying to hold in the pain that is quickly turning to pleasure.

"What a good pussy you have."

He wants to dominate me and I want to be submissive for him. I don't resist him. I become weight-less, allowing his thrusts to move my body, making my breasts bounce. He squeezes the skin on my inner thigh. It hurts but I like it. I bite my tongue and take it, begin to moan, hoping that the sounds will make him come faster. But it isn't working. So, I begin to talk dirty. "Fuck me harder." *No don't please.* "Come for me baby." *Just hurry and finish.* "Fuck your pussy." *Yes, giving you ownership of my pussy will make you come.*

"Oh yes, oh yessss, fuuuuuuuck!" He catches his breath but isn't finished yet. He gets onto his knees and begins licking my clit. I spread my lips open with my fingers. The tip of his tongue is gently stroking my clit for what feels like an eternity, driving me crazy. He gradually begins to apply more pressure, but still going at a slow rhythmic pace. I fantasize a cock in my mouth while he eats me out and I come. "Oh my god, oh my god, oh my gooooood," I scream, but it's theater, just for him.

"Good girl."

He moves my full body onto the bed and lies next to me. "The voodoo doll."

"Yes, Elias. The voodoo doll."

"Let's take a nap. You must be exhausted."

I am. I close my eyes and fall into a deep sleep.

"WAKE UP, BABY. Wake up."

I roll to my side and open my eyes. "What time is it?"

"It's noon."

Holy shit. Did I just sleep for two hours? I must be exhausted.

"Get dressed. Let's go for lunch."

The one thing I enjoy about having Elias at my place is that I can control the environment. Out in the open, he is unpredictable and I could easily lose control of the situation. I have no desire to be in the wild with him.

"Can we order in?"

"I want to show you off."

I roll my eyes. Why does it hurt so much? I need to change my thinking. *Zoe, Elias loves women. Accept him for who he is. Besides, you are getting your fair share of sex out there.* "What should I wear?"

He goes into my closet and picks an outfit. Jeans, a blouse and pumps. I put them on.

"You look gorgeous."

*Thanks Mr. Sociopath.* "Thanks."

"You ready?"

"Yup," I say. But I'm not ready. I'm never going to be ready to go out with him.

"Let's go."

He drives to Little Italy and parks in front of a restaurant called Da Nino. "Get ready for some wonderful homemade pasta," he says as we climb out of the car.

At this point I am starving from the orgasm. My strategy over lunch is to not care about Elias and his behavior, to ignore him, hoping that he won't be pleased with my company and will re-evaluate our relationship. I need to find the exit fast. I'm not enjoying this at all.

"Nino," Elias screams to the waiter as we walk in.

"Elias, come va?"

"Bene grazie, e tu?"

"Cosi, cosi. Prego." He shows us to our table.

"Grazie." He looks at me and waves his hand. "After you."

I follow the waiter to our table. I am facing the restaurant while Elias is facing the wall. Great strategy Zoe.

Elias turns to his side.

"Baby, can you face me please."

"Sorry, of course."

*Why me? Why am I so jealous? Do I actually love him? Do I just want him all to myself?*

"You okay with linguine and clams?"

"Sounds yummy."

"Great."

He flags down the waiter, who is hovering close by. "Nino, can we get two orders of the linguine vongole and a bottle of Fiano?"

"Si subito."

"Grazie."

Elias takes my hand. "I'm so excited that we are out." He leans forward in his seat, "Give me a kiss."

I lean forward and give him his kiss.

"So, what are we going to do this afternoon? Can I take you shopping?"

"Can we go back to my place and lie in bed?"

"Of course, but even with the voodoo doll I need a rest now and then."

We both laugh.

*Yes Elias. All I want from you are orgasms and strategy.* My brain is always on, it's exhausting.

"Zoe, promise me you won't leave me," he says in a soft tone with a bit of insecurity.

"Should I leave you?" I ask.

"Just promise me you won't."

I gaze into his eyes, "I, Zoe Winstein, promise to never leave you, Elias Machetta." Lying. It's one of my best skills.

He smiles. "I love you."

"I love you too." *Fuck. What am I doing? Digging myself in deeper when all I want to do is turn and run.*

The food arrives and I quickly devour it. I want to get back into the controlled environment of my apartment as soon as I can. I'm in love, but I'm of two minds. It makes me sad and it makes me happy. What a couple: crazy and crazier. Who is which? That's the question.

Elias and I arrive back at my apartment and we quickly get naked and jump back into bed. We get under the covers and he fucks me the way he enjoys. I play submissive and he uses my body the way I like it.

ELIAS FINALLY LEAVES AND I have some alone time. I peek at my phone. A few missed messages.

Stefano: What's the fuckin plan?
Stefano: Well?
Blair: Hey. Dinner soon? I miss you!
John: Want to fuck? I'm not wearing a suit. (wink)
Unknown: Let's talk.

My eye lids are heavy. I ignore all of them, turn my phone off and slump on the bed fully dressed, immediately fall into a deep sleep.

# CHAPTER TWENTY-THREE

*AM I DEPRESSED?* I have been spending too many hours sleeping. I have been ignoring my responsibilities. Elias is causing me to go insane. I try to re-focus. *Just breathe Zoe. Just breathe.*

I make an executive decision to be a responsible person this morning and to return my messages. I'm grateful they are messages and not phone calls. The more distance I keep from people, the happier I become. I pick up my phone and notice one additional message from last night.

Matteo: Interior Design Show after party tomorrow
        night @ Gladstone – 9 PM. Bring a friend.

*Does it ever end?*
I get to work returning messages.

To Blair:
Zoe: How about an after party tonight? Gladstone
        9:00 PM.

To Stefano:
Zoe: Give me a day.

To John:
Zoe: Yes…dinner tomorrow?

To unknown:
Zoe: About?

Blair: I'm in! Dress-code.
Zoe: Super SEXXXXYYYYY!
Blair: Gotcha!

I respond to Matteo:
Zoe: See you tonight. Me plus one.
Matteo: Great. See you tonight.

John: Pick you up at 7 tomorrow night.
Zoe: Looking forward to it!
John: Me too. More than you can imagine.

Unknown: Would rather discuss in person.
Zoe: It would be great to know who I'm meeting in person.
Unknown: Anton Bergman. Tomorrow, Grano @ noon.
Zoe: Anton. With an appetite or not?
Anton: With.
Zoe: See you there!

*I'm fuckin close. I can smell it. Anton is my ticket!* I'm in overdrive. Every nerve is on edge. I feel alive! I returned to New York with a purpose, this is what I have worked for and dreamed about.

There's only one thing that occupies my thoughts at this moment…Anton. Why is he now interested in meeting with me? Perhaps I shouldn't read too much into it, but my instincts tell me the opposite. Does he have a proposition? Rather than draw out the millions of possibilities for Anton's message, I decide to spend the afternoon at the gym and rest my thoughts before what I know is going to be a night of madness. After all, Matteo knows how to party.

9:00 PM AND BLAIR IS PUNCTUAL, waiting for me outside the Gladstone.

"Hey Blair," I wrap my arms around her and squeeze. "You look smashing."

"You look pretty hot yourself."

Holding Blair's hand, I walk to the door. The front of the club is a sea of people, milling about, and we have to elbow our way through the crowd to get to the front. We get the doorman's attention. "Zoe Winstein," I shout above the hubbub.

He scrolls through pages and finally finds my name. "Two?"

"Yes," I reply.

He gives us access to enter the archway entrance, draped with charcoal velvet drapery. The dark metal stairs have circular holes in each step that let light through. My heels echo against the solid wood paneled walls and arched ceiling. You can feel more than hear the bass, it's hot and sexy. The look on Blair's face is priceless. She enjoys being spoiled, and I'm glad I can afford this opportunity to spoil her.

We make it to the bottom of the stairs and look around. The venue is monumental. The floor is made of plexi-glass with a red glow coming through. Men and woman are lying underneath the platform, barely dressed; what little covering they have is skimpy lingerie. They move to the music, doing a horizontal dance. Where do I apply? I want that job, writhing to the beat of the music while the entire club watches me. I am an exhibitionist, after all.

I take Blair by the hand and slither through the crowd of beautiful men and women, attempting to find Matteo.

After a few minutes of wandering the club, I finally find his booth, grab Blair's hand and pull her with me. His booth is located on the platform next to the DJ, the best spot in the house, of course.

Matteo notices me immediately. "Well, well, well. Look who showed up." Matteo is half in the bag.

"So good to see you," I shout into his ear. "Thanks for the invite. You remember my friend, Blair."

Matteo extends his arms, "Nice to see you again."

"Likewise," Blair responds.

"I was beginning to think I was never going to see you again." Matteo smiles.

Blair, without missing a beat, responds, "She likes to keep her trophies locked up, away from the public."

We all laugh.

"What can I get you ladies to drink?" Matteo asks.

I turn to Blair.

"Vodka Red Bull please."

"Make that two," I add.

"Coming right up." Matteo makes our drinks and hands them to us, then picks up his glass and says, "To trophies."

"To trophies."

A group of men walk into the booth to join us. Matteo, being the host, makes the introductions. "Ladies, let me introduce you to few friends who will be joining us tonight. This is Sully, Patrick and..."

*Oh my God.*

"...John."

*Why didn't I notice John? I must have been distracted. And Sully is here also.*

The gentlemen stand and we all shake hands. John doesn't shake my hand. He put his arms around me. It doesn't look good. This can't be good. *What could John be thinking? He is too smart to think this is a coincidence.*

This is the 1st and 74th crew. Sully the investor and John who makes things happen. And what is Patrick's part in all of this? There must be a rainbow ending at the door we just came in, because this is better than a pot of gold!

And the icing on the cake? They are all tipsy.

Matteo leans over and whispers in my ear, "I've never seen you work so quickly before."

I laugh nervously. With the music blaring and the lights flashing, I try to give the impression that John is drunk and I'm just being super friendly.

Blair, on the other hand is giving me an *I'm not impressed look*. I keep an eye on her drink, knowing that re-filling it quickly will keep her happy. Perhaps having her around this evening isn't a smart decision on my part. I can only imagine what this looks like. *John is the rat. Am I going to ruin everything? Am I going to ruin relationships?* John still hasn't let go of me.

Matteo is being Matteo and flirting with all the women in the room. Matteo doesn't commit. He doesn't like to. He likes to keep his options open until the last second. This of course means that there are nights when he goes home empty handed, but he is happy to take that risk, he wouldn't have it any other way. We have had this conversation before. Matteo admits that he enjoys having his ego stroked more than he enjoys having his penis stroked.

John finally releases me to re-fill his drink. It's the first available moment I have to myself and I need to think of a way to leave the table for a few minutes. This is too close. I can't take the chance. *What if Matteo inquiries about Elias in front of John? I can't have these men in the same room with me!*

Matteo is speaking to a hot brunette, but locks eyes with me. I know that look. The women in the room don't interest him intellectually, and he wants to take me home. *FUCK!* I try to locate the exit, but I'm frozen.

Matteo is moving closer and closer, until his arm is around my waist. "I'm a little jealous, Zoe," he says. The smell of vodka is on his breath.

I once again laugh nervously. "Jealous? The man who can have any woman he desires."

He leans into me. "You give yourself to Elias, but I can't have you. How do you think that makes me feel?"

Little does he know that I'm also fucking the guy refilling his vodka. Just when I think things can't get worse, my eyes widen, my knees weaken and my eyes start to water as from the corner of my eye I see Elias walk into the booth with his arm around another woman.

Matteo, having some emotional intelligence, even though he is pretty drunk, notices the expression on my face, looks towards in Elias' direction then glances back to me. He brings me closer to him. "Just relax. Don't say a word. Let me handle this," Matteo says calmly. He appears to have suddenly become stone cold sober.

Matteo is clueless to the relationship I have with John, thank God, but how is he going to handle Elias? How am I going to handle Elias? My blood is boiling. I'm in no state to say anything. If I do, I will regret every last word. Do I care? Hell yeah.

Elias takes the first steps up to the booth, looks up and notices me. His body language is telling, he wants to stop and turn around, but it's too late. *I knew I was right about him.*

"Hey! Everyone is out tonight!" Matteo yells across to Elias. The music is deafening,

I give Elias a glacial look.

"Hi folks," he says, "I would like to introduce you to my friend Samantha. Samantha, this is Matteo and Zoe."

Matteo extends his hand. "Nice to meet you Samantha. If you would excuse us, Zoe and I are going to the dance floor." He smiles, making eye contact with Elias.

My body is trembling, my knees are weak. Matteo grabs my wrist and we walk by Elias to the dance floor.

When we are hidden behind a mob of dancers, Matteo puts his arms around my waist and draws me close to him. He leans in and whispers in my ear. "You deserve better,

Zoe. I did that to you." Then he totally and unexpectedly kisses me, deeply and passionately.

*The man I'm figuratively screwing is doing what is best for me?* I push Matteo away and walk to the restrooms. Out of the corner of my eye I see Sully and John talking. They don't see me but I can see them clearly. After a few seconds Sully turns away and starts heading in the direction of the bar. I decide to follow him, I need to take control of things.

When I get back to the table some 20 minutes later Elias is gone.

"My God, Zoe, where have you been?" Says Blair when I finally return. She is pretending to be angry but I can see she is just having fun with me. "First you and Matteo leave, then Sully, John is M.I.A. Luckily the pick of the litter stayed to keep me company. Patrick and I have become best friends in the course of the last half hour. Next time we're going out just the two of us. We're dumping the rest of you."

I laugh and they join in but I can barely keep it together. I stay at the booth for as long as I can manage while Blair and Patrick continue laughing and joking, but before anyone else returns to the table I apologize to Patrick and tell him that I have an early morning, that Blair has a strict curfew, and that we have no choice but to call it a night. Blair and I beat a quick exit the club.

As we reach the sidewalk the cold New York air hits me and I begin to feel better. Blair, laughing and a bit tipsy, turns to me when we are finally in a cab and says: "What is going on, Zoe? Tonight was better than a reality show. I can't wait to get home and tell Michael all about it. Who and how many men do you have in your life? Matteo and John are obviously very interested, but what happened to Elias and who the hell is Samantha?"

"It's a bit up in the air right now," I respond to Blair with a forced smile, "but Elias is definitely out, and there is a new man in my life. I can't say more than that for now. Stay tuned".

# CHAPTER TWENTY-FOUR

I TOSS AND TURN most of the night. My brain is racing. I finally fall asleep as dawn is breaking and don't wake up until the alarm sounds. I jump out of bed. I need to speak with my lawyer and my accountant and get some details straightened out, but I also need to figure out exactly what happened last night, to do an inventory or maybe a debrief with myself. Last night was a culmination in many ways…personally and professionally.

I can now move on from Elias. I guess I was right about him. I want to let him explain himself but I know that as a lawyer he can argue his way out anything with an impeccable and iron clad argument. He will tie it in a bow and I won't be able to say anything in response. That's no doubt the way it would go except I won't believe him and I won't give him the chance. I'm done.

Next is Matteo. What does he want? I thought I knew but I'm not sure anymore.

Then there is John. I guess I won't be seeing him tonight. He is a smart man. He played it very cool last night, but I know he pegged me. I also know that he isn't going to look for me or want to ask me any questions. He will just blame himself for being a fool; my fool.

Stefano, of course, is there, but in the end, if things go the way I plan, he won't be around for much longer.

Finally, there is Anton. I have lunch with him in a few hours. I'm not sure what he has to tell me, but everything has changed since our last meeting and I certainly have a lot to tell him.

In many ways things are still very messy but I somehow feel a huge weight has been lifted from my shoulders. Corny as it may sound, the fog has cleared. It is a crisp, sunny day and I feel renewed. I decide to go for a run. I need to focus on what has to be done. I sweat the toxins out of my body, the tempo of music pushing each step I make as I surround myself with autumn leaves in Central Park. It's deserted this morning, and my thoughts flash to last night. To John, and Matteo, then back to John. Then to Elias with that hot brunette, Samantha, then back to Matteo and that unexpected kiss, then back to Elias. *Fuck him.* I turn around and head back home and try to put him out of my mind. Forever.

By the time I get back from my run, it's time for me to get dressed for the lunch meeting with Anton.

I may not be in the best condition for a meeting that is going to change my life, but I am perfectly prepared and put on my favorite suit. Navy blue pants and a tailored blazer with a crisp white shirt.

I make my way out of my apartment and the elevator doors open. Just as I'm about to walk in, anticipating a silent ride down, Elias walks out and grabs me. *What is he doing here? Could his timing be any worse?*

"Zoe." He pauses and he looks me up and down. "You look great."

"What are you doing here, Elias?" I don't have time for this. "I have a meeting." *He is not going to fuck this up.*

"We need to talk."

*About what? How you are full of shit? How I actually believe your lies?* I know that if I respond with a question or if I don't respond at all it will lead to an argument and that would not be good, so I play smart. "Yes, Elias, we do need to talk, but now is not the time. How about tonight?"

I let him kiss me.

"I will pick you up at 7:00 PM. We can go to my place. Pack an overnight bag."

"Perfect."

We ride the elevator down to the lobby.

"Can I offer you a ride?" he asks.

"No thank you," I reply, perhaps too politely.

"I hope you aren't dressed this way for a date?"

*None of your business.* "No. It's all business today."

"Is that all you are going to say?"

"We will talk tonight," I repeat.

"Zoe, I love you. Please let me explain about last night. It's not what you think."

"I know you love me," *the way you know how.* "Tonight."

"Fine then, tonight. Hope your meeting is successful." He embraces me tentatively and kisses me on the forehead.

He knows how to handle me. Right now I have to refocus. I see Elias drive off and I walk to the street to hail a cab. Grano's isn't a long ride so I have very little time to regain my focus.

By the time I arrive, I have managed to compose myself enough to walk in with confidence.

I am greeted promptly as I walk in. "Good afternoon, signorina."

"Good afternoon. Reservations under Bergman."

"Yes. He has already arrived. Please follow me."

I follow the waiter to a table by the window and Anton is sitting there, watching people as they pass by on the sidewalk. He is stunning in his dark grey suit, magnificent, perfectly put together in an effortless way. It is obvious he takes care of himself.

"Great to see you," he says.

"I would say the same except our last encounter wasn't very pleasant."

"Then why are you here?" he asks.

"Because you asked me to be here."

"Are you in the habit of doing things for people that you don't like?"

"I most certainly am. That's my M.O., but who says I don't like you? If I can be frank, I think I do like you, and wish we had met under different circumstances."

He smiles, a guarded look in his eyes. "Thank you for that, but if I can be frank, I'm not sure whether you're being very truthful or very manipulative."

I smile and say, "I am being frank, you are being frank. There are way too many Franks at this table Mr. Bergman. But you presumably invited me here to tell me something?"

"Indeed I did. Please have a seat."

I sit, wait for him to begin.

"We have a common interest," he tells me.

"Change of heart?"

"Money talks. But I would need certain assurances." He flags the waiter and requests a bottle of red wine to be brought to our table.

*Good. I need a drink.* "What assurances do you need?"

"I want to sell, Zoe, but not to just anyone. I don't have to sell, so I can chose who I sell to and I want to make sure that certain individuals do not benefit from this property. That's the luxury of being a rich man. I think you will be fine with this, but I'm not leaving things to chance. I will draft the agreements to ensure this."

"Continue." There is no expression in my voice, but I want to jump for joy and do a happy dance. Everything is falling into place.

"First, I need to know why?" he asks.

"Why?"

"Why not a bidding war? A bidding war would benefit you significantly," he replies.

"It might, but I can't and don't want to do that. I have my own plan and it's not just about money." I'm pissed now. "You could start a bidding war just as well as I, yet you don't," I state with a firm tone.

"Okay, let's talk business. My terms are as follows…"

The waiter returns with a bottle in hand and opens it. Anton waits for him to pour before he continues.

"The asking price is 175 million and it's non-negotiable."

I keep my body still, not wanting to show any reaction. "And the other terms?"

"Under no circumstances are Matteo Rizzio and/or Stefano Souzas to benefit from this piece of property. Also, non-negotiable."

"And?"

"I want cash, no conditions, and quick closing. If you can agree to those terms, we have a deal."

I raise my glass, "Deal".

"Just like that?"

"Just like that."

"Zoe, you are either a great bluffer or very well-heeled because even I can't raise that money in seven days."

"I assure you, Anton, I'm not bluffing. I will close the deal next week. I know your reputation and I know you're not bluffing. I know that your word is your bond and that you will do what you say. I am the same. I wouldn't agree if I couldn't close. I won't ask for an extension. Let's get this done." *Deep breaths Zoe.*

We raises our glasses in a toast.

We eat a delicious quick lunch and chit chat.

After our espresso's, Anton stands and reaches his hand across the table. "Pleasure doing business with you. I will have my lawyer draft the paperwork this afternoon and send it to your lawyer by end of day."

He leaves and I sit there beaming. Almost there Zoe! But first, I need help. And fast.

I HAVE DONE MY HOMEWORK. I know that Matteo fucked Anton over. Matteo intentionally de-valued

Antonio's parcel by ensuring he couldn't change the zoning to build high-rise buildings. I also know that someone could change that, but it isn't going to be Anton. John will not help Anton. Finally, I know that Anton wants to liquidate his assets, is tired of running his father's business and wants an out. Hence the cash deal and quick close. And just like me, Anton wants respect, and if you didn't show him respect, he will be your enemy. Will Anton become an enemy? No risk, no reward. I make a phone call and let my secret investor know that we have a deal, that the lawyers will have the papers tomorrow. Elias taught me to go with my gut, that I could connect the dots quicker than most, and to move on my intuition. Thanks, Elias. I'm doing just that. I guess I can thank him tonight at our farewell dinner.

ELIAS ARRIVES, AND AS PROMISED I have packed an overnight bag. I let myself into the car.

"Baby, don't be upset with me," he says, excitement in his voice.

He leans in and I meet him half way and kiss his soft lips. He puts the car into gear and holds my hand tight.

"How was your business meeting?" he inquires.

"Very productive," I say without giving any details.

"You are the hardest working person I know," he says in a sincere tone.

"I enjoy what I do."

We arrive at his place and he carries my overnight bag in. I can't wait to hear his explanation for last night. Little does he know that there is nothing he can say to make me reconsider.

A candlelit dinner for two is set up by the window, the food prepared, the wine poured, the music playing. I presume he arranged this with one of his chef associates. 'A' for effort. 'A' plus for execution.

"Please take a seat," he says as he pulls out my chair.

I sit without a word.

"Zoe, I want to explain about last night," he begins, "but I also think you owe me an explanation."

"You first." At this point I have nothing to lose, so I don't need to walk on eggshells or play nice.

"The woman that I was with last night, Samantha, is a good friend and client. There is nothing going on between us. There never was. I like her. I don't love her. I love you. She invited me. I have refused many times but I ran out of excuses and went last night."

I roll my eyes.

"Zoe, please don't roll your eyes at me."

I take a deep breath, slowly exhale. "Why should I believe you?"

"She is married to a dear friend of mine. He asked me as a favor to bring her to that party. I love you, Zoe. Don't be foolish."

I begin to pick at my food.

"If you aren't going to eat, I'm going to have to take advantage of you," he says, his eyes on me.

All of a sudden, I have butterflies in my stomach. I don't believe him at all. I think I don't want to believe him, but in the same breath, he has that effect on me. As much as I want to be weak and believe him, I am terrified. *Can I trust him? Do I want to trust him?*

He stands, takes my hand and kisses me. I am so weak with him. I didn't want to but I quickly become aroused. He grabs my wrist and pulls me to the bedroom, throws me onto the bed. I land on my hands and knees.

"Don't move," he instructs me.

I stay still as he walks to the other side of the bed, stands there, facing me. He removes his pants. His cock is erect. He gets onto the bed, onto his knees. "Put it in your mouth," he says in a soft tone.

Without hesitation, I do and begin to suck.

He adjusts his position, grabs the back of my head, moans, "Take it all," as he begins to thrust, forcing his hard cock deep into my throat.

I gag, saliva all over me, but I take it. Deeper and deeper he thrusts, his entire cock sliding in and out of my mouth, taking me, dominating me. And I take it, willingly, enjoying each thrust.

I can feel him moving towards orgasm, his cock swelling in my mouth, crave the hot release that I know is about to come, when suddenly he stops, withdraws his cock from my mouth, lies down on the bed. "Sit on me," he orders.

I lift my dress and climb on top of him. My pussy is wet as I slowly ride him, using just the tip of his cock.

He, being impatient, grabs my shoulders, forces my pussy down onto his cock.

It's deep.

He looks into my eyes. "Keep going," he says thrusting his hips into me.

His cock deep inside me, my head rolls back as I swivel my hips, yearning for him to feel all of me, as I wrap my arms tightly around his neck.

I attempt to lift my hips, but the force of his hands counter-balances me. I close my eyes, a soft whimper escaping from my mouth. "Please," I plead. He is not moving. Perhaps he didn't hear me? He has, after all, pulled me very close, his face buried into mine. Licking, nibbling, kissing my neck. "Please!" I say more loudly this time. He has to have heard me. But still no reaction.

He leans in to kiss my mouth, biting my bottom lip before plunging his tongue into my open mouth. I feel a hand leave my shoulder and soon a single finger traces a path up the base of my neck to my hairline. First wrapping my hair around his hand, he pulls my hair softly, a playful tug. I let out a moan. My hip movements deepen and slow. My body is on fire. Sensing my opportunity, I again try to lift my hips. No luck...

The remaining hand moves from my shoulder to my tailbone. I feel his fingers trace the small of my back, intermittent, playful tugs of my hair providing little jolts of lightning throughout my body.

He releases his grip and I sit up, leaning against his bare chest. I lick my fingers and begin to rub my clitoris while he slowly thrusts his long cock inside me. My body stiffens and I shiver. "Oh my God, oh my God! I'm commmming," I yell as I extend my neck and roll my head back. *Fuck, that was intense.* My body collapses onto his as I slowly catch my breath.

"My turn," he says as he tugs on my hair. This time it isn't playful. He rolls me onto my back and kneels above me, looking down at me. "You are going to take it," he says, his eyes intense.

He slaps my breasts, hard. I keep my mouth shut as he inserts his cock inside my wet pussy and begins to thrust into me. His hands are all over my body, squeezing everything he touches, my nipples, my skin, my belly. His breath is steady, his rhythm deep. He lifts my ass and squeezes my cheeks as he thrusts harder and faster, until he comes.

I kiss him as he comes, matching my breath to his.

"Holy fuck," he says, collapsing onto my body.

That certainly didn't go to plan. Today has been a messed up day. But within minutes, I fall into a deep sleep.

# CHAPTER TWENTY-FIVE

I WAKE TO THE SOUNDS of Elias' breathing deeply. I roll over to my side and curl my body into a ball, stare at the red lights of the clock on the nightstand, feeling emotionally unsatisfied. I have everything in position to get exactly what I have worked for, exactly what I want - money, freedom and independence – but I still feel as though something is missing. Is it love? Do I want love? Upon reflection, I believe Elias. I believe that Elias loves me...in the only way he knows how. Do I accept this? A man who requires the attention of multiple women? Do I just live in the moment with him and be happy in a controlled environment of my own creation? Do I do the 'I love you' dance horizontally and the 'I hate you' dance vertically? Dear thoughts, can you begin to take a part-time role in my life? What do you think?

*Zoe, you have fallen in love with a sociopath.*

At the age of thirty-six I have no intention of getting married and having children. And Elias is loyal...loyal in the sense that he won't leave me. Companionship for a lifetime...with great sex as a bonus. Elias, half asleep, rolls over to my side and puts his arm around me, cupping my breast. "Good morning, baby."

"Good morning," I reply with my morning voice.

"Breakfast in bed?" He snuggles up closer to me.

"Mmmm, that sounds wonderful."

"Don't move. I will be right back." He rolls to the other side of the bed and gradually makes his way to the kitchen.

I still have some unfinished business. I quickly grab my phone and send Stefano a message.

Zoe: Meet this afternoon?

Within seconds, he replies.

Stefano: Lunch. 1:00 PM @ Trimi.
Zoe: See you there.

Elias walks in with a breakfast tray in hand, sets it on the bed. There's oatmeal with fresh fruit, and something else – a red envelope. I give him a look.

He climbs into bed. "Go ahead, open it."

Intrigued, I tear the envelope open – two first class airline tickets for Italy.

I squeal in delight, throw my arms around his neck. "I can't wait."

Elias beams back at me. "Baby, I'm so happy," he announces.

Only one thing to say. "Ditto."

"So, what are your plans for today?" He asks with a smile on his face.

Is he curious or jealous? Or is he just asking? "Lunch meeting and then rest from all the orgasms," I laugh.

"You mean to tell me that we can't spend the day in bed?"

"Don't you have to work?"

"It's Saturday, baby," he smiles. "When should I come back?"

I know what he wants to hear. "ASAP?"

"Tonight?"

I laugh. "I need some time to recover. I need some space." *Or spending time with your family?*

He puckers his lips. "Space is for astronauts. I can't get enough of you."

"How about Wednesday night?"

"Done."

"I need to get ready," I tell him, finishing up my oatmeal.

"Not until I taste you."

He takes my bowl from my hand and sets it on the bedside, rolls me onto my back and begins to caress my inner thighs with his fingertips, his tongue deep in my throat. I moan and begin to writhe. He moves his fingertips to my pussy lips, then moves them down my inner thigh. He repeats this over and over, making me moan while my pussy becomes wetter and wetter.

Finally, he sits up and places his firm body between my legs and lies on his rock-hard abs. He nibbles my inner thigh, works his way up to my lips, his tongue barely making contact with my clit, driving me crazy. I thrust my hips, wanting more pressure and more speed, but he refuses. He pins my hips down, his hands gripping my waist. I sigh with anticipation and excitement. His tongue gradually becomes firm and picks up speed, sliding up and down between my wet lips, brushing my clit then sliding back down to tease my opening. I close my eyes and roll my head back as his finger enters my pussy, gently teases me as I thrust up and down trying to get it deeper into me. Finally, he lets me have it all, puts a second finger in, vibrates his fingers inside me while his tongue whirls on my clit.

I can't take it anymore. "I'm coming, I'm coming, Oh my God!" I let out a groan that echoes throughout the penthouse. *Fuck. I needed that. He most certainly has a problem but his tongue and penis are not on the list.*

"Mmm, delicious," he beams.

"Babes, I needed that," I tell him.

"Babes is one of your other boyfriends?" he jokes "I'm your baby."

"I mean baby. So hard to keep all of you straight."

"Try. You know how jealous I am," he grins. "Now you can get your day started."

AFTER THAT EXPLOSIVE ORGASM, I'm ready to meet with Stefano. First, however, I have to make a quick visit to my lawyer. Michael Levitt is an old friend who I trust implicitly - he had a major crush on me in high school. I like Michael, but knew that I wasn't prepared to provide him with what he needed, so I let him go. And now he is married with two beautiful kids.

I walk into Michael's office and he glances up at me with a look of absolute astonishment. "Zoe, how did you pull this one off?"

I throw my purse onto his desk while I take a seat. "I have no idea what you're talking about?"

"I got all the documents from Bergman's lawyer. This is amazing. You must have hypnotized him." He grins. "Zoe, remind me why didn't we get married?"

I lean forward and stare into his eyes, put on my poker face. "Because I don't believe in love."

"Come on Zoe. We aren't twenty years old. By now I would have thought you'd flushed all that stuff out of your heart."

"I'm happy, Michael. Aren't you?"

"We would have been a great team."

"You just want all the money I just made."

We both laugh.

"I won't ask any questions, but I have never seen anything like this before. A deal closing in seven days? And not just any deal."

"I just want to check and make sure I don't have any red flags to be concerned about."

"One of the craziest and cleanest deals I've seen."

"Perfect."

I can't keep the smile from my face. "Where do I sign?"

After signing all the paperwork, I stand up and grab my purse.

"Leaving so soon?"

"I've got places to visit and people to see."

"Can I at least get a hug?"

I walk around his desk and give him a big Zoe hug.

"You know I love you."

"I love you too Michael... like a little brother."

He laughs. "You always know what to say."

"And how much to say. Thanks for everything. Call me when we're closed."

"Will do."


TRIMI IS OVERFLOWING with men in business suits as I make my way to our reserved table. I am the first to arrive and enjoy the pure bliss of people-watching for a few minutes. I can't help but be amused by the number of people who are on their phones while in the company of others over lunch – I actually miss the good old days, when technology had less control over us. Doesn't anyone believe in being in the moment anymore?

Stefano arrives. "Happy fuckin Saturday," he yells as he takes his seat.

"Someone is in a good mood."

"I'm in a fuckin grrrreat mood," he rumbles.

The waiter arrives, and Stefano orders a bottle of Caymus, his favorite.

The waiter disappears and Stefano turns his attention back to me. "You have some good news for me?" He leans forward, his elbows on the table.

I lean in and mimic his behavior. "Anton sold 1st and 74th."

He leans back and locks eyes with mine. "What do you mean he sold it?"

"Apparently, there was another interested party," I reply.

"That fucker. I'm going to make sure he regrets this."

I need to stop this…and fast. Or at least stall. "Don't think that's a good idea."

"I don't give a flying fuck what you think." Stefano always wants what isn't his.

"Remind me again why this is so important to you?" I need to distract him.

"None of your fuckin business," he replies, once again yelling at me.

The surrounding tables are noticing Stefano's behavior, but Stefano couldn't care less.

"I would forget about this project and destroy his next one. The rewards are only going to get bigger." I attempt yet again to distract him from his current mission, hoping it will work.

He doesn't respond immediately. I see the hamster spinning its wheel. "You have a good point. Although I could wait for this deal to close and have my lawyer complete a title search on the new owner," he muses.

*Fuck me!* "I bet you Matteo is already planning his next project. Perhaps your timing has been all wrong."

"I'm going to fuckin figure it out. Why do I pay you the big bucks when you can't fuckin deliver?"

The waiter returns to our table, opens the bottle of Caymus and pours us each a glass.

Stefano picks up his glass and I follow.

He toasts, "To fucking. And I don't mean the kind of fucking that just happened to me!"

Our glasses clink and I take a big sip of the full-bodied wine. I need alcohol to get through this.

I place my half empty glass back onto the table and with confidence say, "I'm done."

"What the fuck are you talking about?" he asks, raising his voice.

"I'm done, Stefano. I got you the information you needed and I don't want to do this anymore. It's not fun."

"Your job's not done yet. You're not done until I tell you you're done."

I pick up my glass of wine, and take a big sip. "I'm finished, Stefano."

"Is it that fucker Elias?"

"What are you talking about?"

"Don't play stupid with me. I know you're fucking him. I don't like him one bit."

"And if I was, which I may well be, how is it any of your business?"

"I will make it my business. You work for me and you are mine. That dumb fuck needs to be taught a lesson."

"I worked for you, but I am not your possession. Your threats don't scare me, Stefano." I stand and walk out of Trimi without looking back.

"Fuck you Zoe, and fuck Elias," he yells across the restaurant as I walk out. "You're both going to regret this, especially you, you fuckin bitch."

I just made an enemy.

# CHAPTER TWENTY-SIX

MY FOOTSTEPS ECHO IN the hallway. I walk towards the solid white door with the square panel glass at eye level, thick reinforced commercial glass that won't shatter when someone takes a fist or even a chair to it. I buzz myself in and the doors unlock. A nurse is sitting at the reception desk.

"Who are you here to see?"

"Angelica Winstein." I sign in.

"She is in room 212." She points me in the right direction.

I haven't prepared for this. I am terrified, exhausted and ill equipped. Will she recognize me? I slowly pass one room after another…206, 208, 210… force myself to slow down. I am terrified to see my big sister. Fifteen years, no Christmas, no Easter, no phone calls. Those were the boundaries that I put in place. The last time I was here she was confined, wrists and ankles fastened to her bed. She was suicidal and the doctors had her strapped down and medicated into a stupor. That image has been in my brain for fifteen years. It's time to exorcise it.

I take a deep breath and walk into the room. She is sitting in her chair, watching television, too distracted to notice me.

"Angelica?"

"Yes." She tilts her head in my direction.

My lips are frozen. She is beautiful, wearing the Prada dress that I shipped to her a few months ago.

"Where have you been?" she asks me. "Mom and dad are worried about you."

"I'm fine." *Freaked out, insecure, neurotic and emotional is what I mean.*

"I missed you."

My eyes begin to water as I walk towards her. I wrap my arms around her and hold her and try to make up for fifteen years of missed hugs. I kiss her on her forehead. "I missed you too. So much. " I take a seat next to her and hold her hand to take away her pain, like I did when we were kids, but the pain seems to have faded. It's not the same as it was. Is it the drugs or she in a better place? Probably a bit of both.

"Are you going to leave us again?" she asks me.

I'm shaken to the core by her question so I hold her even tighter. "No, Angelica. I'm back now and won't leave again. I needed to take care of some things and I have."

"What things?"

"Work stuff. Business. Money. But enough about that, tell me what I've missed? How are you? What's new in your life?"

"I'm learning how to paint."

"That's amazing," I respond, forcing a smile to my face.

"I really enjoy it. See that painting over there?" She points to the wall in front of us. "I painted that." I hear the excitement in her voice.

"It's beautiful. A storm at sea? That is absolutely stunning, Angelica." And it is.

"I taught myself."

"I am so proud of you."

I turn to the television set. She is watching *The Mindy Project* on Netflix. "You know, Mindy reminds me a lot of myself."

She smiles. "Yeah, but you don't talk as much."

"True...but I think the way she thinks."

We both laugh.

"You hungry?" I ask her.

"A little."

"Can I take you out for lunch?"

"Sure."

"How about Camorra's?"

"You remembered. It's been a long time, Zoe."

"How could I forget your favorite pizza place?"

I sign Angelica out and we drive to Camorra's.

The place hasn't changed. Red table clothes, black and white photos of Italy, stainless steel parmesan and red chili flake shakers...it's all the same. Perhaps that's why Angelica feels comfortable here? After thirty years, everything is exactly the same, the waiters just a little older.

After her first bite, she puts her slice down and looks at me, emotionless

"What's wrong?" I ask. "Don't you like your pizza?"

"Do you miss Chris?" she asks.

A pang hits me. A name I haven't heard out loud in over fifteen years. "I do." *I hate admitting that. It makes me feel weak.*

"When was the last time you went to visit him?" she asks.

The truth is I haven't gone back since I left fifteen years ago. I wanted to forget, although it was something that could never be forgotten. I focused on all the other pain, because this pain would destroy me. It almost did. "It's been a while. You?"

"Mom and dad took me to visit him last week. They take me once a month. They go every day though. We lit a candle for him." She picks up her slice and takes another bite.

It's easy for her to talk about him. *Thanks, Big Pharma.* I begin to eat faster, wanting to change the conversation. Luckily, she seems to lose interest and just keeps eating at her turtle's pace.

"We miss you. When are we all going to have dinner together?"

"I'm sure it will be real soon. Like I said, I'm back for good."

"Mom and dad would love that." She takes her last bite. "Why didn't you come and visit me? I really needed you."

I thought I was there for her by sending her monthly gifts and covering the cost of care. "Let's focus on the now. I'm here now. I'm not going anywhere," I smile.

"Good," she says and reaches over and squeezes my hand.

"Everything will be fine again now," I smile.

Just as we are finally finishing lunch, a text comes in.

Michael: Deal is closed. Congratulations!

I want to do a happy dance, but I better start acting like a rich person.

After all these years, I have finally accomplished what I set out to do. Adrenaline is running through my veins.

"How was lunch?" I ask.

"Like the good old days," she smiles.

"There will be many more 'good old days' from now on," I promise her.

"I love you, Zoe," she tells me.

"I love you Angelica."

I WALK INTO JOHN'S office unannounced, manage to get through reception. I'm a regular now. They know me. His door is open and he's on the phone. I sneak in quietly and take a seat.

"...I'm going to have to call you back," he says and puts down the receiver.

Before he can say a word, I quickly say, "I'm sorry."

"Conscience got the better of you?" he smiles.

"I need to tell you something."

"How the tables have turned. Confess away."

"When we first met, it wasn't by chance, I had asked Stefano to make the introductions. I needed information from you for him."

He interrupts me. "I was born at night, Zoe, but not last night. I always strongly suspected that and acted accordingly."

"I want you to know, I regret not being honest with you from the beginning."

"As Machiavelli says, *Politics have no relation to morals.* I am willfully blind when it comes to you, Zoe. I knew, or half knew, that you were a mercenary, but I didn't want to believe it. I know you have a good heart. The darkness in you will not win, the light will." He sighs. "Perhaps it already has?"

I sense that he already knew what I was going to tell him and had prepared his answer.

I pause before responding. "I crave nothing more than to be vulnerable and loved," I tell him, "but I have seen and experienced too much."

"Not everyone is bad. You just happen to have had a few bad situations, more than your fair share. It has skewed your perception of things."

"Occupational hazard."

We both laugh.

"We're still friends, Zoe."

"That means a lot. I'm making things right...I hope." I stand up, prepare to leave.

John walks around his desk, opens his arms and holds me. I crawl right inside them and squeeze tight.

"You're going to figure it out. I have confidence in you," he whispers in my ear.

"Ice cream?" I ask.

"Soon. A few loose ends to tie up."

I release my grip, and he does the same.

"Thanks, John."

He has a puzzled look on his face. "Thanks for what?"

"For being my friend."

"Anytime kiddo."

I grab my purse and head out the door. I turn around, find John's eyes still on me. I wave good-bye. He smiles and turns away.

As I walk out of the elevator I pull out my phone and text Matteo.

Zoe: Are you available for a 9:30 meeting tomorrow morning?
Matteo: See you then.

I have one more visit to make this afternoon before seeing Elias this evening – more accurately I have another apology to make.

I make my way up to Blair's office with two coffees in hand. The elevator opens and I see Blair standing behind the reception desk, a look of shock on her face.

"Coffee?" I offer.

"Come to my office."

I follow her to her office and hand her the coffee.

"You were right," are the first words out of my mouth.

"Right about what?"

I take a sip of coffee. "About everything."

"Zoe, I care about you and I'm worried."

"Stop worrying, it's all coming to an end."

"I hope so…. You don't need those people in your life."

"I agree, but don't paint them all with the same brush. I was foolish to think that all of those people cared about me, but some have proved themselves."

She smiles.

"Can I get Cy's number?" I ask her.

She laughs. "Good for you, Zoe. I liked that guy. I will have to get it from Michael. I'll text it to you later."

"Thanks! I assume he is back in Montreal?"

"Yeah. Apparently, he is doing well in his new business. CY Consulting…or something really original like that."

"I'm happy for him."

"Didn't take you for a long-distance relationship type?"

I give her a stern look. "I'm full of surprises, aren't I?"

"You are." She takes a sip of coffee.

"Are we good?"

"We are great."

We both stand up and I walk over to her and give her a hug.

"See you soon."

I have one more meeting for the night…Elias. I need to know what he has planned.

> Zoe: Baby! Hope you are having a great day! What time should I expect you tonight?

I make my way home and decide to have a glass of wine and watch *The Mindy Project,* it feels like a connection with my sister. An hour passes and I haven't heard from Elias. That isn't like him.

Don't overthink it, Zoe. I pour myself another glass, celebrating my victory, my new life. It seems so surreal.

At 8:00 PM Elias still hasn't contacted me. Should I start to worry? It is strange. He has never been too busy to contact me before. I watch TV for another hour then do a final check of my phone, but I know already that he hasn't called. I decide to pack it in early. Something important must have come up. I put on my nightgown and read in bed, pleased to be alone for once. I fall asleep thinking about Elias.

# CHAPTER TWENTY-SEVEN

9:30 AM SHARP AND still no word from Elias. I will worry about it later. The elevator doors open and Rebecca, who is on the phone, waves hello and motions for me to go right in. I'm now familiar with the routine, so I make my way to Matteo's office, returning Rebecca's wave and mouthing "good morning" as I walk in. Matteo's back is to me as he stands gazing out of the window, on a call. I can see myself in the reflection and I know he knows I'm here. I lock the door and take a seat, waiting for him to finish.

After a few moments, Matteo turns around and signals that he is almost done.

He finally ends his call and takes his seat next to me, swiveling my chair closer to him.

"You locked the door? I hope this visit is about pleasure, but I'm sensing that it's all about business."

"I have something for you,"

"What?" He is intrigued, leans back, opening the space between us.

I'm nervous, but confident. "Anton Bergman," I tell him.

He has a puzzled look on his face. "Anton? How do you know Anton?" He isn't smiling any more.

"Let's just say that Anton and I have become friends," I say.

"That's not really my business." He pauses. "As long as it doesn't become my business…"

I shrug. "You're looking at the person who…" but just as I am about to finish my sentence, Matteo interrupts me.

"I'm looking at someone who is getting mixed up in a very big deal. My deal. If you fuck up my deal…" He stops and looks at me, his eyes suddenly dark, probing. "I can see the veins in your neck, Zoe. You look stressed. Have you crossed the line?"

I laugh nervously. "I wasn't expecting this reaction out of you."

He says nothing, waiting for me to reveal myself.

"There is something I need to tell you," I say with a soft tone. "We didn't meet by chance."

"Wake up, Zoe. You think that me letting you in was by chance? Not even close."

"I thought you couldn't resist my charm?"

"That was just a bonus."

"Did you know who I was working for?" I ask bluntly.

"No I didn't, but it wasn't top of my list to figure it out. Just because it looks like I don't care doesn't mean that I don't. I file a lot of stuff and only remember it when there is a contradiction or something doesn't fit. Eventually I knew it was Stefano – people talk."

"Why does Stefano want to fuck you over?"

"Stefano is an uglier, less sophisticated, more crass version of me. We do the same thing, both of us chase after the same slice of pie. I consistently get the bigger piece of pie and he is tired of it. Basically he wants to be me."

I think for a moment. It's show and tell time. "The other night," I tell him, "when I went to the ladies room, I met the Sultan. We talked for a while, and I made a – "

"Sully?" He stares at me. Now it's Matteo who looks tense. "Zoe, you come into my office, ask me for advice.

And what do I do? I give you advice, open up to you, tell you shit that I shouldn't tell to anybody. You know intimate details of my business and personal life. And you do this? I'm upset. I'm very fucking upset. The other night I was there for you. I always have been. I feel comfortable, want to be with you. I want to share with you – then this? Anything but this. This is just not right, Zoe!"

"I'm sorry," I say, looking into his brown eyes.

"Never mind sorry. You knew exactly what you were doing," his volume increases.

"Matteo, hold off. Hear me out…Please?"

"I'm not sure I want to. You did what you had to do Zoe, and I will do what I have to do," he snaps.

"Anton wasn't ever going to sell to you…"

"What makes you so sure?"

"Because he told me. I don't know what you did to him, but he wasn't going to sell to you. Never."

"Is that what you want me to believe, or is that the truth?"

"Did you not try?"

"Of course, I tried. And he wouldn't sell to me."

"That's right. He would never sell to you or Stefano. So I saw an opportunity and I took it."

Matteo stares at me, says nothing, but I can see his anger bubbling just below the surface. I have to tread lightly if I am to get out without completely burning my bridges.

"Of course, I got my consulting fee, which I discussed with Sully before-hand, and which I'm very happy with, but I think you should be thanking me right now."

"Thank you? For me to say thank you, I have to be grateful for something. So, what am I grateful for? What am I supposed to be thankful for?"

"I met with Anton to help you. I wasn't doing it for Stefano. You are my friend, which you proved that night with Elias. I did this for you. My fee would have been paid by Stefano, so I had no monetary reason to favor you, I just couldn't let Stefano screw you and be part of it."

Sensing that he was listening, I ploughed on. "The other night, I told Sully that Anton had reached out to me. He had arranged for a meeting the following day. Unsure as to his motive, I ran a few scenarios by Sully. He was on board. One condition was that we not tell you until later – we didn't want to get your hopes up. Sully is smart, very honorable. He financed the purchase of the piece, but it belongs to you."

His eyes widen as he starts to understand.

"It wasn't about the money," I continue. "I couldn't give a damn about money. And it wasn't about ego. It was about respect. I respect you and want you to respect me. It wasn't easy. I have made enemies along the way."

His wheels are spinning. "I need time to process this."

"What is bothering you? I gave you what you wanted, something you wouldn't have got any other way."

"You betrayed me, lied to me."

"Is that what this is really all about?"

"Zoe, I let you in."

"I never betrayed your trust. Every intimate detail you have shared with me has stayed between us. And I have never taken advantage of you even though I know what makes you vulnerable. I couldn't do it. You were the only one I trusted."

"My gut tells me you fucked me, Zoe!"

"Matteo, your deal was going nowhere and I saved it. So why don't you tell me why you're really pissed? Is it because you have feelings for me? You thought you were in control, that you could stay detached, you knew it all and that Matteo was king? All of a sudden you find out that you have feelings for me and that I have not only impacted your life, I have landed the big deal for you. That's tough for your ego, isn't it?"

He doesn't say anything. He just sits across from me, staring into my eyes.

"I know you will never admit your true feelings for me or anyone for that matter. But you can't deny that what I'm saying is correct and that I'm the one who got this deal done."

He finally smiles. "Maybe you're right, Zoe. And who gets you?"

I allow myself to relax, smile in return. "No one. I'm a free agent. So isn't is time to crack open that bottle of 59 Château Margaux!"

Matteo considers for a long moment, finally stands up and walks to the bar.

"You are a one of a kind, Zoe Winstein," he says, a note of admiration in his voice. He picks up the 59 Château Margaux, considers it for a moment. "Half of me thinks that all you ever wanted was to share this bottle with me."

"I'm a simple girl," I laugh. "A fifteen million dollar payday and a bottle of 59 Château Margaux are all it takes to keep me happy."

Matteo slowly, carefully, opens the bottle, takes a long sniff of the scent as the cork slides out. "Beautiful…"

He carefully pours two glasses, taking care not to spill a drop. I make my way to the couch and he sits next to me, hands me my glass. "I wouldn't call you a simple girl," he tells me. "Complex, infuriating, and very high maintenance would be more like it."

"What about loyal?"

"And yes, loyal." He looks into my eyes and makes a toast. "To loyalty."

I take a sip and savor the wine while I fold into the couch. I inhale from my nose, hold it and exhale from my mouth before finally saying, "To loyalty." I sneak a glance at Matteo. His face has relaxed, he looks calm at last. "So, are you going to tell me why everyone wants revenge on you?" I ask.

He laughs. "You are a persistent little operative, aren't you?" He takes another slow sip. "When I first started up, I was, how can I put this, basically a punk. I was from the streets, a fighter. I didn't play fair. I took a lot of short cuts and pissed off a lot of people. It's inevitable in this line of work, but as you grow older, as you learn, you try to burn as few bridges as possible."

"Amen to that."

"Let's just savor this bottle of wine right now."

I nod.

We take our time, enjoying each other's company, not needing to say much, but eventually we finish the bottle. Feeling on top of the world, I am ready to leave, happy that I have a few bridges left unburned.

"I will have my lawyer send the agreement to Elias later today," I tell him as I set my glass down.

He gives me a surprised look. "You don't know?" He says in a serious voice.

His tone concerns me. In an instant the atmosphere has changed. "I don't know what?"

Matteo takes my hand. "Elias is dead, Zoe."

"What?" My eyes begin to water, and Matteo wraps his arms around me.

"I don't believe you," I gasp.

"Zoe, I'm so sorry."

"But how? Why?" But as I say it, I hear Stefano's voice inside my head. 'If I can't have you, no one can.'

"Elias burned a few too many bridges. Do you need some water?"

"No."

"Would you like my driver to take you home?"

My body is in shock. I have to escape, be by myself, process this in my own way. I stand up. "I have to go."

Matteo tries to stop me, to comfort me, but I run out of his office and hurry to the elevator.

As soon as I am alone I text Michael to send Matteo the agreement, fighting back the tears the whole time.

I hail a cab and go straight to my apartment.

I am completely alone.

## QUEEN'S DANCE

HE LEFT ME JUST as I was beginning to accept him and his love, accept him for who he was. I open a bottle of wine, thinking of Dido, Queen of Carthage being abandoned by Aeneas. He abandoned me. I drink some more until I am numb, mourning the loss of my first love. The fuckin sociopath. My sociopath.

# CHAPTER TWENTY-EIGHT

GUILT HAS BROUGHT ME here. Is it necessary to atone for my sins? Do I need to be here? *I hate being here.* It's raining. It's cold. Droplets of freezing water drip from the tip of my nose. I don't move, my feet glued to the wet ground. I feel like I'm in the confessional: "Bless me father for I have sinned, it has been 15 years since my last confession...."

It has been fifteen years since my last visit. My eyes are closed and my face is pointed up to the sky, inhaling through my nose and exhaling through my mouth as if I'm about to start a conversation with the Gods. I feel numb.

*I hate being here. Why did I come?* I'm in no rush to leave. His tombstone reads: *He who follows me in the light will never walk into darkness.* I call bull-shit. We may follow the light when we see it, but we can't always see it. We have moments when we walk into darkness; darkness that we can't come back from. That was me. That is me. I can't walk back. I will remain in the darkness. I don't want to leave the darkness. It's too much fun in here.

I want to cry. I'm supposed to cry. But I can't. How do I force myself to cry? All I can think about is how my parents picked the worst photo of my brother to put on his tomb. My mother, most likely, picked up plastic flowers from the dollar store and placed them next to his stone. I hate them. I hate everything about this place. Yet, here I am.

The priest began to read *"As for us, brother, we are separated from you for a little while – not in our thoughts, but only in body – how we will miss you and how hard we will try to see you again."*

His casket was lowered into the ground. I looked away as the soil covered him.

I stood apart from the crowd that gathered close to the grave. My ears couldn't hear noise but I saw the strangers crying. Why were they crying? Perhaps they were tears of fear, knowing that they too will one day be covered in dirt.

The rain stops. I open my eyes and see that the clouds have broken and slivers of light begin to peek through the openings. I see the truth. He did this to himself. His hands did it. His thoughts did it. It was my sister's diary that told me the story. All I remember reading was my brother saying, *'I'm suffering, I'm suffering…I want to be dead'*, while crying with his body covered in ashes.

That is the pain that I carry today. His painful death.

Rather than be at Elias' funeral, I am here. I know my place. I'm not his family; I was his lover. Guilt has brought me to where I belong. *Did I kill Elias?* Did Stefano kill Elias? Was this Stefano's way of getting back at me for hurting him in the worst way? For abandoning him? His death left a void inside me. I am hollow without him. I need him. He was supposed to take care of me. He taught me how to be independent, taught me how to forgive, taught me how to accept someone for who they are, taught me patience. I hear his voice in my head, 'Baby, I miss you!' Elias, the man I loved but never understood. But now he is gone and I never will never truly understand him.

Stefano never called, but I think he sent a message, loud and clear. Will I ever hear from him again? Probably. I am confident I have been replaced with new companions, but he will never replace the love he felt for me. I made him feel safe. I was the only companion he could count on. After all, I was reliable, loved him in my way, and always kept my word, at least until I didn't.

I don't miss him, and I definitely have no regrets as to the outcome of it all. I hope he learned something from this experience. I hope this experience has taught him how to treat the people he cares about. Maybe that's how he treats the people he loves, but either way, I'm out. Either way I don't want to have any more to do with him. Perhaps he will have healthy relationships? Perhaps, but I don't think so. I know he has a lot of hurt and anger. Maybe one day he can let that all go and move on to be happier with himself and those around him.

John and I have become friends. We text often. I didn't need to burn that bridge. He was, after all, the Mayor of New York. I haven't seen him since our last encounter, but I have a feeling that we will be having another scoop of ice cream in the near future.

I was clever enough to make friends with Sully. I did need him after all. He is a smart and shrewd and can think on his feet. My type of guy. He likes me, probably for other reasons, but he did offer me a job, which I politely declined. I am done working for others. I have investment capital and I am going to work for ZoeWins Corp., just as soon as I incorporate that company.

I did learn something from Sully – that you can't tell your business partners everything. I learned that sometimes you just have to be patient and wait for the right moment. Sully kept his end of the deal with Anton. Although the development is going through for Matteo, the project was redesigned to have Anton's piece stand on its own, and although Matteo is a part of the development, Anton doesn't have a clue. One less thing for me to worry about. Anton is happy. Sully is happy. John is reasonably happy. Matteo is happy.

Speaking of Matteo, after leaving his office the other day, I wasn't sure where our relationship was going to end up. He opened up to me about what our relationship was, told me that although he enjoyed the sex, he enjoyed opening up to me even more. A few days later, he sent me a text message. *Thanks for being the only person I can talk with.*

I like to think that in the end, the good guys won. But who is to say who is good and who is bad? Am I any better? Or am I just playing the game like everyone else?

Blair and I are even closer. The love of her life, Michael, asked her to get married and the wedding is planned for the spring. I will be the maid of honor.

With the money I received from Sully I upgraded my sister to a better facility, closer to my parents. I have visited her every day since, checking in on her and encouraging her to continue painting. She is happy.

ANG THEN THERE ARE my parents. Although growing up I expected more from my parents, I now have come to believe that they did what they could. They did what they knew and most of what they knew they learned not at school but from their parents in a small town halfway around the world in another century. I do love them.

I knock on the door and my father answers.

"Hi dad." *I really don't want to be here.*

I see his eyes water. "Zoe." He puts his arms around me.

When I was a child, I wanted him to hold me, but now, I don't want him touching me.

He releases me and tells me to come in. "Zoe's home," he screams, attempting to get my mother's attention.

I hear my mother hurrying down the stairs. "Zoe!"

She runs to the door and just stands there in complete shock, not saying a word. "Hi Mom." I give her a hug and don't let go.

"Are you hungry? Come. Sit," she says with her scratchy voice in broken English.

"I just wanted to stop by and let you know that I'm back in town. And I have something for you." I hand my mother a set of house keys, a large manila envelope.

"What's this?" she asks.

"I bought you a house in Brooklyn."

My mother begins to cry. My father is not sure if I'm joking or not.

"I have worked very hard and I wanted to do something for you. Dad, it was you who taught me hard work. You worked to provide for us. Now it's my turn to provide for you."

My mother gives me a hug, while my father watches.

I can't stay. I have to leave. "I hate to do this, but I have to go," I tell them. "I have a plane to catch. Work never ends."

"When will you come back?" my father asks.

I have set new boundaries for my family, but they don't need to know that. "I will see you soon. Besides, you will be busy with all the packing you have to do. I will see you at the house-warming party," I smile.

I give them both hugs and head back to the city.

As for myself, I am independent. The money is invested and I have plans. We all do things we don't want to do. But the game is done, the Queen's Dance has come to an end. I am ready for that missing piece in my life.

I have come to realize that people aren't who they claim to be. People want to be loved. So they pretend to be something they are not, just to be loved. They are terrified that they will not be accepted for who they truly are, so they become imposters.

And why do men gravitate towards me? They are attracted by my looks. But why do they stay? Is it because I don't judge them, I just accept them for who they are? I allow them to expose their demons without passing judgement. I bring them to a calm place that provides a haven. And what about the sex, you ask? You can get sex anywhere, that was not what kept them coming back for more.

Most people live a fairy-tale. They pretend. I separate the fairy-tale from reality. I am a realist, after all. Love brings madness. I'd rather keep my logical, business-minded brain intact without any distractions. What are distractions? Feelings.

MY FLIGHT LANDED ON time, and I knew exactly where I was heading.

It's 11:00 PM and I knock on the door. He is wearing blue jeans and a form-fitted white t-shirt showing his killer body.

"Hi." I pause. "How are you?"

He gazes at me in complete shock. "I thought I was fine but someone has put hallucinogens in my beer."

"Perfect."

He grabs me and my bags and takes me into his bedroom without saying a word. He slowly undresses me before gently lying me down me on his bed. He undresses himself and I watch. His body is just as I remember, chiseled to perfection. It is the most beautiful thing I have seen in some time. He lies next to me and holds me gently in his arms, kissing my forehead as we lie there on our sides.

He places his hand under my chin and tilts my head up, allowing our lips to touch. Our breath is in sync. No words can describe how my body is reacting to him, to his touch, to his smell, to his skin.

I crave deep, true love. Can Cy give me what I need?

My body writhes as does his. I begin to caress his torso, moving my way to his cock. I feel the tip of his cock. He is hard. I grab his cock with my hand and begin to stroke it. His cock feels different compared to all the other cocks I have held. Everything about him feels different. I let go and allow him to control me…all of me, including my heart.

He rolls me onto my back, forcing me to release his cock as he climbs on top of me. He inserts the tip of his cock inside me. His hips are at a stand-still, but his tongue, on the other hand, is intertwined with mine. My hands, on his back, slowly move up and down, brushing him with my long nails.

I'm panting, moaning.

He begins to move his hips, slowly thrusting in and out of me. It is the most beautiful thing I have felt in a long time. My eyes begin to water. *My God, can I be crying?* He continues to slowly thrust in and out of my pussy. With each thrust I moan, repeating his name. My body begins to twitch and vibrate as I hold my breath and finally when I can't hold it back any longer I scream, "Oh Fuck. Oh, Cyyyyy."

My body collapses and I look at him. "It's your turn. Use my body as you wish."

He draws my body closer to his and holds on for dear life. His thrusts speed up and deepen inside me, just as he releases his come inside me. His body weight pins me. I continue to hold him in my arms and we just lie there, holding onto one another. He eventually rolls on his back and curls me into his arms. I close my eyes as he caresses my hair. Before I know it, it's morning. A new day, a new place, a new beginning.

# ABOUT THE AUTHOR

A.P. Thanos is an accomplished artist in a variety of media. She also has multiple post-secondary degrees including an undergraduate degree in Psychology. It is no surprise that her first novel, Queen's Dance, would be about the behavior and psychology of men in a testosterone-fueled, multi-million dollar industry of real estate and development.

Made in the USA
Columbia, SC
22 January 2019